THE HEIRLOOM BROOCH

Kate Nixon

The Heirloom Series by Kate Nixon
The Heirloom Brooch
The Heirloom Pearls

THE HEIRLOOM BROOCH

Cover image of garnet brooch from Mindi Ribar of MindiLynJewelry on Etsy

ISBN Number:9781500565091
First Edition 2014

For Randy and my girls along
with all the women who wore
the Garnet Brooch

We need to haunt the house of history and listen anew to the ancestors' wisdom.
Maya Angelou

Chapter 1

Part 1

Indianapolis, Indiana, July 18, 2010

Lauren Spencer reread her mother's letter with three words, complete with punctuation, running through her head. Fake garnets! Why?

Next she studied the appraiser's typed note about the garnet brooch and paused over the description. Red glass crystals set in a brass mounting. Value $10. Typical of Victorian-era jewelry and probably manufactured in the United States.

Taking her cell phone, she snapped a picture of the brooch and loaded it into the computer. Then she googled it to see what matched.

Awards for church attendance and sweetheart brooches came up, but none were very good matches. Not a one of them was as old as her inherited jewelry.

She revised the search strategy and added Victorian. The counter listed thousands of images as a result.

Switching 1880s for Victorian dropped the count to 500. Doable. But in a few minutes, she realized she had retrieved a lot of false hits.

Maybe she would just have to accept that there were some things with no answers, as her mother used to explain innumerable times when she was growing up. The answer didn't satisfy her then, and it wasn't doing such a great job now.

Lauren went back to the handwritten sticky note the appraiser added as a post script to her formal report.

I found your family legend intriguing and would love to learn more. Your inheritance is not the first, as you call it, "fake" I have appraised, but seeing how garnets are semi-precious stones and rank fairly low in value, I think we can safely rule out that one of your ancestors switched the original crystals for paste.

Lauren laughed and dabbed her tears. She was so glad her mother never had known the truth about her prized heirloom.

Chapter 2

Richmond, Indiana, January 1, 2000

"Damn it," Margaret Julian muttered. She wished she had not walked down the narrow hallway and spied the roll top desk that had belonged to her grandparents. Occupying the right corner was evidence of her mortality and altered life, the new will. Her attorney had finished and handed it to her last week along with the strong suggestion to sign and return it by the first work day of the new year. Time to accept that she was a widow was the way he phrased it. Then he added, "You know Mark would have wanted you to."

Her immediate thought was that the nuns had certainly drilled into him a firm grip on the power of guilt. Probably by example was her second. But she agreed, "You're right. I'll be back January second."

She must not put it off any longer. Sitting on the incongruous vanity stool left by the apartment's previous resident, she picked up the large white envelope, held it for a few moments, and put it down. Completing the task was more difficult than she had imagined.

Repeating the attorney's words helped, and she found that her resolve was renewed. A promise was a promise, and she had been reared to honor her word. Besides, signing the will was the first on the list of New Year's resolutions. After she pulled the document from its envelope and wrote her signature, Margaret gave herself an "atta girl." The New Year was well begun. She drew a line through number one on the list taped to the drawer. Now with a clear conscience, she could enjoy the New Year's Day plans she and Emma had made. Three romantic movies that widows of all kinds would enjoy. When their husbands had been alive, she and her friends had joked about being "football widows" on those all important game days. Never once had she ever pictured herself as one.

Knowing what she knew now, would she have changed those game days and stayed home if she could go back and redo it? Have a rewind moment as one woman said in the support group?

Margaret shook her head no and was about to lick the glued flap when she remembered the letters. Her daughters needed to know how she had changed the tradition of passing the paisley shawl and garnet brooch to the oldest daughter. Although her estate would not be worth much, she did want Lauren and Beth to understand the importance of their inheritance. Lauren, as the older, would receive the garnet brooch.

Somehow it seemed unfair that Beth would not receive one of the family heirlooms. So the brooch's companion piece, the paisley shawl, would go to her second daughter.

Dearest Lauren and Beth,

I have left you my most treasured heirlooms. Lauren, I know I am leaving you a mystery along with the garnet brooch. It passed to me, since I was the oldest daughter, from Cousin Marie and her mother, Aunt Betsey. I have no idea who wore it before they did. Garnets aren't worth much these days, and I venture to guess they were not worth a whole lot back whenever this tradition began. For me, the value has been in its history, and I have worn it proudly.

Beth, I have changed the tradition and left you the paisley shawl. I hope you'll enjoy wearing it as much as you will treasure its history. It has always been inherited along with the garnet brooch, as far as I can tell. Like the brooch, its true history is also unknown. When you examine it, you might find the different stitching intriguing. The silk lining has been turned and whipstitched into place by hand while the middle seam was machine-made. Why? The only reason that comes to mind is probably two daughters got in a fight over it. So someone with the wisdom of Solomon divided the shawl in half and turned it into stoles. Funny, though, how the name "shawl" stuck with it, if my guess is right.

I also hope both of you have happy memories of the day the brooch and shawl arrived at the post office. It was such a big deal since it wasn't every day a package came to little old Webster all the way from far away Florida. You would have been ten and eight, and we had a tea party with your aunts and cousins. Do you remember the fun we had that day?

Your loving mother

Chapter 3

Webster, Indiana, June, 1961

"Come on, girls, I have to go to the post office," Margaret untied her apron and called through the screen door.

"Was that Harriet on the phone?" Beth asked.

"Yes, I told her we'd be right down as soon as I unplug the iron. Hurry and put on your shoes and straighten your ponytails. She said I've got something special, addressed just to me, from a David Hotchkiss in Winter Haven, Florida. Come on, I want to get to the post office before anyone else does, especially old nosy Mrs. Hendershott."

"Did you hear Petey?" Lauren asked.

"No," Margaret laughed and wrapped the damped, unironed clothes in a plastic dry cleaning bag for their return to the refrigerator. "I'll sure miss that parakeet's singing when he passes on. That's the only way I know when she's got the receiver plastered to her ear."

Lauren complained, "I can't even hear her breathing."

"Oh, she's good," Margaret agreed. "She can listen on the party line, cook dinner, wash clothes, and watch the street at the same time."

After the girls found their flip-flops under the bed covers, Margaret got them started on the short walk to the post office. Lauren whistled for Fifi to come along. That dog never refused to go with them even though she was at least ten pounds overweight. She gave a small yip of excitement, jumped off the chaise lounge on the porch, and waddled their way.

"What's in the package, Mom?" Lauren asked before the trio cleared the gravel driveway.

"I don't know. I'm not expecting anything."

"Who do you know in Florida?" Beth asked.

"Just Cousin Marie."

"And she died, didn't she?" asked Lauren.

"Yes, it was, let me think, about four months ago," Margaret said.

"Mom," Beth said, "Do you think this guy sent you some money in a big box, like Scrooge McDuck has in the comic books?"

"You're such a baby," Lauren said.

Margaret could see the peaceful walk turning into a moving argument and ruled, "Lauren, that's enough."

Two houses farther on, Margaret caught sight of her sister Miriam's laundry hanging on the clothesline. When Margaret and her daughters got to Mary Rose's house on the corner, she waved at her baby sister who was taking down a load of sheets from the clothesline.

Lauren broke the silence. "Does everyone do laundry on the same day? Is it a law?"

Margaret had never thought about it that way before. "Your grandmother did her wash on Monday. I guess that's why we do it on Monday, too. You'll probably do the same."

"Not me," Beth said, "I'm going to be rich and pay someone to do mine."

"You'll have to have lots of money to get out of housework," Lauren said.

Beth must have had her answer all ready as usual. She didn't hesitate a moment. "I'm gonna marry me a rich Texas oilman."

Margaret laughed. "I guess that's one way. How about you, Lauren? Any changes from last week?"

"Nope, I'm going to be a career woman, a lawyer like Perry Mason. I'll solve cases. In my spare time, I'll train dogs and be Webster's postmistress after Harriet retires."

Margaret knew how her daughter felt about such grand career goals and worried about her. The world just wasn't ready for what her older daughter wanted. "Better stick to the dogs and the mail. Don't see any lady lawyers on the TV, do you?"

"No, but I could be the first one in the county."

"You'd make a good one," Margaret said.

"Yeah, and you could help out my rich husband," Beth added.

A few minutes later, they had walked halfway around the block and reached the center of Webster, the combination post office and general store. The friendly bell jingled over the door when they entered. Margaret was not surprised to find the store empty of customers. The town came to a complete stop from 1:30 to 2:00, the thirty minutes Lisa and Bob of *As the World Turns* held the town's inhabitants hostage.

She inhaled the scent of peaches that lingered by the front counter where half-bushel baskets overflowed with her favorite fruit. Her mouth watered at the thought of peach cobbler, hot and bubbling from the oven, and topped with hand-cranked vanilla ice cream. Maybe this weekend. Not now. They had come for the mysterious package.

Harriet looked up from her *Photoplay* magazine. "Didn't wait to find out about what Lisa's up to, huh?" she said.

Margaret said, "My sisters will tell me all about the carrying-ons in Oakdale."

Harriet took off her store jacket and folded it carefully by the cash register, and Margaret watched Lauren eye the pony express patch on Harriet's sleeve. She knew that horse was one of the main reasons Lauren wanted Harriet's job. The other was the wanted posters, which captivated her daughter every time she came there.

They followed Harriet to the back of the store where the post office was tucked into the space opposite the meat counter. However, on that day, Lauren ignored the posters. Margaret was also relieved she didn't have to tell her to move away from the bank of glass-fronted mailboxes. The girl was so nosy. She'd usually try to crane her neck so she could read the return addresses.

Harriet raised the hinged counter marking the entrance to the post office and reached down to some shelves behind the mailboxes. "Do you think this package is from your cousin?"

Margaret didn't feel like contributing to the gossip pool and gave Harriet her most innocent look. "I won't know for sure until I open it."

Harriet pulled out a small pile of letters held together with a rubber band and a wrapped package the size of a dress box. "Could be connected with your cousin from down there. You remember, you showed me a picture of her leaning on a cane beside her very own orange trees."

Margaret waited. After Harriet put the box on the counter, she retrieved a pair of scissors. "Do you want to cut the string and tape?"

The jingle of the bell caught Margaret's attention. She turned to see Constance Wheeler walk through the door and said no to the offer. Harriet replaced the scissors on the mail counter. Margaret understood why Harriet didn't look too happy when she moved out of the post office and went to wait on Constance at the cash register.

"Come on girls, let's go home," Margaret whispered, and they beat it to the door. "Thanks, Harriet, for your help," she called and waved with her free hand.

Harriet had her store jacket on again and nodded once before the bell signaled their exit. As they retraced their steps toward home, Fifi sniffed one side of the street and then the other.

After they turned the corner by Mary Rose's, Margaret said, "That was sure lucky, girls, Mrs. Wheeler coming in when she did. Harriet didn't have a chance to grill me about what might be in the package. Of course, by two o'clock, everyone in town will know. It's not every day a box arrives all the way from Florida."

"Everyone?" Beth said.

Margaret described how Mrs. Wheeler would scurry out of the store and back across the street like a big spider in a rush to grab her phone in three minutes flat.

"If you listen, you can almost hear the phone wires buzzing. Mrs. Hendershott'll be the first call. Glance at her front window when we walk by. You might even feel her eyes staring a hole right through us."

"Eww, creepy," Lauren said.

"That's small towns for you," Margaret said. "Everybody knows everything. Your grandfather used to tell me that it was real important to get your mail early before your neighbors came in to spy and gossip about you for the rest of the day."

As soon as they walked into the house, Margaret said, "Well, girls, the laundry's not done, and you haven't finished your chores either."

Lauren and Beth gave each other a disappointed look that Margaret could read like a book. They had been hoping she had forgotten about the agreement made earlier in the day. They had promised that their room would be picked up after an hour of play on the front porch.

So she said, "We'll let that go. Today's a special day."

Margaret put the box on the kitchen table, and asked Lauren and Beth, "Do you think I should open it now or wait until Dad comes home?"

"Now," the girls said together without a bit of hesitation as they moved in for a closer inspection.

"Dad can see later," Beth added.

"Okay."

They climbed into chairs at the kitchen table while she took the scissors from the tool drawer. It seemed to take forever, but at last, Margaret had cut through the large amount of tape and stiff brown paper wrapping and had the lid off.

The first thing Margaret saw was an envelope addressed to her. After that, she noticed that a white jewelry box rested on dark fabric with red and yellow threads twirling through it.

"Why, I'll be," she said in a half-whisper. "Cousin Marie remembered her promise after all. She did send me the garnet brooch and paisley shawl."

8

Beth elbowed to get closer first and looked into the pasteboard box. Lauren soon muscled her way in. "Keep the letter for later please," Lauren said. "I want to see what a brooch is."

Margaret opened the box and showed them. The small garnet stars anchored in their gold settings looked the same as when she had seen the brooch on Marie's Christmas picture a few years ago. She held up a pin about as long and thick as her index finger. "Pretty color, isn't it?"

"This is what Cousin Marie promised?" Lauren said, and her tone hinted how disappointed she was.

Beth seemed just as disappointed. "There's no sparkles," she said.

"Lauren," Margaret said, "you take Beth and run to Aunt Miriam's house first and tell her the news. Ask her to come as soon as she can. And then go to Mary Rose's. Tell her about the package and invite her too. I'll mix up some chocolate cupcakes. We'll have a tea party."

Before the cupcakes were out of the oven, her sisters and their children had arrived. Once the babies were plopped down on blankets with enough toys to keep them occupied, Mary Rose, along with Miriam and the older girl cousins, came to the kitchen table and looked over the inheritance.

Miriam, wearing her favorite robin egg blue housedress, asked, "Margaret, goodness gracious, have you seen this pin before?"

Margaret said, "Remember that studio picture Cousin Marie sent for Christmas a few years ago?"

They shook their heads. Both had the same shade of strawberry blonde, but Miriam preferred the French roll made popular by Princess Grace while Mary Rose wore her hair in short ringlets.

"The one where she wore a dark crepe dress and this brooch?" Margaret prodded their memories.

Mary Rose nodded. "I remember that. She looked exactly like what she was, an old maid schoolteacher. A real sourpuss."

Miriam whispered, "You'd be one too, if you had lived her life."

The spark of curiosity in Mary Rose's eyes increased when Margaret said, "Not now, little pitchers have big ears."

Mary Rose nodded and peered into the larger box that contained the shawl. "Did you ever see Cousin Marie wear this?"

"No, I don't think so." Margaret answered.

Mary Rose ran her fingers over the material. "How about her mother ?"

Miriam leaned forward for a closer look and shrugged. "Can't recall ever seeing Cousin Marie or Betsey wearing either one."

"Exactly how are we related to Marie?"

Margaret looked at Miriam who shrugged and said, "All I know is Mom called Marie a shirttail cousin and she and her sister had something called the summer complaint when they were little."

"I thought Mom had mentioned polio. What is summer complaint?" Mary Rose asked.

"Who knows?" Margaret said. "It was the thirties. Spoiled food, bad water, stomach flu. Children got sick and ran temperatures. If they kept vomiting, they got dehydrated or worse. There wasn't a whole lot they could do for children back then. Grams always said we had it easier with our children. What with shots for polio and fluoride and all."

"So no one ever talked about where we came from?" Lauren asked.

Margaret had been so caught up in the family talk that she forgot her previous warning about the children hanging on every word. "No, Grams didn't tell me much." Margaret added as she worked on fastening the brooch to her green blouse. "She refused to give me much more information than her family came from Ohio and Gramps from Indiana. She always preached that the future was what was important, not the past." She wrapped the shawl around her and twisted to show the effect to her sisters. She hoped the girls would be distracted.

Miriam said, "They're not something you'd wear every day."

"No, I agree, especially since the shawl makes me itch. Must be wool."

After Margaret repacked her inheritance in the box, all eyes were on her when she opened the envelope and scanned the letter. A few seconds later she shared the contents. "It's dated May 21st, and he says he's a lawyer and has been a friend of Cousin Marie for years. They attended the same church. As a kindness to her, he agreed to honor her instructions and sent these heirlooms as a bequest."

Margaret looked up from the letter and said, "How sad, seems she didn't have enough assets for an estate."

"How those lawyers talk," Mary Rose snorted and gave her curls a little shake. "Takes them twenty words to say something most normal people can say in five. What he meant was he sent these things himself because Cousin Marie was poorer than a church mouse."

Miriam looked at her and rolled her eyes. Margaret decided to change the topic and said, "All her remaining personal items such as clothing and books went to the church for their annual rummage sale."

"Did he say anything about the brooch and shawl?" Miriam said.

"Not much. Marie had told him that they had been in the family for some time, and she wished to follow the tradition of passing them on to the oldest daughter. Since she was childless and I'm now the oldest female cousin, they're mine. That's all."

Margaret started the letter around to her sisters. "I'm glad she had some good friends and wasn't lonely down there in Florida without any family around."

"Too bad Cousin Marie didn't tell any of us what she knew," Miriam said.

Lauren squirmed in her seat and blurted, "Maybe she did leave some clues like in the movies or mystery books. But her friends missed them, and now all of her stuff is gone."

Margaret thought it was time for the kids to leave the table so the grown-ups could talk, especially about her brother Tim's wedding invitation that arrived in today's mail. Evidently her sisters hadn't seen theirs yet. Mary Rose could never keep news to herself, and Miriam would have been crying over his announcement that he was staying in California after his twenty years were up. The news was going to break their hearts. Through the years, the three of them had concocted scheme after scheme to get him to return to Webster. Was he still upset over that horrible argument she had with Poppa? Time to let that go. It was water under the bridge.

Margaret sensed from his letter that his fiancé had a lot to do with the decision although he did mention he couldn't see how he'd ever return to the gray skies and snow-drifted roads of Indiana. She wished she remembered the name of the girl he brought with him last year for Mom's funeral. The last name sounded something like MacDonald, maybe? No, that wasn't right. She'd ask Miriam and Mary Rose if the name McConkey on the invitation was also that girl's name.

What upset her the most was he was marrying so soon. There was no way she could save up enough money in six weeks to buy a plane ticket to California, and she knew her sisters couldn't either. The three of them were selling Avon to help pay off the medical and funeral expenses for their parents. "Girls, go wash your hands and sprinkle the powdered sugar on the cupcakes before you all go have your tea party on the front porch."

Marie Hussong circa 1960

Chapter 4

Webster and Richmond, 1947

Engagement and Wedding Announcements

Mr. and Mrs. Russell Dakin of Webster, Indiana are proud to announce the engagement of their daughter, Margaret Castella Dakin to Mr. Mark Stephen Julian, son of Mrs. Martha Julian and the late Mr. Stephen Julian of 614 Kinsey Street, Richmond, Indiana.

Miss Dakin, a 1944 graduate of Webster High School, is a secretary at the Gifford Insurance Agency here in Richmond.

Mr. Julian graduated from Richmond High School in 1943 and has served in the Royal Air Force, Canadian Branch, from 1942 to the present.

Upon returning to civilian life, he will join the NATCO Company, Richmond, Indiana.

The wedding ceremony and reception will be held June 7, 1947 at the Julian residence. Service begins at 2:30; reception is set for 3:30.

The happy couple's residence will be 614 Kinsey Street after a wedding trip to Cincinnati, Ohio.

Palladium-Item, April 23, 1947, Section B, p. 2.

Chapter 5

Webster, Winter and Spring, 1944

<Hattie and Robert Brown
<Castella and Russell Dakin
Margaret, Miriam, & Mary Rose

The emptiness in the house gnawed at Margaret. It had a living, breathing presence because suddenly her brother Tim had shipped out. Since they were only eleven months apart, Irish twins as Grandma Hattie put it, Tim had used his older brother status to be her agitator and protector. Sometimes at the same time. Now she didn't quite know how to navigate her world without him.

Margaret hoped she could ease her loneliness by doing more for the war effort. The family already saved soap slivers in jars, used saccharine, and canned the crops from their victory garden. She also volunteered to roll bandages for the Red Cross. However, it didn't come close to what her brother had signed on to do.

When she noticed the WAC recruitment flyer at the post office, it was the slogan that touched her. Not the model's smart khaki uniform and matching hat. The phrase "I'm in This War Too" reached into her head and heart and whispered her name. The uniformed woman pointed to a service flag with such pride and determination that Margaret transposed herself into the scene, down to her auburn pageboy and short stature that had no curves. So that night, she made her announcement at the kitchen table.

What Margaret had imagined would happen, proud looks from her parents and tears from Miriam and Mary Rose, didn't take place. Instead, her sisters stared at her with worshipful eyes. Momma flew from her chair so quickly, it tipped and banged on the floor. Poppa pounded the table with his fist, and the water glasses teetered.

His shouts erupted at a volcanic level. "Do you think I'm out of my mind? There's no way in hell you'll ever step foot on an army base with all those men. Where for Christ's sake, do you get these hare-brained ideas of yours?"

Margaret, undeterred by his wrath, met him head on. "Poppa, it's my war too."

His face turned bright red as he leaned toward her. "What a load of crap. Nice girls don't do things like that."

"But..." was all she got out before he gave her the look that meant no backtalk.

"Don't you 'but' me. End of discussion." He picked up his knife and fork. "Now go tell your mother you've regained your senses."

Margaret glared at him. He said nothing more and only pointed toward the door with his knife. She seethed as she obeyed. That man was always telling her what to do. But soon she would be a high school graduate and could make her own decisions.

A few months later, the perfect plan fell into Margaret's lap. While she listened to the Civil Service recruiter during advanced bookkeeping class, it came in a flash that she didn't need her father's permission to take the test and she didn't have to ask him for any money to take it either. Best of all, she could serve her country once she earned a passing grade. The recruiter promised jobs, even careers, in government offices in exciting places like sunny California and powerful Washington, D.C. But doubt soon set in. She might not be good enough.

Her teacher, Mrs. Reed, must have read the indecision on her face because the older woman pulled Margaret aside and said, "You're the only one who can do justice to that test. You need to sign up for it right away. I know you'll earn a high score." Mrs. Reed pushed up her glasses and gave a brisk nod. "I have a lot of confidence in you."

"I don't think I can do it." The whole idea of a national test intimidated Margaret. "I'll never score high enough."

"You're the best business student I've ever had in thirty-seven years of teaching. You can do it."

"I don't know." Margaret twisted a strand of hair and considered. She wanted to take that test so bad she could just cry. How good was she? Besides, it would be one way to show her father what she could do.

Mrs. Reed said, "Look at it this way. You take the test and do well, and you will have an offer to work in Washington, D.C. If you don't take the job, you can always use your test score when you apply for jobs in Richmond after you graduate."

Richmond did not sound as glamorous as the nation's capitol. But it was better than Webster. "I guess I could try."

"Good. I will proctor the test for you and the other senior girls. Trust me; I'm sure you'll have a high score."

On February 25th, she took the test. It was nowhere as hard as Mrs. Reed's first semester final. Though Margaret had no idea why the federal government asked the questions they did. Especially why she had to figure out how long it would take two families traveling by train from opposite directions on the same track and at different rates of speed to meet. She had no desire to work as a railroad dispatcher.

Margaret gave her exam paper a starring role in the movie in her mind and wished it a fast journey. First, it rested snug in its envelope in the dirty white canvas mailbag with the drawstring securely locked. Next, it left the Webster post office and waited for the freight conductor to hook the mailbag as the eastbound morning train to Cincinnati slowed at the town's railroad crossing. Cincinnati was the first city that came to mind. It was the largest one she had ever been to when one summer a few years ago, they had all piled into the car for a family reunion and headed there.

After Cincinnati, the easterly route to Washington, D. C. got a little murky. A quick check of the atlas in the school library gave her the rest of the way through Ohio, Pennsylvania, and Maryland to D.C. and the return trip to Webster.

March dragged its heels. Every day she had walked into the kitchen after school with her sisters and gave a quick glance at the mail stacked by her father's place at the table. By March 31st, she still had not heard, and her mood darkened.

When April was almost over and there had still been no reply, Margaret surrendered to her fate. She'd never leave Webster. Either her results had gotten lost, or else she had failed, and the government didn't even bother to send a letter.

On the last Friday in April, Margaret won the race with her sisters through the back door and noticed her mother standing by the head of the table with her arms folded. She wore her worried look.

"Tim, is it Tim?" Margaret asked.

Miriam wailed, and tears pooled. "He got sent overseas?"

Margaret saw her mother's worried eyes lock on her. "It's not Tim, it's you."

Was she in trouble? Margaret's memory played through the past few days of school and came up blank. When she glanced around the kitchen, she read the word OFFICIAL blazed near the postmark on the letter by her mother's hand, and her heart soared.

Momma rubbed her forehead. "What'd you do? You didn't go and try and join the army, did you? Poppa and I didn't sign no such papers."

"No, that's not it. Momma, let me see what it says."

Margaret watched while her mother considered. Poppa always opened the important mail but this was different. The letter had her name, Miss Margaret C. Dakin, on the envelope.

At last, Momma handed it over. Miriam and Mary Rose crowded around her as Margaret read the words "For United States Government Business Only."

She ripped open the envelope and slid out the letter that held her future. At the end of the first paragraph, the words "pleased to offer you a position with the Civil Service Commission" leapt from the paper and left her feeling lightheaded.

"I passed, I really passed." Margaret held the letter high. Miriam and Mary Rose danced around her. "I can't wait to tell Mrs. Reed. She was right after all."

Miriam said, "You did it. We knew you would. You're going to Washington."

Mary Rose caught the chant. "Washington, Washington, here you come."

The three girls reached for their mother and tried to include her in the celebration, but she shooed their hands away.

"Girls, be still. Stop that foolishness right now. What do you mean, you passed? Margaret Castella, look at me. What have you gone and done?"

Margaret and her sisters fell silent before their mother whose face had paled against her dark home-permed hair, making her look older. She swayed a little before she wilted into a kitchen chair.

Momma said, "I can't bear it if you leave. I've lost Tim to the war. I don't want to lose you too."

Margaret slipped into the nearest chair. She had to make her mother see how important this was in her life. She would just die if she couldn't leave Webster. "Momma, that's not fair. I'm not going to war. Washington is safe. You should be proud of me. Think of how the government needs me."

Her mother shook her head. "Why do they want you? You're from this dinky little town."

"Because I'm good, Momma. I'm really good at typing and bookkeeping. Just like Mrs. Reed said. You know I get straight A's in all my classes. I've got the typing record for the school, and not for just this year. I'm the best typist the school's ever had."

"Webster's not the real world." Momma pointed to the window. "What's good here isn't that good out there."

"See, I've got proof, here, look." Margaret shoved the Civil Service results towards her mother. "I'm good enough for Washington."

"You can explain it to your father, girl." Momma let out a withered sigh and stood. When she moved toward the stove, it seemed to Margaret that the weight of world had crushed her mother.

"You didn't stop at Mrs. Hendershott's and call him at the plant, did you?" Margaret worried aloud.

Momma said over her shoulder, "Didn't have to. You know how fast news travels in this town."

Margaret understood at once. "Today's payday," she squeaked, and her throat grew tight.

"That's right, he'll know the moment he steps foot in the general store to pay down the bill and get his cigarette paper and tobacco." Momma clanged the spoon against the pot of creamed corn.

Her mother's words hung in the kitchen and left Margaret stunned. Before she could review once more her plan to deal with Poppa, she heard the car's tires spew gravel. He was home.

Poppa charged through the back door, his blue twill uniform stained with sweat, his black metal lunch box in his left hand. Everything about him telegraphed anger. His face flared a bright color. The red hair in his crew cut seemed to stand on end. Silently, he pointed his index finger directly at her and jabbed the air in short, hostile movements. His eyes glared.

"What the hell did you do, young woman?" Poppa shouted before the door slammed shut behind him. "I'm telling you right now you'll never enlist. You're not going anywhere. End of argument." He struck the kitchen table with the lunch box for emphasis.

"Poppa, I didn't enlist. I'm not joining the army..." Margaret tried to explain over her father's words.

"I heard you got a letter from Washington, marked Government Business. Hand it over now."

Margaret passed the letter with pride. "You'll see it's my scores for the Civil Service exam. I'm good enough to go to Washington and serve my country."

Poppa transferred the paper to his left hand before he pulled a pair of glasses out of his front shirt pocket and jammed them on. After he scanned the letter, he wadded it into a ball and threw it on the floor. Crestfallen, Margaret watched the most important mail of her life roll to a stop on the yellow linoleum.

She pleaded, "You don't understand, Poppa. I want to help in the war effort. You know I'm old enough. Besides I'm every bit as patriotic as Tim."

Margaret watched her father's face grow even redder and worried he might have an attack of some kind and keel over.

The volume of his voice rose even higher. "No daughter of mine is going to live in such a godless city. You have no business working that far from home."

"The Civil Service recruiter explained it's important. Everyone has to do their share. That's what I'll be doing, my fair share."

Poppa glared and tried to interrupt, but Margaret had rehearsed this speech so many times. Her words were so logical she felt no rational person could possibly disagree. "There's not enough people to work for the government since so many boys have joined up. My country needs me. I'll be getting paid a good wage too. I can send some money home to help out. And think of the future, Poppa. After the war, I come back, I can have any office job I want. Because I'll have more experience than all the other girls."

"You're not going. That's all there is to it. You have no business out there all alone. Why off you'll go, and the first thing you know you'll be in trouble. Soon you'll come back here and want us to help raise your bastard."

"Russell," Momma moaned. He dismissed her with a wave of his hand and kept his eyes nailed on Margaret.

"But," Margaret couldn't believe how stubborn he was.

"Don't you but me. You're not used to the real world. It's a cruel place, not like Webster. Lots of men, young and old, just lay in wait for young innocent girls like you to get off the train. They're fast-talking strangers, and believe me, they'll move on once they get what they want. You'll be another notch in their belts."

His words shocked her. He had never talked to her that way before. Margaret tried to think of a comeback when he took a deep breath.

He got there before her. "Is that what you want, to be one more girl in a long string of fools? Answer me."

"No, but…"

"But nothing, who'd marry you after they knew you've become a loose woman. I won't have it, and that's my final word on the subject."

Poppa stomped past her. Margaret, however, was not finished. Two different thoughts raced in side by side tracks. She had thought she really wanted to go to Washington. It sounded so exciting to finally get out of this one-block town. At the same time, she wanted to tell her father she didn't even know if she wanted to leave. The important thing was she had proven how good she was.

Margaret knew she was all grown-up. She would graduate next week. She was old enough to decide what was best for her. Even if that meant leaving her family. Anger along with pride took over. She would not back down.

"What do you mean I can't go to Washington? You don't understand. I passed the Civil Service Exam," she shouted at him.

Margaret knew it was a mistake the instant the words flew out of her mouth. The way his eyes squinted and his mouth went straight told her she had gone too far.

"Margaret Castella Dakin, you know I don't hold with talking back in this house. If I've told you once, I've told you a thousand times. As long as you live under my roof and eat my food, you'll do what I say."

"I'm going to Washington, and you can't stop me." Despite her brave words, Margaret realized that she had just stepped off a cliff.

Poppa folded his arms and smirked. "And how are you getting there?" His words were so cold she shivered. "Money doesn't grow on trees. You're not getting any of my hard-earned cash."

"You didn't talk this way to Tim. You were proud of him and even took him to the tavern for a beer. I heard you brag to the neighbors after his uniform picture arrived. Why can't it be the same for me?"

"He's a man. You're a girl. And," he leaned closer to her, "just so you know, you leave this house, you can't come back. I won't have you corrupting your sisters."

Her heart constricted. Margaret went past red-hot rage. Somehow, she had moved to ice-cold anger, a land in her personal geography undiscovered until that moment.

She blurted, "I won't stay here then."

When Margaret heard her mother and sisters gasp, she ignored them. "I'll go live with Grams and Gramps, get a job, and save up enough money to get to Washington. I don't need your money or your permission. I'll get there one way or the other, and you can't stop me."

"All I've got to say is good riddance," Poppa snorted and stomped to the stove for some coffee.

A miserable week limped by, and guilt buried Margaret. She regretted her mother's pain. Momma withdrew the minute Poppa walked in every night and filled the house with tension. More than once Margaret had heard her mother whisper a plea for the Lord to give her strength when her second child left home.

The worst was supper, the only time all of them were together. Every minute stretched to an hour. Poppa refused to talk or even look at her. Margaret had no appetite and picked at the food in stony silence while her father ignored the silent undercurrents eddying around the table. He talked about his day at the factory. No one else spoke unless he spoke to her first. Momma ate a few bites between dabbing her eyes and nose. Miriam and Mary Rose hurried through their meals. When the evening chores were finished, they pleaded schoolwork and spent every spare minute in their bedroom.

Two nights before school let out, Margaret lay in the bed she shared with her sisters. The evening had gone the same as the others had. She struggled to find sleep. Remorse over what the family had endured battered her core, yet her resolve didn't weaken. However, her anger had stilled enough that she could think instead of react.

Once more, she ran through the argument and decided, yet again, that is was all her father's fault. His words had backed her into a corner.

On second thought, Margaret realized that wasn't quite true and turned onto her side in frustration. She had to admit she was too hotheaded. Everyone always said she was a chip off the old block when it came to matching her father's anger. In the past, Tim had always jollied them out of their disagreements.

The thought of Tim brought her to tears, and she eased out of bed. She moved to the window and looked at the moonlit cornfield across the road. She prayed he was safe. The cornstalks stood as silent, still sentinels and offered no peace. So she took another view of the argument and examined it as if she was above the scene in the kitchen. From that perch, she could at last see what had niggled at her brain all week.

Without her brother there, she and her father had revealed sides she didn't know existed. It had gone beyond stubbornness. Something unknown lurked under their anger and spite and made her squirm.

Margaret backed off from that last line of thought. It was too scary. But she had to accept that the awful argument would remain forever unresolved and unforgotten. How could she ever forgive her father?

Yet the hope lingered that he regretted threatening to banish her. Maybe he'd take back his words and their life might be normal again.

The next morning when she looked at Poppa, much like she had examined her bookkeeping practice sets, he didn't seem to have any remorse or second thoughts. Her heart broke. He had watched her grow up and was supposed to love her. Her hope that he might retreat melted. Her resolve strengthened. She could be just as stubborn as he was.

The evening before graduation, the conversation between her parents rose so loud she heard them through the bedroom wall.

"Russ, please give Margaret a chance to say she's sorry," Momma said.

"That girl is too headstrong for her own good. I can't back down now. She'll take it as a sign of weakness, and the next time it will be something even worse than this Civil Service crap," he snarled.

"Can't you see, it's tearing me apart. I don't want to lose her too."

"She has to learn her place, otherwise she won't be a fit wife."

"I haven't asked much of you in all these years. Can't you, just this one time, meet her halfway, for me?"

"Don't ask me that, Cassie. She's made her bed, now she has to lay in it."

Margaret heard the bedsprings squeak and her father say he had wasted enough breath on the subject. He needed his sleep. Unlike some people, he had to work the next day. Soon his snores rolled over her mother's hushed sobs.

Sleep eluded Margaret as her mind weighed different solutions. Her mother had hinted earlier in the day that Poppa might accept an apology. However, Margaret felt if she caved in, she'd never have any power in her life again.

The reality was that tomorrow night the last train would carry her to her grandparents' house in Richmond if she and Poppa didn't mend their rift. From then on, her mother would eat every meal with another empty place at the table.

Visions of her future sped through her mind. Margaret would be a ghost at the family dinners with her sisters and their husbands and children. Her wedding, the birth of her children, all the Christmases would be so lonely without her family. It would be like they were dead. It didn't seem possible that one outburst could cause this much damage. Her words weren't that terrible. The heavy price of her banishment weighed upon her and crushed her heart. Her father had cut himself and her mother out of her life. How could he fail to see what he had thrown away? Or didn't he care?

And how about Momma? How could she live with that man? Could she ever forgive him for driving their daughter out of the house?

Right then and there, she vowed that her marriage would be different. She would not put up with any kind of hurt and stubbornness. No man was worth it.

The next afternoon, Margaret had almost finished packing when her mother came into the small bedroom where movie star photos covered the pink and green floral wallpaper. Pictures of school friends edged the mirror of the waterfall dressing table. Margaret caught her mother's glance at the empty spots on the wallpaper where her pictures of Frank Sinatra had recently hung. The raw pain in Momma's eyes forced her to look away. She continued to fold her clothes into the open suitcase on the bed, which lowered where Momma eased herself down.

"Margaret, are you sure? You don't have to leave. Remember your father just wants what's best for you. He wants to keep you safe."

Margaret straightened and crossed her arms over her chest. "He wants to control me and keep me a child."

Momma slowly inhaled and let her breath out. "I'm not saying you're not all grown-up. Come on. Sit down here beside me, so we can talk." She patted the bed.

As Margaret joined her mother, she said, "There's nothing to talk about. My mind's made up. It's not fair. Boys like Tim ship out all the time."

"You have to understand one thing. Tim would've been drafted soon. They told him if he enlisted he had a better chance of fixing airplanes. Maybe even staying stateside."

"But he and other boys can get hurt or even die, and no one says they can't go. If I was a boy, Poppa would've taken me out for a beer like he did with Tim. You know it's true."

"Girls don't get drafted. It's not the same."

She weighed the truth in her mother's words. "Okay, I won't get drafted. But I've got just as much right to do what I want. That's what the Bill of Rights says. And," she paused before going on, "I don't want to live in Poppa's house anymore."

Tears spilled down her face and made her angrier. Margaret turned away. "It's not right that he gets to make all the decisions."

"The Bill of Rights and the pursuit of happiness have nothing to do with you getting to decide where you want to live." After a heartbeat

24

Momma continued. "Your father works hard to provide for you and your sisters. That gives him the right to some say so. He gets up every morning and goes to work. It's hard work too. Work you and I can't do."

Margaret turned back and saw tears join the pain in her mother's eyes. Momma went on, "I'm not sure I agree all the way with your father on everything. Sometimes just one person gets to decide. Since he's the man of the house, your father has that right."

"You live here too, Momma. Why can't you have the say so?"

"It's not like that. Maybe some day, just not now. All I know is men have always been in charge." Her mother held up her hand like a policeman and said, "I'm not saying that's the way things should be. It's just the way it is. Someday when you've married, you'll know it too."

"No, I won't." Margaret stood and put her hands on her hips. "I'll never marry a man who won't let me make my own decisions. When I have children, I will tell my daughters they can do the same things their brothers get to do. It's not fair that girls get told no all the time. It's just not fair."

Momma rose and hugged her. "You're fortunate that Grams wrote you can live with her and Gramps. You be a good girl and don't cause any trouble for them."

"She said I'll have the same rules you had. She said unmarried girls have to be careful."

"Those were good rules."

Margaret disagreed with her mother's wisdom. Times had changed since her mother had been young, but to keep the peace, she said, "Those are the only rules she knows, and she said they worked when you were my age."

"Do you have enough money?"

"Yes, I've saved a little, and Miriam loaned me some from her piggy bank. I've got enough for the train ticket."

"You'll write me that you got there okay? And every week to let me know how you're doing?" Margaret, too broken up to speak, nodded faintly.

Momma reached into the pocket of her yellow floral housedress. "I had put a little back in the egg money jar. Here's eighteen dollars." She folded wrinkled bills and change into Margaret's hand. Shame over her mother's generosity took her breath away. Margaret wondered how long Momma had scrimped to save that much.

She looked from the money to her mother. However, Momma had already started for the door with heavy steps and her head down.

When the door closed, Margaret realized she'd need courage to face day-to-day life without her mother's support. She didn't know what the next day would bring and tried to picture tomorrow and failed. Scared, all at once she knew she was responsible for the situation. No one else was to blame.

Chapter 6

UNITED STATES
DEPARTMENT OF DEFENSE
OFFICE OF THE SECRETARY
WASHINGTON

April 26, 1944
Miss Margaret C. Dakin
P. O. Box 44
Webster, Indiana

Dear Miss Dakin:

The War Office is pleased to offer you a position as a typist and stenographer with the Civil Service Commission, grade GS 1, $5.76 per diem.

Margaret C. Dakin   ID# 39609127-90045
Typing   70 WPM   2 errors
Dictation 130 WPM 1 error
Total score   95.9

Report for duty June 16, 1944 at The Willard, 1401 Pennsylvania Avenue, NW at 8:45 a.m.

Enclosed are a personal history statement, an oath of office, and a personal information sheet. These are to be notarized and returned to this office by June 15, 1944.

Also enclosed is a list of suggested boarding houses.

Sincerely,

Robert W. Reader

Robert W. Reader
First Assistant Secretary

RWS:cl
Enclosure 56903521865

Chapter 7

Richmond, Indiana, June 1944

<Hattie and Robert Brown
<Castella and Russell Dakin
Margaret Dakin

Hattie Brown shifted her weight to ease the lumbago gnawing on her right side and yelled up the stairs at her granddaughter. "Margaret, your curling irons are past done. Get down here and get 'em off my stove. You hear me, girl?"

"Yes, in a few minutes."

"No, now. I need the stove for your grandfather's supper. You know he wants his food on the table the minute he walks through the door."

Drained from the heat, Hattie tugged at her housedress, damp and clinging. Perspiration trickled down her hairline, and she took a few more swipes at her forehead with Robert's work handkerchief.

She smiled as she remembered her own grandfather's words. "Remember, Hattie," he had said when she was about twelve and complained about the sweat pouring down her face, "Horses sweat, men perspire, and ladies glow." She laughed at the memory of having the same conversation with Castella.

Her good mood lowered a few notches though when she saw the withered lilac bushes through the front window. The newspaper had predicted that June would break all temperature records, including last year's drought. She didn't understand how they could know about those things, yet the evidence sat right out there, growing more pitiful by the day.

Maybe next year, if she was still on the good side of the sod, she'd have their perfume back in her house. For the first spring she could remember in all her married life of over four decades, each room had to do without the fresh lilac scent she so enjoyed.

Fatigue and pain regrouped and overtook her. She shook her head in disgust and muttered, "What do you expect?" She leaned against the newel post in hopes that the ache would magically go away. "I'm sixty-four years old, thank you very much, and being tired is just part of being sixty-four."

When the next bead of perspiration dripped off a loose strand, she didn't even try to smooth her hair. By nine o'clock that morning she had given up on keeping the frizz from her coiled braid. It seemed the humidity made her hair worse each year. Probably because the gray was setting in so fast. She recalled her mother's hair had done the same.

Hattie tried to ignore the next rivulet that took the same path as the last and reviewed all she had done that day. She'd put up twenty-five jars of strawberry jam, cold-packed two chickens Robert had taken in trade for the work on Jim Snedicker's old '38' Dodge Coupe, baked two pies, and washed and stretched Mrs. Westcott's fancy Irish lace parlor curtains.

Those curtains were probably the culprit that had done her back in, but she needed the money. It was a bald fact that business at the service station was never going to improve. Robert's eyesight would soon be gone, and the only customers left were his faithful ones. Moreover, the war had turned them into misers with their gas and tire rations.

Hattie returned to the moment and cocked her head to listen. Drat. Margaret hadn't moved a bit. "Young lady, don't make me come up there."

"Please, just a few minutes more."

"I'm done talking. It's too hot. You'll just have to be the one to deal with your grandfather."

Hattie gave the drooping lilacs one more scornful glance and returned to the kitchen where she moved the curling irons off the burner and put the new potatoes on to boil. As she wiped the counter, her rant about taking the girl in hadn't even built to a full head of steam before guilt gave her pause. After all, each of the four grandchildren knew she treasured them. Yet having Margaret underfoot was more than Hattie had bargained for. She felt responsible even though the girl had graduated. Nevertheless, Hattie had to remember all that spark had come from Russell Dakin's side and not from the Browns or Garretts.

The older woman had tried to make Robert understand how Margaret's moving in had made life difficult. She thought she had done a good job of it the night Margaret and her friends, with their carrying ons, had driven her out of her own home to the front porch. "It's just not the money for her keep. Those friends of hers are more than I bargained for. I got used to Emma. She's been visiting Margaret since they were knee high to a grasshopper. Franny has just made it worse. The three of them giggle and whisper all the time. They run around all hours night and day, in and out the front door, up and down the stairs, making such a hullabaloo that I can't hear myself think straight. Why can't they do that at their own folks' homes? Why didn't their mothers teach them to walk like ladies? Those girls don't glide. They sound like a herd of elephants charging on my stairs."

He sat there patiently and waited until she had wound down a bit. "She did get a job," he said in Margaret's defense.

"True, but those girls mess up things when they get fixed up to go out. What with curling their hair in the kitchen and leaving makeup in the bathroom sink. The worst is their dancing to the radio in the parlor. And they call that Frank Sinatra a singer? The three of them sing and jump around in the parlor and shake my glassware something fierce. It's not ladylike."

Robert chose that moment to bring up some examples of her youthful foolishness. His favorite was her streetcar rides, and Hattie had to stop her rant and laugh.

Perspiration dripped from her scalp, and Hattie reminded herself that she had work to do and couldn't lollygag. However, the memory of those rides made her stop wiping the table. She gazed at her ankles. They looked about as sorry as her hair and the lilacs.

But oh, when she was young. Her ankles were reputed to be the tiniest in town, and she'd show them off once a month at Fourth and Main. The boys would cluster on the corner for a peek when she'd lift her skirt a bit higher than she needed to and place her foot on the lower step to board the streetcar. She chuckled when she thought of how she'd forgo penny candy after school in order to save enough money to buy the tickets.

The lid on the potatoes rattled and brought her out of her reverie. She turned the flame down and winched with each step as she returned to the base of the stairs to yell at her granddaughter. "Margaret, don't make me climb up there. Answer me."

"I'm on my way."

Hattie heard Margaret take her time as she walked toward the head of the stairs. Horsefeathers, the girl still had that infernal hairbrush in her hand. Hattie watched her count each brush stroke as she came down the steps.

The girl would be the death of her yet.

"Two hundred thirty-nine, two hundred forty. I have to be ready when Emma and Franny get here."

"You make sure you get something to eat before you go. The prices they charge for refreshments at those places is nothing short of highway robbery. It's a-"

"A racket," Margaret spoke over her and continued the count.

"Glad you see it for what it is. You just eat here and save your money."

At the three hundredth stroke, the girl turned her long chestnut hair into a pageboy and pocketed the brush in her blue housecoat.

"I promise," Margaret said with a smile that melted her grandmother's heart and mood. "We'll probably go to the Blue Note. Maybe there'll be some cute boys who can dance and won't chew gum in my ear and talk, talk, talk. I just want to have a really good time tonight."

After Margaret picked up the curling irons, she gave Hattie a quick peck on the cheek and hummed on her way back upstairs.

"Not too good of a time, young lady," Hattie called after her. "You better watch out for those roamin' soldiers. And I don't mean the ones from Italy. I hear you laughing at me. You know what I mean. They can't keep their hands to themselves."

"And I also promise to stay away from those rushin' soldiers too," Margaret got in the last word.

Hattie moved on to set the table. The banter about soldiers brought back thoughts of those young men she'd loved and known before the Big War. She almost dropped a water glass when her memories led to her only grandson, Tim, and worries about him swept over her. As with every other time she thought of Tim in danger, her heart skipped a beat.

Thank God, he was still safe at Patterson Air Force Base and had not met the same fate as those wounded soldiers she saw come to church every Sunday. They all had eyes that hinted they'd seen much too much for their young years. At least they had returned home to their families.

Hattie knew that good manners called for her to ask about their service tours, but her courage didn't extend that far anymore. Too many painful stories.

Her customers shared their news and stories when they came in for their weekly Marcel wave set. Ida Lancaster's was the most haunting. Her son Wiley's plane was shot down behind enemy lines in France, and it was weeks before Ida learned his fate. The young man had survived though he was still recovering from burns over most of his body.

While the wives and mothers drank tea in her kitchen and waited for their hair to dry, they told how they pulled back their curtains when they heard a strange car make its way down the street. If it was the black sedan from the War Department, they were ashamed that they'd held their breath and willed the car to pass by and stop on another block.

Every time Hattie heard one of these stories, she imagined the heart-stopping terror the women must have experienced when the car parked and two uniformed strangers got out. To stand by their windows and watch the soldiers walk to their front doors called for its own kind of courage.

A courage familiar to her because even after all of these years, memories of her brother Charles still colored her opinions about war and sacrifice.

Upstairs, Margaret pressed some pancake powder to a shiny spot on her forehead while she sat at the old dressing table she had painted white and skirted with some second-hand lace curtains. She did love her grandma, even though the old woman came off a little gruff at times. Margaret realized how lucky she was to have a place to go after that terrible argument with her father.

Actually things had turned out really swell. She worked with Emma every day, and the two of them included Franny in their running around after the new girl had started at the insurance office a few weeks ago. Margaret also realized her plans had changed. Her job was supposed to have been the first step in saving enough money to get to the Civil Service in Washington. But that had been before George and his letters.

Hattie got up from the table when a knock on the front door disturbed their dinner. Maybe by the time she got back, Robert would have moved off his complaint about having no new inner tubes for John Wheeler's car. Wiping her hands on a dishtowel, she headed toward the hall. She could hear Margaret's friends on the front stoop and snorted at the noise as she opened the door.

"I knew you were out here even before you knocked," Hattie said to Emma and Franny. "All that giggling and shrieking."

She took a bit of pleasure when the girls looked a tad crestfallen.

"Don't you know it's six o'clock and still dinner time in decent peoples' homes? Mr. Brown likes to eat in peace and quiet."

"Yes, Mrs. Brown, we're sorry," they said in unison.

"Now get in here and don't you be messing up my house. Margaret's already set the bathroom to rights. And don't go bothering Mr. Brown. He's enjoying his pie."

They didn't even stop to greet him and rushed upstairs in a swirl of black and white skirts and petticoats. Despite her annoyance, Hattie did have to admit they looked real smart in their cotton sundresses and matching black and white spectator pumps.

Margaret chided herself for taking so long to make up her mind and chose the new rhinestone earrings. She checked them out in the mirror and nodded. No doubt about it, they made her look sophisticated and at least two years older.

The quick steps on the stairs told her Franny and Emma had arrived. The door opened, and her visitors bounced into the small bedroom. Emma, thin as a rail, full of giggles, and constantly in motion. Even her bright red curls seemed never to still. Franny was the opposite in so many ways, sedate, slow to anger, pleasingly plump, with brown straight hair that refused to hold any wave or curl. Margaret had at first thought that Franny was shy until she saw her wait on some elderly customers with more patience than a saint and recalled that her new friend was an only child born to parents late in life.

The girls dodged the iron bed covered with a white chenille bedspread and made a beeline to the dark chest. Margaret smiled from the stool in front of her mirror as her friends sorted through the perfume samples she willingly shared. She had so many since Grams' friends worked at the dime store and passed samples along with a wink and smile.

"You know, we gotta wear the same, so we don't smell like Jarrett's front door. I almost get sick every time I walk in there. All those different scents in the air upset my stomach something awful," said Franny.

"Why is it that a high class place like that puts perfume right there?" Margaret said.

"I just love Jarrett's," Emma laughed and took the lid off another bottle and sniffed. An impish smile marched over her face. "Remember, Margaret, when for your thirteenth birthday, we got a full makeup session at the Max Factor counter?"

"Yeah, we sprayed every tester in the place on our arms and necks," Margaret said, "and we thought we were all grown-up?.

"Your grandmother didn't," Emma stage-whispered.

The image of her grandmother's face that Saturday afternoon made Margaret smile. "She said we looked and smelled like two-bit whores and then had to explain to us what a whore was after we asked."

"And that they only charged a quarter?" Emma giggled.

"Yep, I guess we did grow up that day," Margaret said. The girls dissolved in laughter.

"Let's wear Evening in Paris. It comes in such a beautiful bottle," Franny suggested. "It's possible that someday we might get to see the Eiffel Tower."

The other two girls agreed and dabbed the samples on their wrists, throat, and behind their knees.

"Take care you don't smudge your seams." Margaret cast a meaningful glance at her friends' legs and the lines drawn with eyebrow pencil. "I'm down to my last pencil, and it has to last until next payday."

She inspected her own leg makeup. The lines still looked straight and solid. "I'm so mad at you two," she tried to keep a stern tone in her voice. "You're both dressed to the nines. You changed after work. Now I can't go out wearing the same blouse and skirt I wore today. I look like an old maid school teacher next to you two." Margaret made her face take on a sour, pinched look.

Emma looked at Franny and laughed. "Mom ironed this dress for me today and-"

Margaret interrupted, "You're all decked out in new shoes too? Where did you get enough ration cards to buy them?"

Emma shook her head. "I didn't. Mom let me wear hers so I'd match Franny. Put on your graduation shoes and a snazzy sundress. It's gonna be real hot in there tonight."

"Nuts, I'll have to redo all my makeup, even the lipstick," Margaret said.

Franny looked at her wristwatch. "Not enough time."

"We gotta leave soon, you know," Emma said. "No way we're getting to the Blue Note last again. I want first dibs on the new dreamboats."

"Okay." Margaret gazed at her friends and understood their hope of finding some really cute boys.

She undid her blouse and skirt, and after folding them on the bed, she pulled a brown and white polka-dot church dress from the small closet. With a few quick, careful moves, she pulled it over her head without mussing her hair, lipstick, or leg makeup.

After Emma buttoned the dress, Margaret turned and said, "I'm going along with you two children to keep an eye on you. I promised George I'd go out and have a good time, once in a while." Margaret fought back a smile and winked.

Franny stopped smoothing her dress. "You and George eloped!"

Margaret felt a blush grow on her face and shook her head.

"You better not of!" Emma broke in. "We promised back in junior high that we'd stand up with each other."

"Yes, I remember." Margaret gave her best nonchalant look. "George and I did discuss getting engaged the last time he was home. That was before he got sent to Taft Air Force Base."

"But," Emma drew the word out and nudged Franny in the ribs. "What you haven't told us yet, is…" She paused for dramatic effect, "is if you sealed your engagement with a kiss or if you went all the way?"

Margaret sensed the blush bloom down her neck and into her ears.

"Holy mackerel, you did, didn't you?" Franny exclaimed and plopped down on the bed.

Emma joined her. "Forget the Blue Note. Tell all, we want details, every one."

Margaret tried in vain to regain her composure but gave up the effort. She pushed her bangs off her forehead and returned to her stool. "I won't tell you everything. But remember George's favorite pickup line?"

Margaret's audience of two panted together, "Indian blanket."

"We were out at Glen Miller Park in his uncle's car," Margaret began.

"The one with the fold-out rear seat?" Franny said.

"Yeah, that's the one. We were in the front seat. On such a wonderful spring night," Margaret stalled.

"Spill the beans," Emma waved her hand to hurry Margaret along. "Get to the good part."

"His leave was up in a few days, and he kept telling me how much he'd miss me. After we kissed a while, he whispered if he got killed, he'd die without ever knowing what loving me was like." Margaret's heart raced at the memory. "I started crying. I felt so guilty for telling him no. He looked at me just like Humphrey Bogart and said, 'Maggie mine, want to take a chance on an Indian blanket?'"

"And then?" Emma urged Margaret.

"I said I'd love to, and that's all I'm going to say except it was so romantic."

"Did the earth move and violins play like in the movies?" Emma asked.

"No, but afterwards, he proposed while we snuggled."

"Oh, your dad's going to kill both of you if he ever finds out," Franny said.

"I'm not going to tell him. Are you?" Margaret's glare warned her friends.

"No, cross our hearts and hope to die." They raised their right hands and crossed their fingers.

"And?" Emma said.

"George and I talked about it again the next day, and we agreed that it'd be best to wait until the war's over. Grams and Mrs. Hartman and now the two of you are the only ones who know we've even talked about getting engaged."

Margaret stared at them, and they both showed her their crossed fingers in another silent promise. With a nod, she went on, "We decided not to tell a lot of people because we can't do anything until he gets back home. I haven't even told Momma or my sisters. They still think I'm writing to keep his morale up." The next thought brought such joy she had to share. "He's shopping for a ring."

The word ring seemed to have a magical effect on her audience. They sat in stunned silence. From downstairs, Margaret heard someone knock at the front door followed by her grandmother's slow steps headed in that direction.

Franny and Emma looked hard at Margaret, and Franny said, "Is that Marilyn at the front door?"

"You didn't ask her to tag along with us, did you?" Emma said and crossed her arms. "Okay, she's new to the office. But no guy's gonna face the four of us. We'll never get to dance with a boy."

"No, I didn't. But next time we should." Margaret stood. "Let's get going."

"Hold on," Emma said, "I don't want to drop the subject of you and George."

"Emma's right," Franny said. "We knew it. We've seen you practice writing Mrs. George Hartman over and over when you thought no one was looking."

"You've gone and planned your wedding, haven't you?" Emma said.

Margaret accepted that she'd have to share the details with her friends since she had been found out. "I admit it, I have. Something old, something new."

"Something borrowed, something blue," the two girls said.

"Something old will be Grams' gold bracelet, and I've chosen a white lace handkerchief for the something new."

"You know, you can borrow my strand of pearls." Franny touched the promised jewelry on her neck. "Emma, you can too when you get married."

"Thank you." Margaret sighed in happiness.

"So, what's blue?" Emma bounced against the pillows at the head of the bed.

"I've found the perfect shade of blue satin ribbons. I'm going to tie it in lover knots around my corsage."

"And a dime in your shoe," Franny said.

Margaret looked at her shoes and didn't understand what a dime had to do with getting married. "I've never heard that," she said.

Franny said, "My cousin told me. I don't know why. Maybe it's like mad money. You can call for a taxi, you know, at the last minute."

Emma looked at Franny and frowned. "That's crazy. Did you make it up?"

"Just the taxi part," Franny said. "Margaret, what do you think about the green suit in Jarrett's front window?"

"The one with the frilly white blouse? Yep, perfect," Emma said.

"That's what I thought too when I saw it last week," Margaret said.

"We're still in the wedding?" Emma tugged a loose strand behind her ear.

"Of course. It'll probably be very small. I'm hoping rationing is over by then. I'd like to wear hosiery on my wedding day. I don't even care what shade."

Margaret tried to remember the elegant feeling the silky fabric gave her. But she couldn't recall the last time she had worn them, let alone bought any.

Franny's worried tone brought her attention back. "What did you say?" Margaret asked.

"I said, will your dad be there?" Franny repeated. "Will he give you away?"

"I suppose so. I'm still really mad at him." She frowned and considered what George had written in his last letter. Life was short. Live without regrets. "He is my father."

Hattie heard the knocks on the front door from the kitchen and didn't hurry to answer. "I'm coming, hold your horses, I'll be there directly," she raised her voice to her visitor as she took her hands out of the dishpan.

"You don't want me to risk falling and breaking a hip, do you?" she yelled on her way down the hall. "I've got too much to do to be laid up in bed,"

"If it's important, you'll just have to wait," she said and opened the door to see little Jamie Laughlin from two streets over.

He stood there all out of breath and clutched a small white note in his hand. The eight-year-old boy reached out to give her the paper, and using his Sunday manners said, "Good evening, Mrs. Brown. This is for Margaret."

"Thank you Jamie. I'll make sure she gets it. Say hello to your mother for me."

The door was almost closed when Jamie spoke up. "Mrs. Brown, something's doing at Mrs. Hartman's."

Hattie shook the impatience from her voice. "What are you going on about?"

"I was out playing when Mrs. Fields came out and handed me that note." Jamie pointed to the paper in her hand.

"Then what happened?"

"Well, she said, 'Jamie, I've got an errand for you. Take this message to Mrs. Brown's house right away. Tell her it's for Margaret. Right now.' I didn't stop one time."

"You did good."

"Then Reverend White drove down the street and pulled into Mrs. Hartman's driveway, right past me."

A cold heaviness crept into her heart, but she managed to tell the boy to be careful on his way home and shut the door.

Hattie wanted to lean against the wall and not move. "Lord Jesus, not George."

Enough light came in through the window blinds for her to recognize the handwriting of George's aunt. Though the ink had run in places, she could still make out the request, 'Hattie, please give to Margaret.'

Hattie unfolded the note and read.

Margaret dear, I'm so sorry to give you the bad news. Two men from the government brought us a telegram. George was killed in a training accident. Please come soon.

Hattie heard the girls' low conversational hum overhead and pictured them crowded around the mirror for a last minute inspection.

Next, she saw that girlish scene vanish. She feared the note could be enough to destroy Margaret's youth and dreams.

"I can't do this, I'm too old."

It took Hattie a few minutes to reach down, deep inside for her courage. When she found it, she straightened her shoulders and began her reluctant journey up the stairs.

Chapter 8

Richmond, Indiana, Spring and Summer 1944

George Hartman, Officer Training School,
Jefferson Barracks, Missouri

January 5, 1944
Hey Margaret,

It's swell you agreed to write to me. I was feeling sorta left out when I walked away from mail call empty-handed. Maybe some of the gals you work with could also write? That'd show the guys what a ladies' man I am.

Everything is fine here except they don't feed us enough, but you would never know that from the dishes we have to wash. My job this month is the dish room detail. I have to shove pans of cups and saucers along a twelve-foot shelf to the kid washing dishes. Then I have to go back to the end of the line of about six other guys where I grab the next pan and walk it the same twelve feet, over and over again, for hours.

Your friend,

George

May 3, 1944

Hey Margaret,

The candy and cookies you sent were really swell. All the flight crew really went for them. Can you send some more? We don't get much sweet stuff with our chow. Marvin put it best when he said there are still holler spots after he licks his tray clean.

Wish me luck. I've got my eye on the barrack record. I've worn my fatigue suit for two weeks running without sending it to the laundry. Only fifteen more days to go.

Your George

May 25, 1944

Hey Maggie,

I finally got word today about my leave. Maggie mine, I'm coming home in June. You'll be putting your pretty eyes on me by the 15th. Don't send any cookies or candy until I'm back at base. The guys won't save any for me.

Pencil me in your dance card, okay? We'll go trip the light fantastic at the Blue Note every night.

Marvin wants him and me to take up flying for real when the war's over. We make a good team. One thing I can say about the Air Corps is they really do know how to train. Marvin says we'll get hired by any airline company. At least the ones with the sense to recognize good pilots when they see them.

Your George, always

June 30, 1944

My dearest Maggie,

I want to see you again and hold you in my arms real bad. I'll love you forever. As soon as they demob us, I'm coming back for you. We'll marry and live in the neighborhood. Are you sure just two boys and two girls?

Oh Maggie, I can't wait to return to Glen Miller Park and our spot under the big maple trees.

I've got my eye on a ring. I know you said we shouldn't say anything yet until I get home. But you could wear it when you're alone. I want to think of you sleeping with it on a chain around your neck. That way you'll have sweet dream of me. I won't go into my dreams about you, with the censor reading every word you and I write each other.

Marvin knows something is up. Says I have a bounce in my step and a silly grin on my face. Don't worry. I didn't spill the beans. But I did write Ma. Not about the park. Just the ring.

Write me back as soon as you can, my love.

Your George, forever

Chapter 9

<Hattie and Robert Brown
<Castella and Russell Dakin
Margaret

Margaret attempted to shake off her unease. It had started when she recalled George's words that life was too short to bear grudges.

Franny must have picked up on the feeling too because she said, "Time to talk about something happier."

"What's with you? I thought you were in a hurry?" Margaret said.

Emma shrugged and answered for Franny, "There's no rush. No new guys ever show up."

"Are his letters more romantic now?" Franny scrunched a pillow from the bed and settled into a more comfortable position.

"A little. He's real busy."

"He can't be that busy," Emma said.

"He is," Margaret said. "Can you believe that they let him go to the latrine only three times a day? The whole squad marches there, in a line."

"Sorta like when we go on smoking breaks at Gifford's," Franny said. "I'd die, if I had to hold it and couldn't go more often."

"Guess I wouldn't be a good soldier." Emma laughed so hard she snorted.

"Not in the Air Corps, anyway," Margaret said and anchored one of Grams' roses behind her left ear with a bobbie pin. She smoothed her pageboy and was pleased with how her natural highlights caught the red from the flower.

Emma leaned over and touched the rose. "So you're telling all the guys tonight that you're taken, huh?"

Margaret said, "Don't want to lead anyone on. I'm after some dancing and laughs, that's all."

At last she was ready to go. Emma and Franny gave themselves the once-over for the last time while Margaret put her lipstick and a clean handkerchief in her purse.

She had her hand on the doorknob when an unusual shuffling on the other side of the door gave her a start. Her friends stood behind her, and Margaret turned to look at them.

"Ooh, what is that?" Emma said.

"Your grandma?" Franny spoke softly. "I thought she never came up here anymore because of her hip."

Margaret's knees started to go. "Please, please don't let it be anything bad," she whispered under her breath. "Don't let it be George or Tim." Her words became a low chant while she pleaded with time to stand still.

The steps slowly grew closer and stopped. The door opened. Margaret looked first in Grams' eyes full of pain before she noticed her grandma's arms outstretched ready to embrace her. The last thing Margaret saw was the note in the older woman's hand.

"Margaret, I've got some bad news for you. Honey, George was killed in a training accident." Grams cradled her. "I'm so very sorry, Maggie. I'm so very, very sorry."

"No, no, oh no, not my George," Margaret said. When her limbs began to shake, her grandma's arms tightened even more around her. She and Grams rocked side to side.

"Margaret," Grams murmured in her ear, "Come sit on the bed."

She stayed within her grandma's embrace and let herself be led toward the bed. Her breath came fast, and she gulped for air. "No, nooooo. It can't be. It's got to be a mistake. He promised me he'd be safe. He promised me we'd have our whole lives together. We had it all planned."

She collapsed into her grandma's lap and took comfort from the kind, old hand stroking her hair. "How could God let this happen? Why did he have to take my George from me?"

"I know, Maggie, I know." Grams gave Margaret a handkerchief.

"He loved me so much, so very much. He really did, and I loved him. We were going to be together forever and ever." Margaret wiped her eyes. "We were going to have kids, a nice house here in the neighborhood, close to you and his mom," she said through her sobs. "Oh Grams, what am I going to do?"

"Why, you're going to be the brave woman George would be proud of. You're going to wash your face and freshen up and go be with George's folks. Sit up now," she advised.

Margaret felt her grandmother's hands on her shoulders. "I can't."

"They need you," Grandma said in her unwavering voice. "He was their little boy."

"I've never done this before."

"You're a grown woman, Margaret Castella. You have responsibilities and duties. Just like George had his."

Margaret stood on the doorstep and stared at George's service flag in its pride of place in the Hartman's window. His blue star was centered against a white field and red border. She bit back tears and remembered how her heart had soared when Adeline placed the symbol of George's honor in the window. All the world could see she had a son serving in the armed forces. As the war intensified, the girl had watched too many of the blue stars change to gold and black wreaths hang on the front doors.

Margaret raised her hand to knock on the door, then hesitated. George's death was not only about her. Digging down deep, she found her strength and swore that when she entered the house, she'd be a grown-up woman, not a silly teenager.

She knocked. When George's aunt opened the door, she said, "Honey, I'm sure glad you're here. Adeline was just asking after you."

Margaret entered the familiar house. When she heard weeping in the kitchen, she hurried past the parlor and bedrooms to the back of the small one-story house.

It unsettled her because she saw Adeline in George's place at the kitchen table. His father, Nathan, still in his factory work clothes, occupied the chair beside his wife. Reverend White had taken the seat opposite.

Adeline looked up. "Child," was all she could say between her sobs and wiping her tears.

"I'm here for as long as you need me," Margaret said.

Adeline grasped her hand and pulled her close. "I just can't believe he's gone. He was supposed to be safe out there training others to go overseas."

"Maybe it's a mistake?" Margaret asked. That hope had been with her every step on her two-block walk to George's home.

"No," Nathan said. "They found his dog tags. The plane crashed on landing. The other boy was the pilot. That's all they know right now."

Adeline said, "Reverend White is gonna lead us in prayer. Won't you join us?"

Hard as Margaret tried, it was impossible to focus on the minister's words. Her heart spun. The thought of the last time she had kissed George goodbye was too painful, and she raised her head.

Three church ladies in hats and aprons organized the gifts of food. A neighbor directed the other women around the cramped kitchen and tiny dining room.

Margaret had never figured out how the women came with food that quickly, but a mental picture of Grams' pantry gave the answer. The older woman always put a little something by for emergencies. Bread, jelly, home-canned peaches, and beans.

Touched by the women's thoughtfulness, new tears washed the others from her cheeks. Margaret looked around the room. African violets in the windowsill brought a little more color into the kitchen. A small icebox occupied the corner by the back door. The sink had been tidied, and dishes put to drain by the pump.

Bit by bit, the truth registered. She would never again feel George's arms around her or his touch. He would never see home again. This prompted her to list the other never agains. He'd never walk again through the back door and give his mom a hug. He'd never again hear her or his mom's voice.

Her next thoughts moved on to the never woulds. They would never marry and live in their dream home. Or have the children they had wanted.

The thought of the gothic H script stationery put in a shoebox under the bed for later chased away all other thoughts. Even her best friends had no idea she'd mastered the grand style H and embroidered it on pillowcases for her hope chest. And for what? She'd never get to use them.

The crash in the desert had ended so many things. Margaret had her yesterdays with George. Suddenly the todays and tomorrows were gone. That awfulness made her heart hurt, actually ache, and she pressed her fingertips to her chest to stop the pain. She wondered if all those yesterdays would be enough for the rest of her life.

A touch on her hand made Margaret look up. Adeline held out a cup of coffee. Margaret thanked her and remembered the blue star in the window. If she had married George the last time he was home on leave, she'd have one of her own, and she'd be sewing the gold star over the old one until no blue showed.

She got up and knelt beside Adeline. "I'd like to help sew George's gold star on his flag."

United in grief, they embraced.

Hattie watched her granddaughter mourn with a near-Victorian intensity. Immersed in her loss, Margaret wept and sobbed that her life was over and there was nothing to live for.

A week after the funeral, Hattie grew concerned because Margaret still refused to return to work. The girl had become so wan and ghost-like. Finally, Hattie decided enough was enough. She fixed a breakfast tray and took it upstairs where she made Margaret sit up and show some sign of life.

After Margaret took a few sips of tea and shoved the fried eggs around on her plate, Hattie moved the tray to the dressing table. Instead of leaving, she sat on the bed and began her rehearsed speech. "Saying good-bye takes time. But you can't stay this way forever. You are still alive. You have to rejoin the living."

Margaret looked like she was paying attention and had not turned away, so Hattie pressed on. "It will get better."

Margaret nodded.

"A little bit each day."

Margaret gave a small smile.

"You'll start to notice the world again. It might be a bit of sunshine or bird song. That means your heart has started to heal and you can open your heart to love again."

Margaret's nostrils quivered. She flung the bedclothes aside and jumped out of bed. Drawing herself up as tall as possible, she stood with her hands clenched. "How can you say that? I love George. I'll always love him. I can never love anyone else."

She stormed out through the bedroom door and wailed as if her heart had crumbled into bits.

Hattie heard her stomp to the bathroom and slam the door.

"Stupid, stupid, stupid," Hattie let the castigations fly a few moments later when she eased into a chair at the well-scrubbed kitchen table. "Just plain stupid. Should've known better. She's not ready. The child can't think of her future yet. It's the first time she's seen how precious life is."

She stirred some drops of honey into her second cup of tea for the day and remembered her own first experience with death. The answer came to her at once.

An hour later, Margaret moped into the kitchen. At least, Hattie thought, her granddaughter had dressed and combed her hair for the first time since the funeral. Hattie put down the knife she was using on the potatoes for the evening's cold salad and didn't say anything until the girl sat down and faced her.

"I'm sorry, Margaret."

Her granddaughter reached out and touched her arm. "I hurt so bad. I don't want to feel this way anymore."

"It won't last forever. I know. Look at me."

Margaret raised her eyes. Hattie braced herself to relate events from long ago. "I'm going to tell you a story. There's not another soul alive today that knows it. You'll be the second one."

"Is it a true story?"

Hattie was pleased when she heard a hint of curiosity come into Margaret's voice.

"Yes. When I was eighteen, the person I was closest to in the whole world died, my twin brother Charley."

"Grams, I'm so sorry. I didn't know you had a brother. What happened?"

"He died in the Spanish American War.

"In battle?"

"No." Hattie felt her composure slip and fought to keep her lips from trembling. A few seconds crept by before she could go on. "That's what has riled me the most. Even after all these years. You see, just a few of our soldiers died in battle. Some, like Charley, died for nothing. The government fed those young men rotten canned meat. Rumors flew that it was left over from the Civil War. You see, Charley died from eating spoiled meat."

"Our government killed their own soldiers?"

Hattie picked up her handkerchief and noticed Margaret went after hers. "Not deliberately," Hattie said after her eyes were dry again. "They were just trying to save money. However, that doesn't change the fact that Charley's death was plain unnecessary. I've lived long enough, Margaret, to see many young men march off to war, time after time. I don't think any war is good though sometimes it's needed. But I've always remained angry about Charley's death."

"How long before the hurt stopped?"

Hattie barely had the strength to couch her words. She feared the truth would be too much right now. "You learn to hide it away, but sometimes you take the hurt out, hold it, and cry."

Margaret sat silently for a few minutes while Hattie turned back to her potatoes. "Thanks Grams," she said and kissed Hattie on the cheek before she left the room.

It soon became clear to Hattie that Margaret still wrestled with her grief and was making herself sick. Margaret was down to skin and bones, and her pacing overhead in her room at night often kept Hattie awake. Hattie decided it was time to intervene once more.

Margaret was swinging on the glider in the back yard when Hattie brought out iced tea and ginger cookies after she'd finished the morning chores. Margaret got up and took the tray. Hattie watched her place it on the table under the big maple tree. It took Hattie a few moments to get down beside Margaret. Once she was in place, she helped set the glider back in motion.

"Child, we've got to talk, and you need to listen. Everybody loses people they love. There's not a soul on God's green earth that hasn't had to part from a loved one. You must remember every love is a tragedy just waiting to happen."

"I don't want to hear this." Margaret shook her head.

"I know, but you have to."

Margaret gave her a look that said she wished her grandmother would get up and leave her alone.

Hattie paused because she wanted to get it right. She was so nervous that her throat dried up. After a sip of tea, she started again and prayed the words would find her.

"You cannot run away from life. Maybe your future holds a husband and children. No one knows for sure. But I can tell you this. George loved you. There's no way he'd want you to live your life alone and unloved. He didn't have a jealous or selfish bone in him."

Margaret stilled the glider. "No, he didn't. He was perfect for me."

Hattie stopped herself in time from protesting that no such person had ever breathed air and decided instead to pick up on Margaret's love for George.

She said, "True love isn't selfish. When you love someone, truly love them, you want them to feel loved, don't you? Even if it was before you met?"

Margaret turned and stared at her. Hattie could almost see her puzzle out her thoughts.

"I don't understand," the girl said. "Usually you talk about the dangers of love. How if a girl's not careful, she'll get into trouble and end up disgracing herself and family."

"That's true enough." Hattie eased the glider into a slow rhythm. "Love is also good. Listen to what I'm telling you."

Hattie forged ahead while she still had her granddaughter's attention. "You wouldn't want someone you love, truly love, to be unloved for the rest of their lives, would you?"

"I guess not," Margaret considered. "I can see that."

When her granddaughter started to get up, Hattie pulled her back. "Grief is a gift, Margaret. Remember that. You must accept the trials of life. Use your pain. Find a way to make the world a better place. Help someone else. Once you get your mind off of yourself, you'll be happier."

In late August, Margaret knew the big news was the liberation of Paris. To her, though, the larger world served only as a backdrop to her personal tragedy. It struck her that so many windows held gold and blue service flags when she walked home from work. Her grandmother's words flowed through her mind. Margaret realized many other people must be grieving just like her. Somehow, she didn't feel so alone anymore.

Later that evening, Margaret had a new purpose when she met Emma and Franny on Emma's front porch. Her friends, dressed like her in shorts and sleeveless blouses, sat on the cool concrete ledge around the porch and listened to Frank Sinatra.

When the needle reached the last track of "Close to You," Margaret walked to the record player. Instead of flipping it over to play the B-side, she told her friends she had an idea she wanted to run past them. They looked up with their nail polish bottles and brushes frozen above their toenails.

"I noticed you have a lot of blue and gold stars in your neighborhood."

"Don't know." Emma shrugged and worked her pink gum into a big bubble. "Never paid any attention. Seems they've been there, for.." She shrugged again and made another bubble. "I don't remember when." She bent forward and changed a toenail to a bright red. Bits of cotton showed between her toes.

Margaret started the flip side on a lower volume, and Sinatra sang "You'll Never Know."

"I counted twenty-two on my walk over here tonight." Margaret sat between her friends. "There's eighteen more in the few blocks around Grams' house. How many around your neighborhood, Franny?"

"A bunch. I haven't kept track. Why?" Franny painted her little toe a seashell pink.

"I'm thinking about something Grams told me a little while back. Lots of our neighbors have lost their sons or husbands. But I'm young and don't have any children or other responsibilities. Don't you think they might need some help?"

"Help?" Emma stopped the work on her second foot.

"Running errands or something?" Franny said.

"Something like that," Margaret said and lifted the hair from the back of her neck and twisted it into a knot. "Remember at Mrs. Hartman's house after George's funeral? When people said how sorry they were for her loss and for her to let them know if she needed help?"

"Yes," her friends answered.

"What did George's mom say?"

"Thank you, I'll let you know." Emma's words had a rising inflection at the end of her answer.

"Right. And I don't think she's asked anyone for help. She's too numb to know what she needs."

"So," the two friends said together and waved their hands for her to get to the point.

"She can't be the only one. Here's my plan. We take a street at a time and knock on the door and visit. You know, stay a little while and talk. Find out what each one needs and volunteer to do it," Margaret said in closing.

Emma and Franny put their polish down on the ledge. Margaret could tell they weren't convinced. Why didn't they see it?

At last some recognition lit Emma's face. "We're so busy. When will you have the time?"

"You know all that time I wrote George every week?"

"Yes," Emma said.

"I'll start with that." Margaret waited for Emma's reaction and was glad when the girl nodded.

"I wouldn't have to be by myself, would I?" Franny asked.

Margaret promised to always be with her.

"I'll try," Franny said. "You know, it might actually do some good."

On the Sunday before Labor Day, Margaret sat with Grams and skimmed the church bulletin before the service began. She couldn't believe it when her name leapt off the page. Reverend White had written a few lines about her work with the neighborhood families of soldiers. Her surprise changed to pride when people around her turned and asked questions about her volunteer work.

On the church steps after the service, Margaret was stunned when girls, in ones and twos, stopped to talk with her and offered to help.

She was down right astonished when her grandmother invited all of them back to the house for Sunday dinner.

That afternoon Margaret saw her idea become more than she'd ever imagined. Seven young women sat around the dining room table and planned. One of the first decisions was to name themselves We Can Help.

Margaret never learned who tipped off the local beat reporter for *The Palladium-Item*. The young woman caught up with Margaret when she was in the process of cleaning the garden of a neighbor of Emma's before the cold weather set in. It happened to be Margaret's birthday, and that was the lead the reporter took. "Richmond Girl Gives Up Her Birthday to Help Others." A picture of the two women showed them pulling the bare corn stalks and bean trellises from a victory garden.

Her grandmother's comments after she read the evening paper were what Margaret had expected. They sat in the living room while Gramps listened to the Cardinals take on the Browns.

"Nice write-up," Grams said with a stern look on her face. "However, a true lady has her name in the paper only three times in her life. Her christening, her wedding, and her obituary. This would never have happened in my day."

And with that, Grams stood up and headed to the kitchen to check on supper.

Chapter 10

"Richmond Girl Gives Up Her Birthday to Help Others."

By Suzy Harris

Margaret Dakin, of 401 West Main, is a stellar example of how women of all ages are serving at home. Not only is she the driving force behind creating a group named We Can Help, she also puts her foot to the shovel when helping Mrs. Martha Julian of 614 Kinsey Street clear her victory garden for the winter.

We Can Help's members are all local girls who identify families in need by the blue and gold service stars in their windows. They visit the families and ask how they can help. Some girls babysit or run errands. Miss Dakin and her friends Miss Franny Wolfe and Miss Emma Hopping began the group before Labor Day and have watched their membership grow to thirty-four helpful and willing young women.

Miss Dakin and her two best friends say the idea came to them after they noticed all the service flags in their neighborhoods. Mrs. Julian is one such example. Her only son, Mark, is serving overseas in Germany.

Mrs. Julian tells this reporter that she will certainly let her son know about this terrific young woman in her next letter. She also had a birthday cake baking in the oven since Miss Dakin gave up her birthday to pull weeds and corn stalks.

Mrs. Julian is happy to share her cake recipe since it came from the County Extension Office in the Court House.

The Palladium-Item, October 8, 1944, Section B, p. 1.

YOUR VICTORY GARDEN
counts more than ever!

WAR FOOD ADMINISTRATION

Chapter 11

Part 2

Winter Haven, Florida, September, 1960

<Sarah Jane and Isaac Guymon
<Betsey and John Hussong
Marie & Louise

Marie thought she had put all the spiraling emotion from her mother's death to rest until the sight of the garnet brooch in the jewelry box proved her wrong. A rush of grief with the intensity of a flash flood overwhelmed her, and the shouts of the neighborhood children playing ball next door suddenly muted. She grabbed the jewelry box and urged by an internal beacon pointing the way, walked the few steps from the bedroom to the fountain burbling in the garden.

Part of her realized that she had to get herself together. The whole faculty and their spouses were expected in a few short hours, and she had little time to spare for a good cry or whatever the rising emotional tide was threatening to release. But the other part of her realized that it was better to deal with the storm now instead of later, when her fellow teachers were present. She could not start the school year as a basket case.

The soothing ripple from the fountain and the sight of calming blue plumbago flowers drew Marie deeper into the riot of color. She took a deep breath and headed for the red and pink awning stretched over her favorite hanging chair. In the almost twenty years she had rented the house, the garden had provided a quiet spot to sort through her problems, large and small, and a source of inspiration for her painting. Every moment spent there was valuable.

Marie gazed at the sunlight playing off the red firecracker shrubs and hoped that the garden would work its magic again. A hummingbird darted among the long grass stems, and she lost herself in following its swerves and dips. A pair of casius blue butterflies joined the aerial parade. The late afternoon sun awoke her as if from a spell as it crept a bit lower in the sky and warmed her face and hands. Overhead, several vultures caught the thermals and performed a swirling ballet. The world seemed normal and calm, very unlike her emotions.

She forced her attention back to the box, and within moments a picture of her mother sitting before the vanity mirror crystallized. She had put her short dark hair into a Marcel wave. The garnet brooch decorated the V of the fancy white-lace frill of her blouse.

Momma was telling Louise the family story of the brooch. Marie had, by chance, walked by and eavesdropped from the hall. "As long as anyone can remember, the oldest daughter of the oldest daughter has inherited the garnet brooch."

Marie moved a little closer to the side of the doorway and glanced in. Louise sat on the bed, and though she appeared to be listening and following their mother's reflection in the mirror, she was busy arranging her long blonde curls. "So why did it come to you?" Louise asked.

Momma gave the brooch a gentle tug to make sure the catch worked. "Because Grandma Sarah Jane inherited it from her mother…"

"Grandma Esther," Louise said.

"That's right." Momma turned and slid the garnet's companion piece, the paisley shawl, over her shoulders.

"So you're the oldest daughter in the family now."

Her eyes met Louise's. "Right again, and one day both will be yours since…"

"I am the oldest daughter of the oldest daughter."

Another memory ran seamlessly through Marie's mind. She could almost hear her sister's voice once again from that time Louise had sneaked her into their parents' room and found the family heirlooms in the chest of drawers. "Momma told me that I will inherit the garnet brooch and paisley shawl since I am the oldest daughter. You can't because I will always be older than you."

Marie was nervous and had wanted to leave, but Louise was determined to show off her inheritance. "When I'm all grown up, I'm going to get all dressed up and go to fancy parties with my rich husband. I will be the only one there with a brooch this pretty."

Marie remembered being so jealous that day because she was not born before Louise and she had accepted that nothing would ever change that fact.

A girl's giggle from the other side of the fence brought her back to the present. It was strange, Marie thought, that out of all the memories of her mother wearing the brooch, she would remember that one. Poor little Louise, Marie thought, she never had the opportunity to wear her inheritance and attend grown-up parties.

Marie looked at the jewelry box in her lap. Its contents seemed to call from deep within. She opened the lid and took in a breath and let it out slowly before she removed the brooch. It dimly reflected in the bright sunlight. The three flower red glass settings seem smaller than Marie had remembered, but the piece remained in good condition. All the crystals were still in place. Marie tried to recover a happy memory from when her mother had worn the piece. Snippets of memories from the past rushed through her mind and stopped on the most painful segments. That was not what she needed.

So instead, she went back one more generation, to Grandma Sarah Jane. As if Marie had spun a bingo cage, her store of memories rolled out the day her grandmother came to visit, a short but happy time before what she had called "the bad time" as a child.

The movie in her mind played, and what Marie remembered most was how happy Grandma Sarah Jane had looked. Her face glowed and reminded Marie of the angel pictures in the Bible storybook Poppa read to them at night. Her bright green dress must have been made of silk and matched the intensity of her green eyes. The material shone in the light from the chandelier in the dining room and felt softer than Louise's hair ribbons. In pride of place, above the self-covered buttons on the bodice of the green dress, rested the brooch that nested in her hand.

Marie remembered being fascinated at the time with how the color of the dress made the brooch stand out. She had looked at the color combination and switched Louise's favorite shade of blue for the green. Somehow she had known it would not match as well.

Her heart thudded as she recovered more details. She suddenly realized that the lines and wrinkles crosshatched on her grandmother's face revealed the hard life and worry the woman had experienced. Marie tried to guess how old her grandmother had been and arrived at somewhere in her early fifties, based mostly on old-fashioned clothes and hair pulled to a bun at the nape of her neck. It was hard to tell.

The image of Grandma Sarah Jane vanished, replaced with one of the friendly man who arrived with her. He had taken the time to ask each of them questions and truly looked delighted to talk with her and

Louise. She had rushed home from school and was so disappointed when her mother explained that Grandma and that man, as her mother always called him after the visit, had to return home to milk their cows. Marie remembered only one time after that she had seen him. But he had changed so much and was not the same man who had pulled peppermints from his pockets to give to the little ones as he had nicknamed her and Louise.

Something about that time pulled on her, but all that came to mind was beautiful, highly polished darkly patterned wood. Shaking her head to clear it, a sense of peace glowed within her. But soon that feeling dissolved when it struck her how little she knew of the brooch and her family history. The only real facts she had were the oldest daughter story and the hint that the family came from real landed wealth as Grandma Sarah Jane had boasted. Marie pinned the brooch to her bright orange blouse and could not help but wonder why it was so important to the family. Garnet Brooch, Paisley Shawl, and Landed Wealth were all spoken with the same emphasis, as if they were proper nouns.

Marie judged from the sun that it was about time to prepare for the party. A quick look at her pendant watch revealed that she had spent almost an hour in the garden. But it was an hour well spent. She was calmer and mentally reviewed the tasks still unfinished while limping back into the house to remove the pin. All were doable in the time left. She added a new one: exchange the green dress for the pink one she had planned on wearing to the party.

While she was in the closet, Marie also retrieved the box containing the paisley shawl. After hanging the dress in the shower so the wrinkles would fall out, she took the box, and easing onto the bed, removed the lid and lifted the layers of white tissue wrap. As she did so, a piece of faded pink construction paper glued with red hearts and a torn white doily fell loose. Upon retrieving it, she saw that it was a fragment of some elementary school artwork. Marie turned it over to see where so long ago, she had messed up her first attempt and started over again on the other side. Somehow Bridget had kept the card that Marie had made for Grandma Hussong the first Mother's Day she lived with them. How thoughtful of the hired woman to have kept it for all those years. She took a few deep breaths and fought to get a hold on her rising tears. When her composure returned, she silently thanked Bridget and vowed she would include a thank-you in her weekly letter up north.

Marie pulled the shawl from the tissue paper and draped the shawl around her. The immediate effect was that the woolen cloth was itchy even with the silk lining. But something clashed with the memories of her mother and Louise wearing the shawl. It had seemed larger back then. Could be because she was smaller, yet something was off.

She refolded the shawl in the box and wondered where she would ever wear it. Between the Florida heat and her sensitivity to wool, it stood a good chance of remaining in the box before it went to Cousin Margaret in Indiana.

It would probably be a good idea to share with her cousin the little history of the brooch and shawl that she knew. Why were the heirlooms so important to her mother and grandmothers?

The question ignited a spark of interest. It seemed a mystery had come her way. Curiosity started to eat into her mixed emotions of grief and anger. She would find out what she could and pass the family history along with the heirlooms, in honor of her grandmothers, not her mother.

Three weeks later, Marie realized that it had been some time since Bridget's last letter. She checked the postmark of the other letters to make sure, and yes, Bridget had not written in almost a month. But she had said in the last one that she and Poppa were planning a winter visit with her and Bridget's sister who lived in Sarasota. She had also asked Marie to send her a list of items she would want from the family home. Bridget was clearing out the house on Poppa's orders and didn't want to throw out anything Marie might want. Bridget reassured her that she would bring some old letters and pictures for her. Marie's response had been there was really nothing she wanted from the house.

Marie wondered how could three weeks have passed since the last letter and she not notice that, for the first time since she had left home for college, she had not received a weekly letter from Bridget?

But before the thought had fully formed, Marie knew the answer. She had found the disagreements brewing among the staff disruptive. It was disagreeable to see supposedly intelligent and educated adults become so petty and revengeful when running into opposing viewpoints. To her there was a time and place for airing political and social differences, and it was not in the classroom or in front of students. Another round of rumors had spread that some Negro parents had filed lawsuits to force Winter Haven to desegregate their schools. Dade County had lost their law suits last year, and now tempers flared on all sides of the debate throughout the staff.

Marie tried to keep her opinions to herself at school. She knew most people still looked upon her as a Northerner, but Florida was now her chosen home. Back in Ohio, there were more integrated schools, but not because the whole state suddenly woke up one day and decided that was the way things were going to be. Economics drove what little social change her home state had acquired. Industry needed more good workers who could read and write.

Yet segregation did not monopolize Ohio's legislative discussion as had happened the last two years in Florida. Marie made her opinions known where it counted. She voted. She wrote letters to the governor and legislature and shared with them her summer experiences when she volunteered to tutor the children in the turpentine camps.

At school, the splits were mostly between the young and old and ones from the north versus staff from the south. All committee work ground to a halt. No group could reach an agreement or pass a budget or decide on a policy.

When the joint arts and athletic committee had dissolved into a snarling snake pit and charges of Communist were flung against countercharges of racist, Marie had had enough.

"Mr. Chairman Pro Tem, I move that this committee suspend the bylaws and table the election for officers."

She, along with Elizabeth Stebbins, Christine Lane, and Allen Farmer, formed a majority. Elizabeth seconded, and the motion passed.

Then Elizabeth gained the floor, "I move that this committee disband until further notice."

Marie watched recognition flicker across the quarrelers' faces. But she went ahead with the plan the majority had made even as the others increased their rising murmurs and grousing. "I second the motion because you are all wasting my time, and I shall never have any of those stolen moments back. Worse than that you are openly arguing in front of the students. I do not care what your opinions are. There are other venues far more appropriate, let alone effective, to vent them. Write letters to Governor Collins, talk to your representatives, write letters to the editors. In sum," and she stopped to make eye contact with the three warring members, "voice and share your opinions wisely."

"Aren't you concerned that you'll lose your job when all the white parents pull their children from our schools?" Caleb Fish stood and shouted at her. His jabbing finger resembled the baton he used to conduct the band.

"It is morally imperative that we protect the civil rights of all children, regardless of the color of their skin," Hugh May, the assistant band director and head baseball coach threw out.

The third one, another art teacher with the name of Hiram Stone, "All both of you are interested in is protecting your departments. You're not looking at this from the historical perspective of the pupil assignment law. It's been working in good faith toward following recent court rulings."

"What about last year's Dade County's case?" shouted Hugh over the other two.

With the three involved with each other, Marie's seconding the motion carried with the arguing men not even noticing what the rest of the committee had done. When Marie and her friends left the room within a few minutes, she closed the door on the trio, still deep in their verbal war.

Marie was delighted when the other committees followed their actions. School became more peaceful, and the students did also.

"I couldn't find much to carry down to you, Marie," Bridget said to her within a few minutes of arriving for the long-anticipated December visit. "Nothing that I remembered belonging to you, but I did include a few nice things from herself." Bridget handed over a shoe box after she and Poppa settled into the garden. Each had changed into their summer clothes. Bridget was in a bright yellow sundress that looked very new and blended so well with the crotons beside her. Poppa's shirt appeared so new it still had the creases from the package. That shirt with its swirling print of palm trees had not been bought in Akron. It resembled the merchandise she had seen at Stuckey's.

Marie held the shoe box and remembered her vow that she had made when she moved away to college. She would never return to live with her mother again. But she gave Bridget a reassuring smile and opened the lid. "Don't fret about it. I'm surprised you found enough to put into a box."

Ever afterwards, Marie recalled how innocuous the letter looked, with the familiar handwriting of her mother. But she should have known better. The letter rested on top of folded scarves. A few pieces of her mother's good jewelry twinkled in the sunlight.

Poppa's snores from the hammock made Marie smile. It had been a long time since she had heard the comforting sound.

Marie glanced at Poppa with pale arms folded behind his head and even paler legs stretched out. She was struck by how much younger Poppa looked and decided retiring from the bakery had done him good. A fleeting expression on Bridget's face caught her attention. When she turned her head for a better look, Marie was surprised at Bridget's new youth as well. Bridget lowered her eyes, and a blush raced from her neck to cheeks.

Marie gasped as the pieces fell into place. Then she winked at the woman who had helped rear her and in many ways was far more loving than her own mother.

"Is this a wedding trip, by any chance?"

Bridget's blush deepened. "I warned him. Johnny, I said, that girl of yours will figure it out before you get a chance to speak to her. Don't let on that you know. He wanted to tell you himself, in person. This isn't something that can be said on the phone. He was worried you would be upset, what with it being nowhere close to a year since your mother passed, God rest her soul." Bridget crossed herself.

"I am pleased for both of you," Marie said and reached for Bridget's hand. "Have you set a date?"

"Maybe while we are down here a-visiting you and my sister Ethel, if we get both your blessings."

"You most certainly have mine. Would you like to hold the ceremony in my garden? Would that be okay with your sister?"

Marie felt a reassuring squeeze before Bridget let go. After glancing at Poppa, Bridget lowered her voice," I need to talk with you about your mother's letters before himself wakes up. I don't possess all the facts, but it seems your mother's mother..."

"Sarah Jane," Marie provided.

"That's the name. Well, seems she kept some love letters hidden away from your mother. They were written to her during the first war," and Bridget took time to cross herself again, "and maybe it was a childish love. But the long and short of it was your mother somehow finally got her hands on both the letters she had written so long ago along with the ones the cousin wrote from over there. Your grandmother made sure she never read them." Her eyes brimmed. "I didn't mean to poke my nose in something that was no business of mine, but first I saw the letter written to you and then all the others scattered about your mother when I found her dead. I just swept the whole pile aside, and it wasn't until I started sorting through things that I realized what they were. It didn't feel right to burn them, somehow. I haven't told himself over there.

Seemed no reason to. So I just gathered a few things to put on top to cover them up in case Johnny would look in the box." Bridget took a deep breath. "You can decide what you want to do with them."

Marie looked again at the letter addressed to her and wondered why there was no stamp or return address on the envelope. Was her mother interrupted before she could finish? Something she would never know, she thought, along with a whole lot of other answers, some part of her said. Thanking Bridget for her thoughtfulness, Marie grabbed her cane and excusing herself, leaned forward and rose from the chair.

"I think I shall open her letter now." As she took each step with care, she crossed the garden on her way to the letter opener on her desk in the front room. Just before she stepped over the threshold into the house, she noticed that the rabbits had returned to nibble the perennial peanut down to the roots. She made a mental note to check the fence to see where they were coming in after she read the letter.

"It just occurred to me, Bridget. Was this the only letter she left?"

"Never found another one. Who else would she have written to?"

"I guess I have been watching too many movies. I guess it depends on when she would have written it. Maybe to Louise," Marie's voice caught on her sister's name. "Or maybe that cousin from the first war?"

"Oh, I see what you mean. Was herself saying goodbye or telling them how much she loved them?"

"Exactly."

"Now that you mention it, doesn't seem like her, does it?"

"No, well, the mystery will soon be solved."

Marie pulled the letter opener from its dedicated slot in her antique roll top desk and carefully slit the fragile envelope open. When had her mother written it? There was no date to give the answer. At first, the words in the very short note did not fully register. Marie had to read it again, this time by picturing her mother from so long ago, the angry woman in the silent, dark downstairs room. The finger pointing at her and the shimmering rage in the voice completed the picture. Every word dripped with scorn and hate.

You have outlived me, Marie and that which should have rightfully been Louise's and her oldest daughter's goes to you, the garnet brooch and paisley shawl. I take great satisfaction in knowing that the legacy of the oldest daughter inheriting will end with you since you are rightfully a spinster and childless.

The words pierced her heart with cold stabbing jabs. Other painful times she had experienced her mother's anger unearthed from where she had buried them so long ago. Marie was once again a little girl, grieving from the loss of her sister, trying to navigate the upheaval in her daily life. Snatches of images flooded her brain. Louise crooked in her mother's arms, Momma kneeling on the floor and keening, Poppa's worried look, Grandmother Hussong perched on the bed telling her that Louise was gone to a better place, the silent grief that wrapped everything in the house in a heavy cloak.

Marie placed a hand over her stomach as her womb contracted and the world telescoped to a tiny prick of light that faded along with a scream full of anguish.

When Marie came to, the coolness of the tile made her long to never move. Then she saw that Bridget was there, just as she had been on that terrible day so long ago when Marie had entered her mother's downstairs room.

"Marie, whatever happened to you? Is it your knee again? Are you hurt? Did one of those awful snakes bite you?" Bridget's worried eyes looked at her for answers at the same time her hands were searching for blood and broken bones.

At that moment, Marie knew she would be forever in this woman's debt for as long as she lived.

Marie sat up and leaned against the desk. Her head was clearing, and the cruel words came back to life. "It was the letter. My mother and her shocking, horrible hate."

Poppa's voice boomed from the garden. "What's going on in there? Can't a man take a nap around here?"

His voice froze them for a few minutes before she felt around for the letter. Bridget's and her hands bumped into each other as they searched for the letter.

Then Poppa appeared, and when he had taken a good look at her, he joined them on the floor.

"You don't look so good. Did you eat some bad fish for lunch?"

Marie straightened even more and saw the edge of the letter under the desk. Bridget must have seen it at the same time because her hand reached for it faster than Marie's. But Poppa was closer, and his fingers grabbed it first.

"What's this?" He held up the letter with one hand and pulled his glasses from his pocket. "It looks like your mother's handwriting."

"Poppa, you don't need to read that. It's so far in the past that it no longer matters."

"Bullshit, Marie. Anything that can knock the stuffing out of you like that is important." The march of emotions raced across his face as he read. Puzzlement, disbelief, followed by the deepest anger she had ever seen him broadcast from his eyes. Last was a pain so intense she could no longer look at him.

"I am so sorry, Marie. I thought I had protected you from her hate. I tried every way I could think of. For a few years, Dr. Purcell kept telling me that your mother would recover. It would just take time to heal. He was wrong," he said as tears streamed down his face. "But I am more at fault. Can you forgive me?"

"Poppa," Marie said, crying as she embraced him. "You were everything to me. Don't you remember how I'd jump into your arms when you came home from the bakery? I drank in the scent of fresh baked bread and cookies from your clothes and hair. When I smelled them, I knew I was safe."

Marie heard Bridget struggle to rise from the floor and broke away to pull her back. "You've always been part of the family, ever since the first day you arrived to help when Louise and I were so sick. You belong here. You don't have to leave."

Bridget nodded and caught a few tears with a handkerchief. Poppa searched in his other pocket, pulled out a white dress handkerchief, and blew his nose. Marie found a wrinkled one in the pocket of her dress and wiped her face.

"She changed so much after Louise died, Marie. That doesn't erase the harm that she did and evidently continues to do." He held up the letter. "But do you have any happy memories of her? The games and songs she made up to entertain you and Louise when you were stuck in bed?"

When Marie shook her head, both Poppa and Bridget began to speak at the same time. In the jumble of words, Marie heard pretend and rubber-legged Ruth. Then they took turns telling about her mother before the bad times.

Chapter 12

Akron, Ohio, March 1960

<Sarah Jane and Isaac Guymon
<Betsey and John Hussong
Marie & Louise

Betsey inwardly railed at her family doctor. How dare young Purcell come here uninvited? She hadn't asked the ninny to come, especially not into her favorite room during the all-important morning time. That was when the light captivated her even on a cold day. The soft sun played across the highly polished maple dining room table where they were seated beside each other. She sat in her wheelchair, he in a carved dining room chair.

"Mrs. Hussong, as I was saying, it's not at all uncommon for older folks such as yourself," Benjamin Purcell advised as he reassuringly patted her hands folded in her lap, "to lose the ability to talk if they don't use their voices.

In her mind Betsey told him he had no idea of what elderly truly was. His grandfather, the first Dr. Purcell, was elderly. At fifty-eight, she was not old even if the recent twenty pounds she had put on and the wispy graying hair that escaped from her bun had made her look older than her years.

Dr. Purcell wore a somber black suit. To Betsey's eyes, he was pitiable in his attempt to appear more mature and professional. His fair hair and light hazel eyes combined with his slight stature of five foot, six inches made him look twenty-five instead of his actual thirty-five. She had heard unfavorable gossip at church that he was nowhere as good and easy to talk to as his grandfather. The parishioners believed that if he had not stepped into his grandfather's practice when the old man retired, he'd have no patients at all. Some wondered aloud if he would ever build up his own caseload.

Betsey relished tormenting him every time he called. The warmth in the house made sweat seep from his hairline. At her insistence, the house temperature was set so she could wear thin, faded cotton housedresses. She saw him look through the window at the cool outdoors and noticed his shirt collar was damp.

The invalided woman silently ranted and questioned why anyone would believe anything he said. He didn't seem to enjoy the practice of medicine the same way his grandfather did, and she had perfected a look that made him squirm. Each encounter she had with him reaffirmed her opinion. He didn't quite measure up to her idea of what a doctor was. She remembered when he followed his grandfather around. Even back then, he acted as if he knew more than he really did.

"I want you to talk out loud a little more each day." She nailed him with her steel blue eyes. "I understand that Mr. Hussong's living next door at the bakery and your daughter moved to Florida some time ago. Teaches school, doesn't she?"

Betsey peered at Dr. Purcell as if he were a cockroach scampering across her kitchen counter.

"Bridget's here every day. Talk to her," he suggested.

She bridled at his words. She did not want to talk to anyone.

Benjamin Purcell nervously rubbed his cheek and avoided her piercing blue eyes. He seemed to refocus on her nose instead.

"Do you have a pet?" His voice squeaked at bit. "I didn't notice one. Some people talk to their pets."

Not since John took her sweet little kitty away with him was her unspoken reply. She remembered with bitterness the day Marie left for college and John, with the cat under his arm, moved out to live in the back room of the bakery.

"Or would you like visitors, maybe from church or a garden club? My mother still talks about your green thumb and yard full of flowers. Your roses and peonies were always award winners at the flower shows."

She inclined her head and glanced outside. Instead of the frozen stalks, a vivid picture of her gardens at their riotous best filled her mind's eye with reds, pinks, and yellows. They had brought her tremendous joy. Back when Louise was alive, long ago. Everything good had died with Louise. Most of the time now Betsey didn't know why she was still alive. Even that damn hall clock taunted her with its infernal ticking. Each beat reminded her that she lived and Louise was gone.

"At least she's listening," the doctor muttered under his breath. "Wonder if she also has dementia."

Betsey snorted in another unspoken reply that her hearing was still good as he returned his gaze to her eyes and asked again in a louder voice, "Is there anyone at all you would like to talk to, Mrs. Hussong?"

"My daughter," she managed to sputter loudly enough to be heard.

"Good, Mrs. Hussong, that's two words. Try to talk with Marie today for a few minutes. Ask her how the weather is down there for me, will you?" Benjamin Purcell gave her a weak smile and got up to leave.

"Louise, you fool, not Marie. Louise is the only one I want to talk to," Betsey muttered. He didn't look like he understood what she said.

"Good-bye, Mrs. Hussong. I'll see you next week." He waited for her to say good-bye. When she didn't, he left.

Betsey sat very still in her chair and listened to the young doctor's departure. He said his farewell to Bridget. At last he was out the door and gone, and good riddance to him. His grandfather had forgotten more than that young nincompoop would ever know.

A few minutes later, she cocked her head to listen to the noise of Bridget running the Hoover upstairs. Betsey slowly rolled her chair to the hutch cabinet. From the middle drawer she removed her treasured picture of Louise on her fifth birthday. With her dead daughter's image in her lap, the long-grieving mother moved her chair over to the east window's light for a better look.

"Louise, my princess," she whispered. Her fingers lovingly caressed the little girl leaning sweetly on the white wicker nursery chair draped with lace. "As delicate and beautiful as that lace," her words came out in a marginally stronger voice. "I loved dressing you up so much that sometimes I changed your dresses and pinafores three times a day." Betsey fell silent and covered the photo with both hands when she heard Bridget's steps come down the stairs.

"I'm going out for some groceries, Mrs. Hussong. You'll be fine while I'm gone?" Bridget asked with a voice that still retained a whisper of the Irish lilt.

"Yes," Betsey forced the single word.

With Bridget gone, it was safe to revert to her internal conversation with her dead daughter. Lonely, she spoke to the image of her precious Louise as if the child had stepped from the photograph.

I remember that day. I dressed you in a bright blue frock, just the color of your eyes. Grandma Sarah Jane made that dress for your birthday.

Do you remember the lace around the puffy sleeves and hem? You looked so beautiful. Mr. Sperry agreed too. He wanted to display your picture in the front window for others to see. He had even promised a discount.

The visit with Louise stirred a brief sense of contentment, and Betsey brought the photograph to her lips before she continued her one-sided, internal conversation.

Your long bouncy curls. Such a beautiful little girl with those curls and sparkling blue eyes. It was worth the time to wrap your hair in rags before you went to bed. I put a blue band with a white flower in your hair and told you it was your princess crown.

You stood very still for Mr. Sperry. Do you remember how he made taking your picture a game of statues. He caught you with one foot forward and one foot just touching down. You smiled sweetly at him and stood still.

Betsey sighed before she rolled back over to the hutch where she replaced the photograph in its accustomed place.

Her next stop was the opposite side of the dining room. She maneuvered her wheelchair to the large picture window that overlooked her neglected flower gardens that remained iced in winter. Maintaining her plants and painting her prize flowers on bud vases had provided her with many contented hours. When she reached back to that time, Betsey understood she had lived for those three precious morning hours reserved for painting. She had guarded them jealously while the girls played upstairs or attended school. John knew not to expect her in the bakery until eleven at best to begin her lunch and afternoon shifts.

Her leg throbbed and forced her back to the present. What a damn fool she was for letting them see her weakness. Her fall on the ice and the broken hip were accidents, and that vile wheelchair was a nuisance and couldn't be helped. She should've kept talking. That old busybody Bridget must have told John she hadn't said a word to anyone, except her and probably exaggerated when she told him it had been months since anyone had called.

At times Betsey considered firing the Irish woman even though she had long ago realized it'd be too much work to replace her and too hard to break in a new girl. Besides, Bridget had been with her for such a long time, and Louise had enjoyed her stories about Ireland. If Bridget left, another link to the past snapped and left her with one less person who had known and loved Louise.

While the gentle warming sunlight crept across the room, she silently castigated Bridget one more time for calling in that damn fool doctor before her head grew heavy and she slipped into a light slumber.

Betsey knew how to play the game. By June she talked precisely enough and satisfied Bridget and Dr. Purcell who, naturally, appeared more pleased with himself than his patient's progress.

It took tremendous effort for Betsey to hide from him what his insistence of talking aloud had unleashed. Her dark musings had gained form and substance and given birth to visits with three long-lost family members. Her one-sided conversations slowly became the best part of her day. Her mind receded to where she would hear all her loved ones' familiar voices and see their forms. Soon she spent hours in her past where she repeated the same conversations every day with the unvarying round of visitors.

In the morning after Bridget finished the breakfast dishes, she cleaned the upstairs and did laundry. Her absence was the cue for Betsey to call five-year-old Louise to her. After Louise skipped into the dining room and climbed into her lap, Betsey gave her whole self to the delightful visits.

"Momma misses you so much. Do you miss me?"

"This much," the little girl said and spread her hands out as wide as she could.

"How's my little English rose?"

"Just fine."

"What were you doing? Just now before you came?"

"Grandma Sarah Jane and me, we were in the rose garden."

"She's not supposed to be out there," Betsey said. "Next time, tell her to go away, back to where she belongs."

"Don't be cross, Momma. Grandma brushed my hair." Louise put her child's hands on her mother's chin, "Do you know why she kissed my dimples?"

"Why, sweet Louise?"

"Cause the littlest angels in heaven gave them to me on my birthday."

"That's right. Because you're my littlest angel. Soon we'll have all the rest of time to play and sing. But I still worry about you. Is the shawl keeping you warm?"

Louise nodded her head. "Thank you, Momma. Half for me and half for Marie."

"You deserved your share. I knew my mother and grandmother would understand. Did you know they came to me in a dream the night you died? They told me, 'We take care of our babies.' I did, didn't I, dearest?"

"You're the best momma in the world." Louise gave her mother a kiss on her cheek.

"I tried, sweet girl, even after Poppa let them take you away that night and I begged him not to. I told him you were a child, and a child needed to be with her mother. He didn't listen. I'm so sorry you had to spend a day alone before you were returned to me."

Betsey paused in grief as powerful as the day her child had died. It was so important that Louise understand. "When they brought you back to the house, you weren't the same. I bent over and tried to pick you up, but you were so heavy in my arms. I didn't understand. I looked at you, a stiff doll, and fainted. When I came to, you were back in your casket, alone. That's when I knew you were really gone from me."

The memory of Louise's funeral still caused her heart to break apart, and tears traced their familiar route down her cheeks.

"Momma, don't cry. Heaven's a wonderful place."

"That's a comfort to me, my precious baby."

Tears she didn't even attempt to dry washed down her cheeks. Worn out and tasting the salty tracks on her lips, Betsey felt fatigue overtake her.

After lunch while the hired girl went to the grocery and ran errands, she wheeled to her bedroom and prepared for her first love to pay his afternoon call. She brushed out the tangles, left her hair unbound, and remembered how her long-lost beau would lovingly curl his fingers through her loosened, golden-brown hair.

At the old clock's chime of one, Jeremiah, her cousin named for their grandfather, strode into the dining room. He wore his World War I infantry uniform and his hair shorn in the military style. He always had red and pink roses, her favorites, in his hands.

"My little Betsey," Jeremiah winked and gallantly said, "You look beautiful," and sat down in the big dining room chair next to her.

"Jeremiah, I love your special name for me."

"It was something for only the two of us."

"I remember the day I changed my name. I did it to protest that awful letter Mother made me write to you."

"Our parents were wrong, very, very wrong. We still love each other." He took possession of her hand.

"I didn't want to marry John. I really didn't. Now though, nothing can keep us apart." Betsey gazed at Jeremiah.

"I understood and vowed that I'd never marry. I would always wait for you. And at last, you've let me come visit."

"I couldn't let you come while John lived here, Jeremiah. It wouldn't have been proper."

"Remember the night we promised ourselves to each other, even before I knew I was going to war?"

"That night filled with moonlit moments? We were going to a barn dance at Cochran's." Betsey's voice had taken on a tender tone.

"I worried about your dress and shoes, but Papa said I couldn't have the wagon."

"Instead you borrowed Willie Cochran's canoe and rowed us to the dance."

"I worked all afternoon cleaning that damn boat," Jeremiah said with a winning smile to show that her comfort was worth the effort.

"Music drifted across the lake." Betsey's hand moved in time with a song long buried in her past. "And the light from the barn laid a path on the water."

"The air was still, and we heard people laughing before we got half way there."

"How we danced." The present fell away. She felt his arms, strong, as he embraced her. Together they waltzed while *Till We Meet Again* played in the background. Long forgotten youthfulness returned to her along with a brief moment of happiness.

Then the memory of her mother's treachery stopped the music and splintered her joy. "Mother showed up the next day in a huff."

Jeremiah gave her his arm and walked her back to her chair. "She said she needed you back in Sabina for the rest of the summer."

"She lied to me in so many ways. She told me her ladies needed their dresses finished right away. I had to take out the seams and sleeves in those dresses over and over again. I can still hear her words, 'Boys are like streetcars. One is by every fifteen minutes.' She was sure that even with the war, I'd find my special someone."

"But I was already your special someone," Jeremiah half-whispered and knelt beside her. "When I kissed you on the cheek like this, the last kiss I'd ever give you and whispered."

As he spoke, she said with him. "How I yearn for your happiness."

Jeremiah's visits and his wooing primed Betsey for her mother's bedtime appearances. She groused at Bridget if the woman was late, even by a few minutes in helping her to the bathroom and bed. Once she had settled under the covers, she waited for Bridget to retire to her room by the kitchen.

That was her long-dead mother's cue. She'd stride into the front parlor, converted yet again to a bedroom, and sit in the rocking chair. Betsey fired the first shot as soon as the older woman smoothed the skirt of her green silk dress over her knees. The next act had begun.

"Mother, go away. Don't you realize you're not welcome?"

"Mollie Elizabeth…"

"Betsey, my name is now Betsey. I demand that you address me by that name." She watched her mother's mouth open and snap shut into a tight line.

After letting out a tired sigh, Mother said, "Why do you talk to me this way?"

"Because you cheated Jeremiah and me out of our perfect love."

"Nonsense," her mother stopped her rocking and sat ramrod straight. "After all these years, surely you know it was for the better. You were children, only children, and first cousins."

She glared at her mother. "He was no child. He was man enough to fight for his country, and he was old enough to know we loved each other very, very much. You and Uncle Cornelius never understood."

"Mollie, it was for your own good."

"He never wanted to marry anyone except me."

"Listen to me." Her mother leaned forward. "You were too closely related to marry. I wanted you to have normal children, like Louise and Marie. Not imbeciles like that poor unfortunate Lines family. You must remember them. They were cousins, you know."

"I pictured his heart breaking when he read that letter because I knew he'd love me forever." Tears gathered in Betsey's eyes.

"Nonsense," her mother said again, "He grew up after he went to war. He realized it was only a first love."

"How can you still lie to me?" Betsey shot back. "You think I didn't find out the truth about you and Uncle Cornelius and your plan to keep us apart?"

"Jeremiah didn't want to embarrass you when he realized you were such a child. He outgrew you."

"Havilla told Jeremiah, after the war, how Uncle Cornelius gave you each letter I had written to my only love. And you, Mother, you thought you had burnt all the letters, both his and mine. But I found your hiding place. I read each one Jeremiah wrote and resealed the envelope. When I realized you wouldn't miss a few, I kept my favorites. Don't shake your head no at me. I know the truth." She sat with her hands tightly clenched.

"We acted for your own good, yours and Jeremiah's. You were too young and headstrong to listen. I did what I had to do."

"You and Uncle Cornelius had no right."

"Every wise person knows first love doesn't last." Mother resumed her rocking.

"How would you know? Were you ever truly in love?"

Betsey knew she had scored a hit when her mother flinched, but the older woman soon recovered. "I had hoped you'd one day realize that being giddy in love is not the love you need for marriage. You were happy with John."

"Not as happy as I would've been with Jeremiah." Her tone changed to wistful. "That summer with Jeremiah was the most glorious time of my life. Angels smiled on us."

That memory calmed her spirit temporarily before she returned to her rage. "You showed up and made me leave Jeremiah, the only man I've ever loved."

"Try to understand." Mother left the rocker to sit beside her. "We didn't want anything improper to happen. You were so young. Uncle Cornelius was concerned the way you felt about each other might get out of hand. He thought Jeremiah was a very foolish young man all caught up in the talk of war and the romance of going off to fight, especially after his friend sent those letters from Germany. He was certain Jeremiah wanted a girl to come back to."

"Uncle Cornelius was right. I was that girl." Betsey refused to look at her mother and sat back with her arms folded over her chest.

Mother tried again. "You were infatuated with a sense of romance about how brave and handsome he was. It happens in all wars. Often girls get carried away. I wanted to protect you. We honestly thought you'd soon forget each other."

"You didn't win." She looked at her mother in triumph. "We wrecked your plans. You never knew we thought the two of you might try to spoil our love. But you did not have the power to stop me loving him. Don't you know love conquers all? Our secret code told him I still loved him and always would. He knew my love was strong. You look surprised, Mother. It was that letter I wrote to him." She paused to let the tension build.

"The codes words were yearn and Betsey," she crowed to her mother. "Did you ever yearn for my father? No, I don't think so. Isn't that why he went away? I know you never yearned for Richard."

"Your father had nothing to do with you and Jeremiah." Mother paused. "I did wonder why you didn't use your first name. I just thought you were being difficult again."

"Because Jeremiah's little pet name for me was Betsey. After that letter, I became Betsey."

The two women glared at each other for a few moments before Betsey reached into drawer of the nightstand and brought out a packet of letters.

"Why'd you keep these so long? To mock our love? To revel in your cruelty. Or did you steam the envelopes open so you could enjoy reading how Jeremiah and I swore our eternal love to each other? Were you so lonely you wanted to know what true love was like because you knew you'd never be loved like Jeremiah loved me?"

Gathering momentum, she went on. "I found those letters a few weeks before you made me write to Jeremiah. That's how we circumvented you. With the words yearn and Betsey, Jeremiah knew. He even whispered them to me on my wedding day."

She roared with delight when her mother retreated into shocked silence and went back to her chair.

"How ironic you were joining our letters together even as you were keeping us apart in life. Our letters are still joined, in my drawer. I read them every day."

"It all turned out for the best," Mother said. "You and John had two beautiful children together. You never went hungry, and John was never mean to you."

"You are mistaken. I paid the price for marrying John. God took away the child I loved best. He took Louise from me and left me with Marie, the cross I'll have to bear for the rest of my life. All because I couldn't love John the way a wife should."

"Nonsense, God had nothing to do with Louise's death. Certainly not with Marie being a punishment."

"How do you know? You never saw the real Marie. She was always such a trial, from the very beginning. It started with the colic. She wouldn't take to my breast and cried and cried in her bassinet. Louise tried to make her happy and even made up songs to quiet her. Nothing comforted Marie."

Mother shook her head in disagreement while Betsey continued to spew her venom, "Even in the photograph we had taken for her fifth birthday, she looked like an ungrateful, obstinate child. By the time we arrived at Sperry's, she had scuffed her shoes and torn a hole in her stockings and ruined her curls."

"Marie could be such a help to you now."

"Not that scornful ingrate. If one of my children had to die, it should've been her. She doesn't appreciate God sparing her, and therefore, she bears the mark of God's wrath. God never forgave her for not telling me quickly enough how sick Louise was."

Betsey's ire had depleted her. She resumed in a quieter tone. "An hour sooner, that's what Dr. Purcell said. Every minute of the fever burned part of my sweet Louise away until nothing remained. Marie won't return until I am dead. She'll be back to bury me and not before. Now leave."

On August 19th., same as every night since she had fallen in February, Betsey endured Bridget's care. The bathing and bathrooming were humiliating as well as the need for help into bed. She was tired and impatient to be left alone. After Bridget left, she was, at last, free to open the nightstand drawer and begin her own bedtime ritual. First, she took out her mother's shawl and brooch and arranged them over her nightgown. Next, by the lamp on her nightstand, she placed her wax-sealed note written to Marie long ago when John left her to her angry grief and moved into the bakery next door.

She didn't need to read it. She remembered every word. She had meant each one as a curse, especially "rightfully a spinster and childless."

The final part of her routine was reading Jeremiah's letters written lovingly long ago. His youthful words of first love calmed her soul's storm-filled clouds of anguish.

However, on this night, she sensed her spirit readying for the long-awaited journey, and the anticipation of joining Louise and Jeremiah on the other side gladdened her heart.

Chapter 13

Well-Known Gardner and Artist Betsey Guymon Hussong Passes

Mrs. Betsey Hussong, age 58 and wife of Mr. John Hussong, died at her house last night. Until her fall on the ice this winter, Mrs. Hussong worked side by side with her husband at their bakery on Claremont Street. She was well-known for her expertise in decorating cakes and the bakery's famous pastries. Others will remember her prize-winning flowers and painted vases.

Mrs. Hussong leaves behind husband John of Akron & daughter Marie of Winter Haven, Florida. Her daughter Louise predeceased her mother and father.

Public calling is tomorrow at Brown's Funeral Home, 52790 Fifth Street, from 7-9 p.m. The service will be held at the First United Brethren Church, Arlington and Fifth, August 23rd and interment follows at Hillside Memorial Park.

Akron Beacon Journal, August 21, 1960, Section D, p. 5.

Picture Jeremiah sent Betsey during his service in WWI

Chapter 14

Winter Haven, Florida, August 1944

<Sarah Jane and Isaac Guymon
<Betsey and John Hussong
Marie

Dazed, Marie hung up the telephone. According to the principal, Nick McCarty was MIA and feared dead. His parachute had drifted behind enemy lines somewhere in Germany. Did she remember Archie's words correctly? Had her former student become entangled in some trees or had she just supplied that information to complete her mental movie?

The mention of the young man invoked a memory of a happy-go-lucky senior who used his afternoon study hall to escape into her art room. His dark eyes hinted that he thought he was putting something over on her. She understood and never let on. She admired the easy grace that allowed him to mix with the athletes, the brains, as well as the loners whose faces always brightened after he drew them into conversation. He was the one who noticed the wallflower's attempt with a new hairstyle and would pass on an heartfelt compliment.

A sense of urgency compelled her to seek sanctuary among her beloved plants. She did not even change into her gardening clothes and shoes. She just turned and walked through the lanai to the far section where the fountain gurgled. Marie tried to make herself focus only on weeding, removing pests, pruning, and celebrating the beauty all around as tears mixed with the soil. The whole time she ignored the rings of the telephone and the outside world until she felt steady once more.

During the retreat in the garden, she wished several times that she had spent some of those afternoons getting to know the boy better. She had never asked him what he did for fun.

There had been some talk in the teacher lounge last year about the increasing number of former students who were in harm's way. But the notion had seemed so remote to her then. But no longer.

As she trimmed a runaway branch of bougainvillea, goose bumps accompanied the epiphany that some of her students' lives would most likely be shorter than hers, regardless of what Dr. Purcell had said so many years ago.

By the time she had reworked the pentas bordering the path, she had planned how the next school year was going to be different. Marie now accepted she was preparing her young people for war and vowed she would find out more about their lives and interests. She would grant her students permission to pursue what made their brains and hearts sing and somehow follow the state curriculum. Those kids would too soon irrevocably enter adulthood and its hazards.

Marie stopped working and gulped back tears when she also accepted that while Nick was the first student she had lost, he would most certainly not be the last.

Three days later, Marie sat in the front seat of Sybil's Buick Special, silent and still a bit in shock. The five-mile trip to Cypress Gardens was her first outing since the news about her student. Marie had tried to beg off when Sybil had called even before she was out of bed. But the older woman would have no excuses. She said last night's storm had done so much damage that all volunteers were needed. If the wind and water had swept through the Garden's flower beds with the same velocity as the storm had through hers, then Marie felt she should help.

Sybil asked, "Did you know the McCarty boy?"

Marie, heart in throat, nodded yes.

"Did you hear what happened to him?"

"Archie Burr called."

From the back seat, Marie could hear the other two women discuss their grandsons in the service. From the bits she heard over the misfirings of the engine, she knew they were comparing notes. Edith, the deaf one, boomed that hers was still in Anzio. The only words Marie caught from Alice's reply was "still laying siege to Monte Cassino." Marie thought for a few moments and recalled what she knew about the young men. Something to do with widely-reported battles in Italy, places she had to look up on the world atlas. Such romantic sounding names for such carnage.

The engine was frankly in great need of repair. Marie uncharitably thought that Sybil did not trust the new group of women motor mechanics formed to replace the young men now gone to war. She tried to rein in her impatience as insects buzzed through the open windows faster than Sybil was managing to creep. The only weapon she had to defend herself was a fan from Ott's funeral parlor. With her free hand, she rubbed her game knee. It was acting up again with the humidity.

Beggars could not be choosers Momma had always said, and Marie accepted she was certainly a beggar when it came to getting anywhere outside of the few blocks she could walk. A trio of white-haired, elderly, forever friends, each old enough to be her grandmother, had come to her rescue and offered to drive after she had placed a notice on the church bulletin board. They would not even take any money to help with the gas.

But the other side of equation was they operated on their own clock, and pick up time was as fluid as the water in River Lake.

She detested being tardy. Always had, for as long as she could remember, but taking a deep breath, Marie counted her blessings. She did not have to return home to live with her mother after graduating college last year. Her rental was fortunately close to school and downtown. The landlord gave her carte blanche with the neglected garden, and her teaching job was safe for another year.

When the entrance to the Gardens came into view, Marie tucked the fan into her oversized purse and brought out a handkerchief. Mopping the moisture from her face, she sent up a silent prayer of thankfulness. The work she did was more than the chance to garden with plants certainly exotic from her Ohio perspective. At first she thought they had come from all over the world until Sybil informed her differently. It seemed that the owners had started with plants from their neighbor's yards and slowly added truly new ones from Asia until the war slowed their delivery.

But for Marie, the volunteer gardening was also rewarding because she enjoyed the friendships she had formed. Most of her fellow volunteers were women at least her mother's age, retired from up north and made young once more by the Florida sunshine. To them, summer break was an all-year event, not just from May to September, as it was for her.

The gardener in charge assigned her and the trio the task of repairing the gazebo damage. Its plantings had suffered from last night's storm. He warned them that the border of new impatiens needed a lot of work. But she was glad. The gazebo was her favorite spot, followed by the South Crossroads Mansion as a close second.

As she walked with Sybil toward the park's signature wedding site, Marie shared the damage her own garden had suffered. "From the way the wind never stopped during the downpour, I expected to find my whole area in ruins this morning. But only the south east corner bore the brunt. It looked as if a giant had trampled everything."

Sybil said, "I was luckier. Not much was disturbed. Just a few powder puff plants. What did you lose?"

"The rain lilies and the pentas. I will have to replant them this week so they will be at their best by my Labor Day party," Marie laughed. "I still find it hard to believe that I volunteered to have both the Christmas and Labor Day parties."

"They like to place the young female teachers on the social committee," Sybil said. "Besides you have such a fine place to entertain."

"Or I am the only teacher who does not have to worry about a spouse or children."

"There's that also. Maybe I can help you. Have you ever tried plumbagos? They'll grow anywhere. But," her friend chuckled, "you'd better be careful where you plant them. They tend to take over. I'll drop some cuttings off tomorrow morning."

Marie accepted the gift though she preferred bolder colors in the garden, but maybe it was time for a change from her usual sun-bright oranges and firehouse reds. "I am sure I'll love them. Someone told me that they are one of the few true-blue flowers that grows here in Florida."

When Marie topped the slight rise, she saw the flooding was not as bad as the gardener had led her to expect. It seemed the head gardener had known what he was doing when he had installed the terraces and drainage pipes. Marie slowed her pace to ease the pain in her knee and catch her breath. There would be enough time to replant the bedraggled plants and clean the debris from the walkways before the sun hit its zenith. She would be back in town in time to bathe and catch the Ritz's new matinee. It never mattered to her what made up the double feature. The blessed air-conditioning was all that counted.

Marie grabbed a camp stool from the workman's cart and unfolded it on a level spot by the border. As she worked and listened to the others diagram their weekly bridge game from the previous evening, she mixed handfuls of peat moss into the soil. It did not take long before a familiar sense of calm swept over her.

Then it struck her so hard that she had to stop working and take a few moments to wrap herself within the peaceful feeling and its origin.

For she had at that moment realized how important gardening was to her well-being. Whenever she touched the earth and became part of the growing process, she almost forgot there was a war raging with its violence and loss of life.

Sybil's voice interrupted her thoughts. "Marie, I can't remember. Did I ask you already about the McCarty boy? Wasn't he in your art class?"

Her calm shattered. She collected herself and accepted that the respite earned through those peaceful moments with the earth never survived long. Reminders of the war came crashing in with the suddenness of stepping on a snake. Sometimes it would happen when Archie announced that school would close the next day so the teachers could help distribute the ration books. Even worse, were the painful moments that arose each time she heard about a war loss or injury of a friend's loved one.

Later that afternoon, something unnerving happened that burst the bubble of good feelings she had carefully crafted all day. She had spent a delightful afternoon watching a light-hearted romantic movie and the musical that followed. On purpose, she had entered the cool theater after the news reel completed showing the week's events. Her spirits remained upbeat on her walk home until she spotted the army transport truck. It was carrying the enemy back to their camp at the Florida Citrus Festival Grounds. The two German prisoners of war she could see at the rear looked tired and dirty from their day's work in the canning facilities. One was about eighteen-years-old, skinny. The other was just as lean, at least fifteen years older, and he gave her an unsettling look. His eyes did not telegraph pity as some others had when observing her limping along with the cane. Instead, there was a hint of concern under his rather clinical stare.

More unnerved by his stare than she would have been by a wolfish whistle, Marie leaned more heavily on the cane and took care with each step home. She felt as if his brief glance had snapped an x-ray.

On the day of her Labor Day party, Marie took stock of the garden. The plumbago had taken root rapidly and was in a full burst of blue. However, by afternoon, the other preparations were running a little bit behind. The humidity kept the floors from drying quickly, and when she turned the ceiling fans on high, the window blinds made such a racket, she could feel a headache coming on.

The last remaining problem was the cheese she had ordered from Conrad's grocery. It was not sliced as requested. But Marie had not called the delivery boy back. She understood why. Mr. Conrad had received notice that his son Merle was reported missing in action somewhere in the Pacific. So she was glad that the first guest to arrive was Elizabeth Stebbins. The woman taught chorus half-days in the room opposite Marie's art studio and had become a very close friend. When Elizabeth took command of the slicing, Marie gained enough time to change into her favorite floral dress of pink and red geraniums and to smooth her permed curls into place. Her mood improved even more when a gentle breeze kicked in just in time to offer some relief from the late summer heat.

Over the next hour, the rest of the faculty and their spouses joined the party. Marie counted fifteen guests in her small garden and two-bedroom home. Everyone had shown up. She loved having her house filled with company, especially with the new staff members.

She had learned last year how important it was to feel a part of the community when she had attended the Chamber of Commerce luncheon for new city residents. Marie had loved every minute of it. The warm welcome from the business leaders made her believe in southern hospitality. The setting at Lake Silver brought out the best of Winter Haven. The fresh squeezed orange juice tasted so tangy she wanted to immediately plant her own tree. And the pink gardenia Mr. Pope had presented brought her to tears. She had never received flowers before. She felt the experience had contributed to the success of her first teaching job.

As Marie circulated among the different groups and hoped that she was helping the new teachers start off well, the topic of conversation remained the same. From the coaches' corner by the fountain to the wives in the kitchen, everyone had an opinion about the prisoners of war. The most vocal were the ones who considered themselves experts since they had been present on the Sunday the prisoners arrived at the train station and then marched under armed guard to the camp. From hearing them recount the day, Marie pictured a parade of the captured men who were followed all the way from town and then watched as they set up housekeeping under the eyes of the locals. The consensus of the coaches was the Germans were eating and sleeping better than America's soldiers serving overseas.

"You just check the Geneva Convention. It states that we gotta give them the same food as our armed forces," said Archie Burr who coached baseball, and much to Marie's amusement, wore his hair in a burr cut.

Reading Collamore, the baseball head coach, said as he ground his cigarette butt by the bougainvillea and managed to escape the thorns. "They even get paid the same as American workers. That doesn't seem fair. They get to buy a cold beer when they return, safe and sound, to camp in the evening. I bet there's no shortage of cigarettes, either. But our boys are certainly running short on both, whether they're in the field or being held prisoner. You can't tell me the enemy's treating their POWs the same as we are."

"But I heard the Army takes most of their pay, except eighty cents a day," said the newest coach who had the most unfortunate surname of any teacher she had ever heard. James Boosey, in Marie's opinion, would not last long if he continued to interrupt and contradict the more experienced coaches, especially since Archie was also the supervising principal for all the town's schools.

In the kitchen, the principal's wife, Muriel, was holding court. "They better hope there's no hurricane this year. Those tents they live in won't hold up after the first big blow."

Joyce, the wife of the new coach said, "Jimmy talked with one of the guards at the grocery store. They don't have any trouble out of them at all." She stopped when she saw Marie and said, "They even grow their own flowers around the tents, though nothing as well developed as your garden, Marie. Seems they have a green thumb just like you."

Marie remembered her mother's words to never discuss politics or religion and just nodded as she removed the last of the solid ice cubes from the freezer.

By 8 p.m., the party was showing definite signs of winding down. The drinkers had grouped into two bands and moved on to Presley's since Marie did not allow alcohol in her house. The teetotalers lasted just a half an hour longer because tomorrow was the first student day. Finally, Marie maneuvered Elizabeth out the door with strong assurances that she could handle the clean up on her own. Marie knew her friend had at least two more hours of work as her elderly mother's caretaker. The older woman needed help taking her medicines and settling down for the night.

The silence of her home was welcoming after the buzz of voices and clink of pottery and glasses. Marie enjoyed her parties, but she also relished the quiet aftermath. That night she looked forward to the first day of school as she cleared the party debris and hoped there would be no blackout during an air raid warning drill. Her advanced art classes were filled with the maximum of fifteen students each. Forty-five had presented portfolios for her consideration. She had expected a few more, but those boys had enrolled in the defense training courses and would be off campus. The thirty selected ones would be the focus of her new plan to enable them to enjoy their last year before adulthood. But she also looked forward to discovering and fostering those in her beginning classes. They did not yet know they were artists.

On the way to collect the last of the ashtrays from the garden, she was surprised when the front screen door opened. Dr. Peyton stood half inside and asked if he could come in. He had never entered her house socially, and he had made only one house call during the brief time she had lived in Winter Haven. The elderly man always sported a bolo tie he claimed was from his cowboy days in Arcadia. Marie had no idea if his stories were true, but they were certainly entertaining. He had planned on retiring and handing his practice over to his grandson. However, the war had delayed his retirement until the young doctor returned from the army.

"Of course, Dr. Peyton. Is something wrong?" Marie asked.

"Not at all, my dear. I just have a delicate question to ask. Can we talk on your lanai? I enjoyed looking at your garden when I was here before."

Marie led the way through the lanai after fixing two glasses of tea with the few remaining bits of ice. They sat at the glass table, and he did not waste any time as he began to explain his purpose for visiting.

"I'm sure you know about the Germans who are, shall we say, our guests out at the festival grounds."

"Yes, that seems to be all anyone wants to talk about lately. But I do not understand why that is such a sensitive subject."

"One of the fellows out there by the name of Brandenburg trained in Austria in something he and I agree to translate into English as "medical gymnastics." He claims he practiced at the best spas in Germany and the Balkans."

All the pieces fell into place. That older POW whose stare had unnerved her after the matinee earlier in the month. The cold appraising look that had failed to take her, as a person, into account. Only his naked stare at the way she limped seemed important to him. She sipped some tea while she decoded what Dr. Peyton was really saying.

"I won't insist if you are reluctant. But I do want you to remember how difficult it was to clear up those inflamed cysts in your weak leg last winter. Do you recall how I was all set to operate if the infection didn't yield to the usual treatment?"

"But the hot compresses and elevation did work," Marie countered.

"Eventually, but you were fortunate this time-"

"But maybe not the next? Is that what you are saying?"

Dr. Peyton stirred his tea, and Marie watched the prized sugar swirl again through the liquid. After he drained half the glass, he said, "He must have caught sight of you. I don't know any of the details, and I don't want to know. What's important is he claims he has treated innumerable, his word, not mine, clients with similar gait difficulties. If this guy is anywhere near as good as he says, I urge you to take advantage of his expertise. He is far more knowledgeable and experienced than I and, heaven knows, far more up-to-date."

"And he speaks English?"

"He's passable, and a dictionary should help the two of you communicate."

"What does this medical gymnastics entail?" Marie asked and was surprised she was both curious and uncertain. It had not taken long for her to translate Peyton's concern about sensitivity. After all, the German was the enemy. Who knew how many Americans had suffered because of his actions before he was captured? Why should she gain while others had lost?

Dr. Peyton's answer interrupted her thoughts. "As best I can tell, it has to do with certain focused exercises." He gave a rueful laugh. "Between my bad hearing and his English, that's about all I can tell you. But my dear, you are so young, with your whole life before you. Why not benefit from his expertise?"

Marie fought back tears. How strange to be called young when her pain was so old. Another thought surfaced for Marie. What if he was a charlatan? Time after time, her father had sought out one miracle cure after another. She had been stretched, massaged, wrapped, braced, and even had electrical wires attached to her leg with one vain hope following another. She had given up long before her father had. Why should she put herself through another treatment? To get her hopes raised once more only to face another failed attempt?

"I shall consider it, Dr. Peyton, and let you know within a week."

"No one else needs to know about the treatment, Marie," he said.

She met his eyes and saw only concern for her within the community, but no understanding about the emotional cost to her if she tried for another cure.

"Thank you, Doctor, for your visit. I do appreciate your efforts."

Marie looked at the notation on the calendar while she waited for the usual breakfast of a single boiled egg to cool and the slice of bread to pop up in the toaster. She had promised to tell Doctor Peyton of her decision by Monday. Only three days to go, and she was still torn. Since the doctor's visit, four more of last year's students had been injured, including a nurse whose ambulance had overturned on a corkscrew road in Tuscany. She remembered how the girl had devoured everything Marie could provide on the Renaissance. The irony that the girl's dream to visit Italy had resulted in a near-fatal accident sent chills through her, despite the warm morning.

Marie's sense of loyalty to the war and America's soldiers challenged her strong desire to end the unrelenting ache behind her knee. Hard as she had tried to remember life before the pain, she could not. Her mind waged its own war. Small but strong rationalizations stung her strong core beliefs like a swarm of wasps. Whom would she harm if she consulted with the German doctor? Maybe his work with her could lead to benefits for other Americans, maybe even some injured soldiers? If she refused this opportunity, she would be the one who would suffer the most. There was no way she could undo any actions others had done or improve the situations of those who had suffered from the enemy.

The next day decided the matter. She stepped off the wet curb in front of the house and leaned into her cane. But her good leg was not planted firmly, and the bad knee wobbled. Something pulled, deep under the kneecap, and Marie hobbled back up the driveway and into her house.

Dr. Peyton arrived within the hour, but Marie had already started on his first recommendation to ice and elevate the knee.

"Well, I see you are still a good patient. Make sure you keep the ice in place for no more than twenty minutes at a time."

"How bad is it?" she asked after he prodded and poked at her knee. The pain from the exam took away all relief she had gained from the ice.

"Bad enough that you need to stay off your feet at last three days." He repositioned the ice a bit to the front. "Five would be better, my dear." He looked at her as if he was waiting for her to tell him her decision, but the moment passed and he left.

The nightmare full of sharks and their gleaming teeth might have risen from the codeine syrup, Marie thought as she willed her heart to slow down and the frightening images to evaporate. Knowing the escalating discomfort and bad dream would drive sleep away, Marie turned on the light and sat up in bed. Within a few moments, she had quickly sketched and filled in two columns on the note pad she always kept at hand. Since the dull ache punctuated with tiny, needle-like stabs was foremost in her mind, pain became number one in the yes column. Second was "obligations?" which stood for the possibility that she could be in the same position as her friend Elizabeth and have to support both her parents someday. If she could not work, how was that possible?

She also added Bridget to the list. The Irish woman had endured so much under her mother's rule that she deserved to also be taken care of. Marie remembered the Irish woman fondly for the times she had been her only source of comfort and understanding. Marie still hurt from the loneliness she had suffered after Louise's passing.

Under the no column, Marie listed enemy first. That was the part of the proposal that racked her conscience the most. Somehow, consulting him seemed like consorting with the devil himself. Next on the list she wrote Am. killed/wounded. After looking at the entry for a few moments, she listed everyone she knew or had heard had been harmed by the war. When she finished, she had a list of twenty-six names. On the last line of the paper, she wrote others.

Rumors and reports were swirling. The people from Germany's growing number of conquered countries as well as England and the German Jews were suffering so much. Some accounts were so brutal she had a difficult time believing them, but the older people who had lived through the first World War were all in agreement. They believed the reports were possible and recounted their own horror tales from when they were young. Who was she to be disloyal to all who had suffered or died?

Marie put the paper aside and walked to the kitchen to replenish the ice pack. Pain sparked around her knee cap with each step. Once she was back in her bedroom, she ripped the list from the notepad and tore it into bits. She did not want to be tormented like this for the rest of her life.

Marie found the next week sailed by while she was waiting for the appointment with Professor Brandenburg. She tried to feel grateful that Dr. Peyton had been able to work through all the military bureaucracy to reassign the German as a hospital worker. The doctor had gone through a lot of difficulty. But after the camp commander had called the hospital down in Venice and found that this was a routine assignment, he relented with the proviso that Dr. Peyton's ass would be on the line, not his, if the whole thing went south. Marie was glad the doctor had told her on the telephone so he would not have seen how embarrassed she was. Even after a few days had gone by, Marie could still feel her cheeks grow warm when she recalled the doctor's frank language.

However, the delay only gave her more time to rethink and wonder over and over again if she had made the right decision. Plus she knew she had set her heart on the possibility that the pain would vanish.

The first impression Marie had of Brandenburg when she saw him sitting next to Dr. Peyton was that she had wandered into a Sherlock Holmes movie set. The German was as thin and tall as the English actor Basil Rathbone while Peyton was as stout as Nigel Bruce. Their temperaments matched as well. Brandenburg sat ramrod straight in his chair beside the desk and managed to wear his dark uniform marked with the large white letters PW with dignity. Peyton, shirt collar open and sleeves rolled-up, was behind his desk and wiping his eyes from the joke Marie had caught the end of through the half-opened door before she knocked and entered. It was the same one she had heard Jack Benny tell last week. She had laughed then as she had now.

"Miss Hussong, this is Professor Brandenburg, late of Austria," Peyton said and waited for her to take the chair opposite them.

"Professor Brandenburg, this is Miss Hussong, late of Ohio."

They nodded at each other. Peyton rose and worked his way around to Marie. Taking her hand in his, he said, "I have high hopes for this treatment, Marie. Professor, I will be in the next room." Then with a smile, he walked out of the room.

Marie could feel the perspiration race in twin beads, one down her front and the other in back. Brandenburg gave her a weak smile and in a voice reminiscent of Mr. Rousch, who made the best candy in Akron when she was growing up, said, "Miss Hussong, I am certain you have questions, yes?" He did not wait for her to answer. "In due time. First, please stand and slowly walk up and down the hall."

He unfolded himself from the chair in one fluid movement and held the door open. She felt terribly embarrassed as she walked away from him, hand on cane. But it was worse on the return. His eyes never left her, but they were not as kind and warm as when she had walked across the bedroom for Dr. Purcell so long ago.

"Once more," he said. "This time, with more speed, but only half the distance." He smiled, and Marie could not help herself. She returned the smile.

Marie found the increased pace more difficult. Her timing was off for using the cane. When she completed the circuit, she saw he was still smiling.

"Now, half the last distance, and without your cane."

Panicked, she had visions of falling and doing more harm to her knee. His nods of encouragement worked however. He did not say how fast so she took one slow step after another. His smile on the return trip was even brighter.

"Now we return to the room," he said and opened the door. "Please take off your shoes and stand this way," he pointed to his feet after he followed her into the room.

Marie noticed his feet were together, no gap between the pant legs. She complied and watched him kneel in front of her and circle around. He stared and said nothing. Next he motioned her to raise her skirt above her knees, and he circled again, this time writing in a notepad.

When she glanced at it, she saw that he had written his instructions in English after what she assumed was German. He quickly entered numbers and other symbols.

"Please be seated, Miss Hussong." He walked to the corner of the desk where she saw a similar notebook. He handed it to her along with a pencil. "This is for your questions."

Marie understood. "Then you will translate and answer for the next time."

"Yes, you will have better quality."

"Anything you can tell me now?"

"Of course." He consulted his notepad, moved a few pages ahead, and read without looking at her, "One, never surrender, two, perform the exercises daily, exactly, and last, trust your body to heal."

Then he lay on the examining table, did a series of leg lifts, and said, "Ten times each day, each leg, knee," he struggled for the right word and resorted to showing her his hand with the wrist straight, "Not this way," and then bent his wrist.

He stood up and said with a motion toward the examining table, "Please to do the same."

She mimicked his movements, and he nodded yes and closed with, "Ice for pain. Next appointment in seven days."

"Thank you, Professor Brandenburg."

He gave a slight bow. "Thank you, Miss Hussong."

Marie felt the fatigue increase with each step up the driveway after the taxi delivered her home from the hospital. But she was not just physically tired. She was emotionally drained as well. She was not quite sure what she had expected when meeting Professor Brandenburg, but his courtly manners combined with his intense interest in the way she moved surprised her. She had also not expected to like him, even a little bit. It did not take much for her imagination to cast him in a romantic period piece movie, set in the castle in the Alps.

As she unlocked the front door, the word foolish escaped out of her mouth, and embarrassment swept over her. She was most certainly not up to Hollywood standards of beauty, even without the limp and tightly permed hair. She had never seen a leading lady as short and thickset as she was or with the sturdy-soled shoes she wore for balance.

Marie brought a glass of iced tea to the garden, and setting the glider into motion, waited for the tea to rejuvenate her. It did not work, and soon she gave into such decadence. She stretched out on the glider and took a nap.

The telephone rang, and through her sleepiness, she counted the rings and waited for the signal to repeat. When she heard two longs and one short, she fell back asleep. The call was not meant for her. But something was going on in the neighborhood. Off and on for the next hour the telephone rang, but never just the two long and two short rings that were her signals.

When Marie returned for the next appointment with her German, as she had begun to call him in her mind, she was surprised to find he had a black eye and his knuckles were scraped.

"Are you hurt? What happened to you?"

He gave her a wry smile. "A few chaps and I had, how do you say, wrestled for the same snake."

"Snake? What do you mean?"

He held out his hands about five feet. "This long," he said, "But I lost."

Marie shuddered. "Good heavens, why would you want a snake?"

Brandenburg laughed. "To make a belt. The guards showed us how. I know, we sound like your cowboys, do we not?"

Marie laughed along with him. That was just what she had been thinking.

"Shall we set to work?" he said and asked Marie to show him how she did the exercises. Then she walked again down the hall and back three times, but she was not as fatigued as last week. He must have noticed because he seemed very pleased.

After she returned to the chair, he pulled a chair next to her and sat. "You have made good progress. Did you place ice on your knees?"

"Every morning after I exercised."

"And did you write your questions?"

She handed over the small notebook. She watched him read and said, "Mostly I wanted to know how much better I will get?"

"It is too soon to tell," he said and closed the book.

Marie felt as if she was being put off. "Have you treated other patients with similar conditions?"

He said up straighter and said, "Even worse, and all improved."

"But how much better?"

"Everyone is different. I cannot tell you yet, but remember what three ideas I told you last week?"

"Don't give up, do the exercises exactly, and trust my body to heal."

"Correct," Brandenburg said and stood. "So now we try something new." He carried what looked like a cabinet drawer to the back wall. She also noticed a shower grab bar attached to the wall. Marie was sure she had not seen it last week.

"I have observed during the brief time I have been in Florida that there are no stairs. Do you have stairs in your house?"

When she said no, he grew very serious. "Stairs are very important to making your legs stronger. You must walk up and down stairs, every day."

Her knee twinged when Marie remembered how Bridget had helped her get better by making her walk up and down the long steps.

"I did that, as a child, after my legs weakened."

"And it helped, yes? So where can you walk stairs?"

"At my school," Marie said and thought of the stairwell going up to the library.

"Every day, including the weekend and vacations?"

"Yes, how many steps?"

"Do you walk stairs now?"

"No, not even into my house."

"Start with ten, maybe in a few days, increase to fifteen, but no more."

Marie nodded she understood and was thinking she could exercise after school.

"Now, we will practice on this step. You must perform the exercises exactly for stronger muscles."

By the third week of stair walking, Marie found she was looking forward to the exercise and was amazed how much better her knees felt. The decision to pursue the medical gymnastics had been the right one after all.

Then the unwanted telephone calls began. A few hung up when she answered and said hello. At first she thought they were wrong numbers. Others had called and stayed on the line without saying a word, but the ones in the middle of the night made her question her safety.

The first night call came at 1:15.

She struggled out of bed to reach the telephone in the front room, When she picked up the receiver, she heard, "Nazi sympathizer," in a deep male voice followed by a click. Standing in the front room with the street lights filtering in through her glass lanai door, she broke out in a cold sweat and her knees weakened. Her heart thudded so loud it gave her a headache.

It was several moments before Marie regained her senses. She was the only one who could protect her. So she walked to each door to check the locks. She also closed the blinds to the lanai. Her home had become a cave, dark and still.

The second night, Marie closed the lanai blinds at dusk and sat at the desk to grade student work, but the silent telephone kept grabbing her attention. Would it ring late tonight? Maybe the caller just had too much to drink and would not call again.

Marie went through her usual routine to get ready for bed and finished a few minutes before nine. But when she entered the bedroom, the bed did not look inviting or safe. It was too far from the telephone. So she unmade the bed, and with pillow and sheet in hand, she remade her bed on the couch, close enough to answer the rings or to call for help.

After she flicked off the table lamp, Marie put her head on the pillow and waited. From outside came sounds she had never noticed before. Neighbors whistled and called their dogs. Music from faraway mingled with laughter and drifted into her house. Car doors slammed. A few cars started, and one, with a distinctive rattle, circled the block five times.

Marie hated how frightened and alone she was.

The clock chimed the hours, and after midnight, Marie lost track of whether the single chime was for half-past or signaled the one o'clock hour. She waited and willed the telephone not to ring her signal.

Then the telephone came to life. Two longs and two shorts. Her code.

Marie argued with herself and tried to ignore the rings as they tempted and drew her closer. She stood and debated with her hand paused above the telephone. But she gave in and picked up the receiver.

The same voice as last night. The same angry words.

Marie detested being a victim. She had refused to be a cripple when she was eight. She had decided to leave home and have her own life when she graduated high school. The bully on the other end was not going to make her feel unsafe in her own home.

She returned to the couch. After punching the pillow, Marie put her head down and planned. There were options. Asking for a new signal might work, but she would have to tell everyone her new number. While the people she would want to have her number did not add up to even fifty, she resented having to do the work involved in notifying them. Ignoring the calls until the man grew bored might work, but she did have to sleep.

Marie turned on her side, and it came to her. She had her answer. She got up, wadded the bed linen and pillow together and returned to the bedroom.

The next evening, Marie wrapped the telephone in several pillows and followed with the winter bedspread used so rarely since her move south. She might not sleep tonight, but at least she might not hear the rings.

Marie was so exhausted by the fourth night that she slept through till daylight. As she brushed her teeth, she decided to continue putting the telephone to sleep every night. Due to the nightly calls, yesterday's session with Professor Brandenburg took on a new importance as she walked into the examining room. His methods were helping. Using a cane might become part of her past and not her future. She would stay the course.

The professor, however, did not look as well as he had last week. He was even thinner, something she did not think was possible. Guilt swept over her. She should have been more considerate. Here he was treating her, and though the rules laid down by the camp commander and agreed to by Dr. Peyton and the two of them disallowed money exchanging hands, no one had said one word about food.

"Professor, have you ever had honey orange upside down cake?" she asked.

His eyebrows went up. "What does upside down mean for a cake?"

After she explained, he laughed and said, "I have never heard of such a thing. You use a tiegel?" His hand moved as if it held something heavy. Then he stuck out the other hand and turned the first hand over.

"If tiegel means skillet, then yes," Marie said and felt very shy when she then asked, "Shall I bring you one next week?"

"Certainly, you will, as you say, put some meat on my ribs."

Marie would never had known how long the 1:15 calls might have continued if the visitors had not shown up at her house after the next week's appointment with the professor. All the pleasure she had received from watching the man eat half the cake before he turned his attention to her evaporated when she answered the door. The sight of two men in suits with telephone company identification badges, accompanied by an unhappy looking policeman, forced the recipe for the key lime pound cake she was planning for next week from her mind.

"Miss Hussong," the police officer said as he stepped first through the door. As Marie edged back, she realized that he was the one in charge and the telephone men were riding shotgun.

After he refused some iced tea and the others unhappily followed his example, Marie sat at her desk and waited for them to sort out who was going to sit where.

"We're here because the phone company's been getting quite a few complaints that you are not answering your phone at night."

He waited for her to continue. She outwaited him.

"Maybe your phone isn't working?" the younger of the other two men asked. His Adam's apple bobbed. Marie felt sorry for him. He could have used some iced tea about now. "Maybe you dropped it?"

"You gentlemen may check. I do not receive very many calls."

"Our records show that, ma'am," the older of the two said and straightened his tie.

"Just one at 1:15 every night, just like clockwork," the policeman growled.

"Well, you see. I do not know that," Marie said and explained how she silenced the telephone nightly.

"Good God, young lady," the young man blurted. "Why didn't you tell someone?"

"I refuse to acknowledge that boorish man's existence."

"But you weren't safe. Conrad was close to blowing up when Officer Lacy arrested him. He was so frustrated with you that he was coming over here tonight to teach you a lesson you would never forget."

Marie went hot and cold at the same time. Heat from the anger that anyone, especially someone she knew, would ever plot to harm her spiked, but icy fear won out. The grocer, who was so friendly before his son went missing, was certainly quite capable of really harming her. How could she have blissfully slept all those nights. He might have broken in at any time. It was possible she might not have lived through the attack.

"Miss Hussong," Lacy said, "You are safe now. We've got him behind bars, and he ain't going nowhere soon. But I have to ask you. You do know that some people are mighty upset with you and your German friend."

"How did you discover that it was Mr. Conrad?"

The older man said, "The company has the equipment to trace calls, and we keep very good records."

"Was he the only one making the calls?" Marie asked.

"Yes, and the company strongly suggests you report any more such calls. We are here to help you. That's part of the service."

Lacy stood up, and the other two followed. At the door, he turned, "We have also increased our patrol, in case some other nut gets it into his head to do you harm. I hope the help the professor's giving you is worth all the aggravation it's causing you."

Marie locked the door after they left and slid the lanai blinds closed. She hoped she would sleep enough to be able to teach tomorrow.

On the third Thursday afternoon in November, Marie decided to celebrate that so far, during November, her life was back on an even keel. The annoying calls had stopped. She had found some German recipes in an international cookbook at the library. The one she was going to make for her next visit with the professor was carrot cake. On page 86, the writers gave a short history of the recipe that went back to the shortages of World War I. Marie was surprised that carrots were considered a sweetener. But the ingredients seemed to lack moisture. Maybe she should add a few crushed orange slices. If nothing else, it might add a flavorful zip. She would half the recipe and also make one for herself that night. Maybe Elizabeth would want a few hours' break from caring for her mother and join her.

One last pat of her dress pocket reassured her that the shopping list had not been lost during the day of teaching. She walked up the stairs so briskly that she was a bit winded at the top. Those intense exercises and the deep massages Professor Brandenburg had begun last month were showing real promise. She did not remember ever climbing stairs so quickly and easily. She would have to remember to ask him tomorrow if it was time to retire her cane.

Marie checked the teachers' mailboxes and very soon wished she had kept on heading for the school's front door. She stood without moving after she read the note from Archie. In the background she could hear the staff wishing each other good evening, setting up bets on the college bowl games, sharing travel plans. None of those conversations applied to her.

Boosey said he was sorry after he walked into her, and his apology got her moving again. She stuffed the note in with the shopping list and started for Burr's office, trying not to feel as if she were a wayward adolescent being summoned to the principal's office.

On the first leg of the trip, down the hallway to the stairwell by the library, Marie thought maybe she had taken the wrong reading on the note. It was possible that Archie wanted to congratulate her on how excited her art students were about "making art their own" as she phrased it on the first day of class.

After she went back down the stairs to Archie's personal office, she turned left at the end of the hallway and saw his door half-open. Perspiration spigoted, between curls, and her palms went damp.

What had she done wrong? The words "before you leave today" did not mean "I put in a good word to the board about your art classes this year."

What kind of knock should she make? A pair of timid sounds or one confident one. Or a friendly tone like a knock-knock joke?

Marie decided on the latter and walked into the office. Immediately a veil of cigarette smoke, old and fresh, settled over her, and Marie knew she would be carrying the odor into her house later.

Archie motioned her to what the kids called the throne of shame. He looked tired and lit a new cigarette from the nub left in his mouth.

Marie watched the glow birth from the old to the new and tried not to breathe deeply.

"Miss Hussong, we have a situation here," he said and waved his cigarette at an envelope on his desk. "This letter, unsigned of course, was sent to the board. You can read it if you like. But I don't recommend it. I'll save you the trouble, seems someone has noticed your choice of cookbooks from the library."

Marie took in how nervous the man was. He was sweating and his hand shook when he wiped his forehead. Archie paced from one side of his desk to another without taking a seat as he said, "Marie, what I'm about to say is not easy, and I want you to know one thing. This did not come from me. I am only the messenger. I tried to get the board to change their minds, but it was no go. I'm so sorry." Then he picked up a second envelope from the desk and handed it to her. He seemed to collapse into his chair. "This one you have to see."

Marie felt the world closing in as she shook the letter free and began to read. The words "consorting with the enemy", "questionable loyalty", and "immediate termination unless" swam before her eyes. She had to blink several times before continuing to read. She had to know what followed the pivotal word "unless." If she lost her job, she would have to return home and live with her mother.

At last she could read the conditions, "must cease and desist fraternizing with the enemy" and "retake the required loyalty oath to remain employed, howbeit, on probationary status."

Marie let the letter fall as she gasped for air. Why was everything so infuriatingly taxing for her? Losing a sister, struggling to walk again, living with her mother, taking the one and only teaching job offered her? Others just seemed to have it so blissfully easy. Nary a bump on their life's path.

But from the other side of her brain, a voice said that everyone had troubles, and each trouble made them stronger.

Well, if that was the case, Marie snarled to herself, she should be the finest tempered steel around. She took a few deep breaths and felt stronger.

Rising to storm out, Marie caused the chair to rock back and crash into the window ledge. When Archie looked up, she caught sight of his face. Embarrassment, pride, and questioning all competed for occupancy. The latter won.

"Don't decide right now, Marie. I'll tell them I missed you tonight. I'm going to be out of town tomorrow. Take the weekend to consider. We'll talk on Monday after school."

The next afternoon, Marie proudly carried the carrot cake past Doctor Peyton's receptionist after eying her and wondering if she were the culprit that had gone to the school board and complained. As she sat in the empty examining room, she waited and debated whether to tell Dr. Peyton and Professor Brandenburg about the board's threat. She wanted to fight her own battles, but history had taught her that even the strongest warrior needed help from time to time. Maybe she did need allies.

A knock on the door broke her reverie, and the nurse walked in.

"Miss Hussong, Doctor Peyton and the Professor have been called to the hospital for an emergency. We'll put you down for the first appointment after school on Monday."

When Marie turned the corner by her house, she was surprised to hear the familiar knocking noise of Sybil's car as it rolled toward the far corner of the street. Sybil usually came to that side of town only on the days they volunteered at the Gardens.

The envelope resting half in her mail box lifted with the breeze and gave Marie a premonition of bad news. Taking it in hand, she recognized her friend's handwriting.

Once inside, she opened the letter with growing unease and offered a short prayer that nothing had happened to Edith and Alice's grandsons. The boys had made remarkable recoveries from their war wounds. It would be heartbreaking if they relapsed.

The letter was brief and very much to the point.

> We ask you to quietly withdraw as a volunteer. You know why.

Marie sunk to the floor. She had no friends left.

Monday came, dark and overcast. Marie ached and could not make herself rise from bed, let alone walk to school. All morning long she listened to the telephone ring from the front room. Something had the party line stirred up again. She was probably the topic of conversation once more.

On her way to the kitchen for a drink of juice, the telephone came to life again. With her signal of two longs and two shorts. Marie lifted the receiver and braced herself for some heretofor unimagined bad news.

"Miss Hussong, I'm afraid Dr. Peyton has asked that you come on Friday and not today. He and the Professor have not left the hospital yet."

"Can you say what is going on?"

"Oh, I thought you would know since all the schools have been closed early for Thanksgiving Vacation. Some kind of brain fever. All five of the Dell children are in the hospital, and the county decided to close schools as a precaution."

The term brain fever caused Marie to become nauseous. Dr. Purcell had used those words at one time to describe both her and Louise's illness.

During the vacation, Marie scolded herself that she had become a hermit. Venturing outside only to walk to Publix, she did no socializing. There were very few opportunities. The Ritz closed down in cooperation with the county board of health and showed no movies. Churches were also urged to limit their gatherings. When Marie walked to and from the market, she saw few people and fewer cars.

Who could she possibly call? The only one who might take her call was Elizabeth, and she did not want to endanger her friend's teaching job.

So Marie turned to her paints and the memories she had stored of the most beautiful plants she had cared for at the Gardens, especially the camellias and azaleas. The painting soothed her, but the inactivity and loss of the school steps cost her. Her legs grew weaker until she gave herself a stern talking to.

She called up one of her former students who was good in woodshop and commissioned a set of three steps. When Ralph brought them three days later, he sat in the garden with her and told all the gossip his mother had heard while cutting and perming hair at her shop.

"It was the strangest thing, Miss Hussong. The German professor from out at the camp, do you know the one I'm talking about?"

When she answered yes, he must have remembered the backstory about her and the German. A dull blush blazed across his face and neck and made his red hair even brighter.

"I'm real sorry, Miss Hussong, I forgot, for a minute, what the town was saying about you and him."

When he realized he had even made the situation worse, he glanced around in panic for an escape route.

"It is fine, Ralph. Please go on with your story."

After a long pull on his Pepsi, he said, "Anyway that fellow, along with Doctor Peyton, took care of the Dells and all the other sick kids. He got their parents in there to pull and tug on their arms and legs something fierce, day and night was what Mom heard."

"Did that help?"

"It sure did. He explained to them that the worse thing to do was to leave them to lay in bed and not move. He even stayed over at the hospital and helped some of the parents when they tuckered out. That's when the coaches got involved."

Marie could not believe her ears. "Did you say coaches?"

"Yes'um. Mrs. Burr told my mom that the German asked for them. Said they should know how to knead, that was the word Dr. Peyton used, knead the soreness out and keep the muscles working. Mom had to explain to me that was how she made bread. Kneaded the dough."

Ralph pointed to the three steps he had made for her. "I met him, you know?"

Marie said, "No I did not. How?"

"At the hospital. Dr. Peyton called me over and told me to do what the German said. He wanted me to make a whole set of these things, for the hospital and for the families to take home."

He laughed and drained the last of the bottle. "You should have seen the first one I made. It was awful. He gave me the measurements in something called metric. I thought he meant inches. I remembered hearing about that stuff in math class, but I never paid any attention."

He laughed again. "What I ended up with looked like doll furniture."

Marie laughed also but said nothing.

"Anyway, that's how I got so good at these step things. Yours is the best one I've made. Maybe after the war, I can get some more training on building other stuff to help old people around their houses. Mom says that would be a good future."

Then another blush ambushed him. "I didn't mean you were old, Miss Hussong."

Poor Ralph, Marie thought, I hope he never gets involved in any high stake card games. He'll lose his shirt.

By the first week of December, Marie had regained most of her strength and had a small collection of paintings, more than enough to send north for Christmas and to give to Elizabeth, Dr. Peyton, and Professor Brandenburg for the holidays. The steps worked wonderfully. She was surprised how stable they were. Ralph had suggested that he anchor them to the lanai. Marie was glad she had agreed. The weather was perfect. The color of the flowers inviting, and the exercise time just flew by as she planned her next paintings.

Even more good news arrived that week. Marie opened an envelope from a gallery in Sarasota and expected to see a notice that they were sending her painting back since they could not sell it. But when a check for $15 fell out, Marie could not believe the amount. The owner had written that the splash of white camellias against a coral Venetian wall crumbling into the blue sea was just what a rich client wanted for their home overlooking the bay. She even asked for five more paintings. Marie collapsed into a nearby chair and offered a prayer of thankfulness. She could pay the back rent. She would not have to move back north, yet.

Marie was in the second bedroom sorting through which paintings to send to Sarasota when she heard Archie's voice through the front door.

"Are you home? Has anyone called? I hope not."

She came down the hall and saw a very happy man smiling at her.

"Why?" she asked and offered him a seat.

"Well, Miss Hussong, I have right here in my hand a letter of apology from the board and an request that you rejoin our teaching staff." He waved a letter her way.

Marie's hands shook as she opened the flap and took the paper out. The letter was on official letterhead and signed by all five board members.

"I don't understand," she said. "I was going to be fired."

"That was before the board heard about the good work of Professor Brandenburg in the hospital. By the time a specialist from the State Board of Health arrived, the Professor had a care plan in place for each patient. The state doctor was so impressed that he wanted to get permission to have Brandenburg follow him around. The big wigs all met and agreed that the state could consult with the German, but he wasn't leaving town. So your guy's a hero, and you are being asked back. I hope you say yes."

For a few minutes, Marie considered devoting her days to her own art. It was a nice dream, but totally unrealistic. Maybe some day, when she retired.

Chapter 15

Akron, Ohio, July 1931

<Sarah Jane and Isaac Guymon
<Betsey and John Hussong
Marie & Louise

A noise drew eight-year-old Marie from her sleep against her will. She fought against the last barrier to wakefulness and threw the thin counterpane over her head. It didn't help. The bright morning sunshine had registered behind her eyes.

"Good morning sleepy heads," her mother Betsey almost sang.

"Morning, Momma." Louise sang in return.

Her older sister's usual good cheer sometimes made Marie grit her teeth. She muttered something untranslatable, stretched lazily from a lump into a little girl, and elbowed Louise while she came up from under the bedcovers.

"Good morning to you, too, Marie," Momma said.

Marie pushed her brown curls from her face and asked, "Breakfast here yet?" Her stomach growled. She hadn't even see a breakfast tray when she sat up and looked around.

Instead, the sunlight flooded the room even more after her mother tied back another yellow curtain. Even worse was the faded pink housedress her mother wore. That meant laundry day and no stories. Bridget and her mother would be too busy to entertain her, as her mother called it. Another boring day lay before her.

"I hate staying in bed, don't you?" Marie whispered to her sister, careful that their mother wouldn't overhear.

"It won't be much longer," Louise said in a low voice and brushed her blond ringlets into a smooth order.

"Breakfast or staying in bed?"

"Both."

"I'm hungry, Momma," Marie said louder.

Her mother didn't stop to look at her while she picked up yesterday's socks from the floor and added them to the laundry basket in the hall. "Bridget will be here soon. Now, quick as bunnies, get up and use the bathroom before breakfast."

"Come on Marie, I think I hear Bridget on the steps." Louise climbed out of bed. "I'm going to be ready to eat when she comes through the door."

"All right." Marie hoped that maybe if she was good, Bridget might tell them a little story. During the three weeks the hired girl had worked for them, Marie never tired of listening to Bridget's words. Her presence was the only good thing about being sick in bed.

Marie and her sister were back under the covers by the time Bridget arrived. "Good morning, young ones. Hungry are you now?" Bridget asked in her voice that sounded like an angel.

At the sight of the dark-haired young woman, Marie gave up all hope of stories. Bridget would not be lingering in the bedroom. The hired girl wore an old blue print dress faded with blotches. She also was garbed for the laundry room.

"Thank you, Bridget," her mother said. "I'll stay with them while they eat. I put the whites by the basement door. Will you add those socks to the first load and bring up some warm water and towels."

"Yes, Mrs. Hussong," Bridget answered and picked up the clothesbasket.

After the girl left, Marie said, "Momma, did Bridget cook us something good?"

Momma gave no hint of what was under the green and white checkered tea towel over the breakfast tray.

"Is it shredded wheat and graham muffins with strawberry jam?" Marie guessed.

"Today, on Dr. Purcell's Protective Diet..." Momma lifted the tea towel with a flourish that reminded Marie of the magician she had seen last month. "The menu calls for oatmeal, stewed apples, and cocoa."

After Momma put the tray on her lap, Marie decided it was good enough and dived into the chocolate first.

"Can we get out of bed today?" Louise asked.

"Soon," Momma said as she seated herself in the rocker beside the bed. "Dr. Purcell says you're now on the road to recovery. Be patient."

"I want to see King," Marie said after she put down her cup.

Her mother stopped the chair. "You know how I feel about dogs in the house. They bring dirt and fur inside. Dogs belong outside."

Marie answered what she always did when her mother said King couldn't come past the porch. "When I'm all grown-up, I'll have as many dogs as I want, and they will all sleep in my bed."

Marie giggled because Momma rewarded her with an exaggerated expression of disgust. "I'm shocked that any daughter of mine would have such unladylike ideas. What is this world coming to? You'd think we lived in frontier times and had barns for houses." Momma shook her head, and a brown curl fell onto her forehead.

"When can we help you and Poppa again in the bakery?" Louise asked.

"Soon, keep thinking soon. You're almost ready to go outside and play again. Soon you can decorate cookies and sweep up next door, just as you did before you became ill. The bakery will still be there when you're better."

Marie ate the last bit of her stewed apples and stuck out her tongue at Louise when her sister wagged a finger at her and said, "You have to rest and not stir around. You don't want to be like rubber-legged Ruth, do you?"

Marie stuck out her tongue at her sister again before she pleaded, "Momma, tell us the story again. I can listen and eat at the same time."

Her mother settled back and rocked to the rhythm of the words. "Once there was a little girl named Ruth. She loved to run more than anything else in the world. She never walked. As soon as she woke up in the morning until she went to bed in the evening, she would run, run, run." Momma motioned for her and Louise to do their part.

"Run, run, Ruth, run," she and Louise chanted.

"At school she ran faster than all the other children. She knew how to run up and down hills and around big rocks and through rivers."

Momma moved her arms to show how Ruth ran. "She ran to school, and she ran home. She ran with the horses in the pasture and the butterflies in the field."

Marie and Louise moved their arms to mimic the motions of the horses and butterflies.

"She ran down to the store to get eggs for her mother."

Marie loved this part. "That's my and Louise's job to go to the store. We always go get eggs when you need them."

"You're right. You and Ruth have the same jobs." Momma laughed. "And then one day, a terrible thing happened. Ruth's legs started to hurt when she ran home from school. Her mother saw her walk, not run, into the house."

Momma pitched her voice higher and took the part of the worried mother, "Ruth, what is the matter? Why aren't you running?"

Momma made her voice grow tiny and said, "My legs hurt when I run, Ma."

"That's just growing pains," Momma spoke as the mother again and shook her finger as a warning. "You'd better rest your legs so you can be strong enough to run."

Marie felt sorry for Ruth. She knew what growing pains felt like. They hurt. Many nights she had awakened because her legs ached a lot. She'd cry, and her mother had rubbed the pain away so she could fall back to sleep.

Momma returned to her storytelling voice, "But Ruth was very excited and did not listen to her mother. She refused to rest her legs the day before the big field day at school. When it came time to run in the first race, her legs felt like rubber, and she could not run. She had to watch all the other children have fun in the races and play games. Therefore, if you don't want to be like rubber-legged Ruth, you'll rest your legs. The end."

"Mrs. Hussong," Bridget said from the door. "Time for the sponge baths?"

After Momma had bathed them and left, Marie squirmed on her side of the bed. She waited for Louise to give the signal that it was time to play Pretend. Though Marie knew the wait for where the game might take them was part of the fun, she had trouble holding her horses, as Grandma Hussong was fond of reminding her. Maybe today they would go to the circus.

First Louise brushed her blond curls again. Next she yawned so big Marie could see her back teeth. When Louise plumped her pillow, Marie thought she would burst before she would hear the magic words, "Marie, pretend you…"

At last, Louise got the bedclothes just right and started the game. "Pretend we're having a picnic by the city lake. What do you see? What do you hear?"

"I see some ducks swimming. Wait. One is a mother with two ducklings. Ooh, I can see it in my head. I just can't find the words. Just a minute, I'll draw it."

Marie reached over to her table by the bed and took her pencil and school-writing tablet. She leaned over the paper and drew the scene visualized in her brain. "Marie has such a way with drawing," she had often heard the grown-ups say after they had said, "Louise has such a way with words."

At lunchtime, Marie pleaded with Bridget to tell them a story while they ate. Bridget gave in to the request and sat down on the bed beside them. Her dark blue eyes gained a faraway look, and she began…

"Niamh, this fair princess, possessed such great golden hair and wore a splendid blue dress the color of the sky and sprinkled with stars. The great love of her life was Oisin."

Bridget's story captured Marie's attention as they traveled with Niamh on the back of her special horse Embarr.

"Her horse had magical qualities. Embarr flew right over the top of the waves and took Niamh and her love Oisin to a land where no one became old or died and every wish came true."

To Marie, the best part of the new story was when Niamh used an enchanted moving picture to visit with the fairies in Brittany. "How did she make the pictures move?" Marie asked. "They didn't have movie theaters back then did they?"

"No, I'm quite sure the fairies had no movie theaters," Bridget answered in her Irish lilt.

"How did she cast that spell?"

"I've wondered that myself, Marie."

"How did she send it to the fairies?" asked Louise.

Bridget laughed like the wind chime in the gazebo. "I've wondered about that too when I was your age."

Marie said, "I'd like to draw like that and tell a story with moving pictures. I could send them to Grandma Hussong."

"That you could, little one, for sure. Now I must be off to my tasks, and you must rest." Bridget straightened the counterpane and untied the curtains before she left them in the darkened room.

"Move over Sissy," Marie complained late that night when Louise's restlessness woke her up. "Give me some room." Marie elbowed her sister. She didn't budge. Marie thought Louise moaned. It was hard to tell since she didn't understand the words.

So Marie used her most commanding voice, "Louise, Momma and Poppa won't like it if they have to come up here again and tell us to be quiet. You'd better move."

Louise stayed still when Marie sat up and touched her sister's shoulder. "Louise, wake up, wake up." Marie drew her hand back in surprise. "Why's your hair all wet?"

Marie wanted Momma because Louise was so hot. Something was wrong. Marie started to cry and called out as loud as she could, "Momma, Poppa."

She waited for their footsteps on the stairs. Nothing. She grew more scared and didn't want to get out of bed because the room was so dark. Those shadows in the bedroom corner held dragons. It would be even worse in the long hallway outside their door. Several times, out of the corner of her eye, she'd caught sight of the scary monsters at the edge of the shadows. They were ready to snap their powerful claws around her ankles.

It was also against the rules. Momma had told her over and over not to get up and fan around. That would bring the temperature back. Deep inside, Marie sensed Louise really needed Momma.

Marie dried her eyes on the sleeve of her nightgown and began her own game of Pretend. "I have to be brave. Niamh's castle is downstairs, and I have to be a strong girl to find it. I'll stomp my foot and tell the dragons in the corner to go away."

Gathering her courage, Marie slowly got out of bed and tucked the covers around Louise.

"I'll go get Momma. Don't be afraid up here all by yourself. You be brave too."

Marie stamped her foot as hard as she could and shouted beyond the door, "Go away dragons. Louise needs me to find Momma."

She crept down the hall and towards the ill-lit stairs. Not once did Marie look at the monsters in the hall. If they remained unseen in the shadows, maybe they'd leave her alone. She kept focused on the soft light coming up the stairwell.

"I'm looking for Niamh's castle. I am brave," she repeated over and over and started down the stairs.

At last, Marie's bare feet hit the oak floor in the hallway. "I'm almost to Niamh's castle," she pretended and ran toward the front parlor.

"Momma, Momma, come quick," she called and passed through the door. When Marie found the room empty, she began to cry. Within moments, she heard the front screen door slam, and her parents rushed in from the porch.

Her mother got to her first. "What are you doing out of bed?"

"What's wrong?" Poppa asked as he knelt down to her level.

"Louise, she…she…" Marie said, pointed, and saw Momma fly up the stairs.

"You're a very sick little girl," her father said and carried her upstairs. Marie nestled into his arms. He stopped patting her back when he came to open bedroom door.

Marie looked up. Her mother had knelt beside the bed and held Louise's quiet body tight. Louise wasn't waking up, and her head hung back at a funny angle.

"My baby, God no, not my baby, not my Louise." Momma rocked as tears streamed down her face.

"No, no," Poppa said. Marie felt his hand leave and saw it go against the doorframe. After a little while, he walked slowly toward the bed and laid her down before he headed toward the door.

Marie watched and listened, too frightened to understand all she saw and heard.

"Don't leave me now," Momma cried out.

"I have to get Doc Purcell or we'll lose them both," he said. "I'll call him and be back as soon as I can."

Marie watched her mother cradle Louise and waited.

When the doctor rushed in, his round face didn't have his usual smile. He looked first at Louise and shook his head at Poppa.

Next, he examined her. At last, the two men came together at the foot of the bed. Their words didn't make any sense, yet Marie understood something very wrong had happened.

"John, I'm optimistic about Marie. Her fever's broken. Just keep her quiet."

He looked over at Momma and Louise and took out a bottle from his bag. "Here's some laudanum. Give a teaspoon in water to Marie and triple that amount for Betsey. It'll help them rest. The next few days will be arduous."

Dr. Purcell removed his glasses and polished them with his tie. "I'll call Groves, and they can come for Louise. John, you'll have to help me. We must get them away from Marie, understand?"

Her father nodded, and the doctor clapped him on the shoulder. "Good man."

Marie swallowed most of the doctor's medicine. It wasn't good though it tasted a bit like cinnamon.

"Little one," Poppa said, "In a few minutes, I have to go downstairs. I'll send Bridget up. Will you be a good girl and go to sleep now?"

Although scared, she had suddenly become tired. "Yes Poppa."

She watched her mother also drink the medicine. As soon as the glass was empty, her father gently gathered Louise and carried her out of the room. Dr. Purcell helped Momma from the floor and guided her from sight.

Marie felt a sweet sleepiness creep over her and hoped Louise would get a dose of the magic drink. Though she was alone and uneasy, everything seemed like it would be okay tomorrow.

Chapter 16

Mr. and Mrs. John Hussong announce that their bakery will be closed for the rest of the week due to the passing of their daughter, Louise Abigail Hussong, yesterday

Akron Beacon Journal, July 8, 1931, Section D, p. 5

**Louise Abigail Hussong is
God's Newest Angel**

Louise Abigail Hussong, age 10, was called to her heavenly home yesterday. She leaves behind her parents, Mr. And Mrs. John Hussong of Claremong Street, a sister Marie, and a grandmother, Mrs. Rebecca Hussong, all of Akron.

Public calling will be held at the First United Brethren Church, Arlington and fifth, Friday, July 10th at 10 a.m., With the service and interment immediately following at Hillside Memorial Park.

Akron Beacon Journal, July 9, 1931, Section D, p. 1

Chapter 17

<Sarah Jane and Isaac Guymon
<Betsey and John Hussong
Marie & Louise

When Marie woke up the next morning, the world didn't feel right. It took a few moments to realize why. Louise was not beside her. Marie struggled to sit up and felt someone's presence in the room. Bridget rocked and looked at her through eyes red and tear-filled.

"Where's Louise?" Marie asked, "I want Louise."

"I know you do, little one."

"Why are you crying?"

Bridget ignored Marie's question. "Be a good girl, Marie. Take your medicine and eat so you can get strong," she said and placed the food tray on Marie's lap.

"Will you tell me a story about Ireland?" Marie wanted company. She didn't like being alone, and she certainly didn't feel like eating or taking that awful medicine again.

"If you promise to eat all your food and take your medicine."

Marie swallowed the cinnamon drink and ate. She was hungrier than she realized. Drowsy from Bridget's voice and story, she had about drifted into sleep when a kiss brushed her forehead.

Sometime later, a disturbance from downstairs startled Marie from sleep. The way the sunlight came into the room told her that it was almost time for lunch. A woman's voice ascended. It was almost like her mother's, but the words were slower.

"No, not my baby. Bring her back. Why'd you let them take her away? Give her back to me. Why can't I hold her?"

The loud cry grew fainter. Marie could hear her father's voice without any words. Only the low and steady way he talked when something was wrong.

At once, Marie knew in her soul Louise had died. She had to go find Momma and Poppa. When she tried to get out of bed, her left leg felt funny. Her mother's story came back to her. Was she about to become rubber-legged Ruth?

"Marie."

At the sound of her name, she turned and noticed Grandmother Hussong rocking by the bed. The old woman looked a lot older than the last time Marie had seen her at the Memorial Day Parade. Her face and mouth drooped, and her gray eyes had sunk into her face. Her white hair, braided and gathered at the back of her neck, made a sharp contrast to her black dress.

Grandmother leaned on her cane and took her time rising from the chair. The arthritis must be acting up again, Marie thought as she watched the old woman pick her way toward the bed.

"Marie," she said again. Her black dress crinkled the whole long time she eased herself onto the bed. "You have to be a very brave little girl, so you can be a comfort to your mother and father."

The heavy pain in Marie's heart made her want to go back to sleep and wake up in a happier time. "Is Louise dead?"

"Yes, my dear."

Marie collapsed into her grandmother's arms and held on tight. The woman's words seemed far away. "Louise has gone to be with the Lord. He decided to call her to heaven where all her pain and suffering will end."

"Is she coming back soon?"

"No, but remember, one day you'll see her when you go to heaven. She's joined Grandfather Hussong. He's telling her stories about what a wonderful place heaven is."

"I don't want her up there. I want her down here. Who's going to play Pretend with me?" Marie buried her face into her grandmother's chest. "Why can't she come back to me?"

When Bridget brought up the lunch tray after her parents had left for Louise's serices, Marie asked her, "Have you ever been to a funeral?" and again noticed the red rim around the girl's blue eyes.

"Aye, back home in Ireland, when I was about your age."

"What's going to happen at Louise's funeral?"

"Have you attended one?"

"My grandfather died after Christmas. See the picture I drew this morning?"

122

Bridget sat down on the bed. "Take three bites of your chicken and dumplings first. Good. Now tell me. What's this picture about?"

"The funeral. Here's the church. That's me and Louise." Marie pointed out two small girls in her drawing.

"I can see you there. A good likeness."

"Momma made us wear those ugly black dresses. We couldn't have any bows or lace ribbons." Bridget's fingers traced the images of the two girls. "I wanted to wear my party dress, the blue one with ruffles."

"It is certainly the better of the two."

"Momma said ladies wear black to funerals. Is it the same in Ireland?"

"Eat three more bites of food. Artists need to keep their strength up. How else can they draw pretty pictures?"

Marie took three tiny bites before she put down her fork and said, "I'm not hungry anymore."

"All right, little one."

Bridget rose from the bed and started toward the door. Marie panicked. "Please stay," she pleaded. "I'm not finished explaining my picture. See all the people crying? Especially Grandmother Hussong? She's crying the most."

Bridget placed the tray on the table by the bed and took a seat beside her. Marie took a deep breath and caught the scent of lilac Bridget usually wore. Having her close made Marie feel a little better.

Marie pointed to her artwork, "That's a lace handkerchief in her hand. She's wearing all black with her pearls. She's promised them to me. Pearls are real pretty, aren't they?"

Marie waited for Bridget's nod before she went on. "See Momma's garnet brooch and shawl she got from Grandma Sarah Jane? They're promised to Louise. It's like the begats in the Bible. The brooch goes to the oldest daughter. Momma got them from Grandma Sarah Jane, and she got them from her mother. And Louise was supposed to get them from Momma." Marie's eyes pool with tears. "I guess she'll promise them to me, now."

Bridget took a big handkerchief from her pocket and dabbed at Marie's face. "Don't you be worrying about that right now."

They sat in silence for a few moments before Marie said, "I've been thinking. When Grandfather Hussong died, we went to the cemetery. Momma said that is how our family honored our loved ones. We bury them because the Bible says we have to. Dust to dust. I asked Momma if that was because Adam came from clay and clay is the same as dust. She shushed me and promised to explain later. But she never did. Do you know?"

Bridget's hand went to her hair where she tucked some loose strands into her bun. Marie waited and loved Bridget so much at that moment because she took her time and really thought about what to say.

"Oh, I never considered it that way. You're probably right."

Not too many people ever told her she was right, and hearing it from Bridget made Marie grow stronger in her heart. "Here's my other picture. At Grandmother Hussong's house. After we returned from the cemetery. The women kept their hats on, just like church. And the men smoked cigars on the front porch."

"Is that because your granny doesn't like cigars in her house?"

Marie nodded and loved the questions and Bridget even more.

"What's this they're wearing?" Bridget pointed to the sections Marie had left uncolored except for some red and pink dots. Marie didn't have a white crayon so she added dots that were supposed to be flowers.

"Grandmother's aprons. They went into the kitchen and put on her aprons. See, they're carrying food the neighbors brought into the dining room. The ladies stationed Louise and me by the front door. Our job was walking the neighbors to the dining room." Marie looked up. "Did Mrs. Haslett bring over some gingersnaps?"

"I believe she did. I'll go get you some."

While Bridget was gone, another thought scared Marie. Maybe Bridget would have the answer to that one too.

As soon as the girl walked through the door with the cookies and a glass of milk, Marie asked, "Do you think God will forgive me?" Her heart made so much noise that her ears were plugged. She had a hard time breathing while she waited.

"Whatever have you done that the Lord has to forgive?" Bridget put the food on the table beside Marie. "You're only eight."

Marie didn't think being eight meant that God would just forgive her. "For me living and Louise dying?"

Bridget dropped to the bed and gathered her close. "We don't know why God chooses some and leaves others here on earth."

The words and arms eased Marie's heart. Yet something else still worked at her. "Is it sinful? I'm not crying and thinking of Louise when I'm drawing. Making pictures makes me feel good inside."

Bridget gave her a little squeeze before she released her. "Look at me." Marie did. "You must remember this." Marie promised. "You'll think of Louise every day for the rest of your life, and you won't cry forever. Do you remember your grandfather's funeral?" Marie nodded.

124

"The men stood on the porch?" Again Marie nodded. "Didn't they laugh some of the time?"

"Yes, I asked Momma about that."

"What'd she say?"

"She said they laughed because they remembered the funny things that happened in Grandfather's life. And they were thankful he had lived a good long time. He'd earned his reward to be with the Lord."

"There you are. Try to remember that Louise is in a better place and you'll be with her one of these days."

"So, I'll see her in heaven?" Marie asked because she wasn't sure she deserved to go there.

"That's right, you're a good girl."

Suddenly a weight lifted from her. She would be with Louise, and they could play Pretend forever. "Would you like to see what else I drew?"

After she showed Bridget the picture of Louise in heaven, Marie explained how Louise smiled and sat with Grandfather Hussong. They both rocked in his favorite chair.

"What's this?" Bridget pointed to a brown object at his feet.

"That's his spittoon."

"Ah, he liked to chew, did he?"

"Yes, Grandmother said cigars were worse than chew."

Bridget took the picture and moved it close to her face. When she gave it back to Marie, she asked, "Who is the woman on the other side of Louise?"

"That's Grandma Sarah Jane. She's making a heaven dress for Louise. It's almost done. Louise loved that color blue." Marie's tears fell on her artwork. "I want Louise back here with me. I don't want to wait until I go to heaven."

"I know, little one, I know." Bridget's arms came around her again and rocked gently.

Throughout the day, Marie awoke several times as the front door knocker echoed within the stilled house. Bridget's voice floated up the stairs each time she talked with neighbors and Grandmother Hussong. Marie did not hear her mother or father's voice. Nor did she hear any men on the front porch or church women in the kitchen and dining room. During her wakeful moments, the pain of being alone rushed through her, along with some confusion. Where were her parents? Had Louise been left alone at the cemetery? There were other times she thought she heard the bedroom door open, but by the time she had struggled through the deep sleep and looked, no one was there.

It was bedtime when Marie's father visited. "Time for a story, my sweet Marie?" he asked.

"Tell me about rubber-legged Ruth," Marie asked.

"How does it start?"

"Once upon a time there was a little girl. Her name was Ruth. She liked to run. She didn't want to ever stop running. No, that's not right." Frustration boiled within her because she couldn't remember all the extra details her mother put in. "Where's Momma? She knows the story."

"She's resting downstairs. It will be a little while before she can come upstairs and tell stories." Since Marie wanted to be a big girl, she tried to hide her disappointment.

Her father gave her a small smile and asked, "Why don't I tell you one of my favorites?"

She looked at him. His dark hair wasn't smoothed back the way she liked. He looked so old and tired. Maybe he needed to rest too. "Yes Poppa, tell me a story."

"That's a good girl. Now do you know the story of how Daniel Boone was real brave when he was your age?"

"At eight?" Marie was curious. She didn't know anyone her age had adventures.

"Yes, back in those days children had to help in grown up ways. He was out hunting with his friends in the dark woods when all of a sudden...."

Dr. Purcell's daily visits were always something Marie looked to. Not because of the jokes. He always told her the same one about the chicken crossing the road. She didn't think it was funny. But she laughed anyway.

What she really wanted to hear from him was she could get out of bed and go outside and play. Finally, a week after Louise's funeral, he gave her the good news. "You can walk around a little after breakfast and a little longer after supper. But," he pointed his index finger at her, "you have to rest in the afternoon."

"Thank you, Dr. Purcell." Marie threw the covers back.

"Do you promise to rest?"

"Yes, yes, yes," she promised and crossed her fingers and heart.

"Fine. Now, up you go and walk across the room."

Marie's feet touched the floor. "I don't have any slippers."

"You don't need them, just this once. Walk to the door and back to your bed."

She took a few steps. Her legs were stiffer than ever, and she must not have done it right. His smile faded, and he said, "Into bed with you and rest. I'll be back soon."

A few minutes later he returned with her father. Marie smiled at him. It was a surprise to see Poppa in the middle of the morning. But the smile he gave her was not a very happy one.

"Marie," he asked. "How are you feeling?"

"Ready to get out of bed, Poppa."

"That's grand," he said and looked at the doctor.

"Marie," Dr. Purcell said. "I want you to walk again. Are you too tired? No? That's a big girl."

She walked to her father. His smile turned upside down. When he picked her up and carried her back to bed, she was surprised to see his tears. "Don't worry Poppa. I'll rest my legs. I won't be like rubber-legged Ruth."

"I know. You're a good girl. I'll come and tell you another story tonight."

When her father returned at bedtime, he had a new story about a little girl named Marie. "Once upon a time, Marie tried to be a good little girl, every day. She always did what her mother and father asked her to do. She helped them decorate cookies in their bakery right next door to their house. Marie loved to put red hots on the gingerbread men and chocolate icing on the cookies."

Marie interrupted her father. "That's just like me. That's my job."

"Why it is. How about that?" and he continued. "One day Marie's leg started to weaken. It hurt to walk, and it hurt to lie in bed. But she was a brave girl. She wanted to go help her parents next door. So she set out for the bakery. She had to rest and stop on each step on the front porch. And there were so many steps."

"How many, a hundred?" Marie had a picture in her mind of a castle with many stairs in front.

"Not quite that many, probably about five. Each step made an awful pain in her leg. She was so very disappointed she could not walk to the bakery. There was nothing for it but to go back up to her room."

"Did she have to stop and rest after every step?" Marie knew how the other Marie's leg felt. She rubbed her own leg in sympathy.

"Yes, she did. That night her father asked her why she didn't come to the bakery and help. She told him her leg hurt too much. Her father grunted and left her alone. A few minutes later he returned with a beautiful

127

black cane. 'This is for you, Marie,' he said as he gave it to her. 'It's a magic cane. It will make your leg feel better when you walk.' "

At this point, Poppa stopped his story. He walked to the bedroom door. Marie saw him reach out for something. When he turned around, she saw it was a cane and realized the story had been about her. She got out of bed and took the light-brown cane from his hand.

"It doesn't look like a magic cane, Poppa. Is it really going to help my leg?"

"You have to put the magic in it. Use it every time you walk."

Chapter 18

Parents! Heed This Advice to Avoid Polio

Polio will soon be with us once again as the days warm up. Every summer polio strikes children as they play and swim. Last year there were over 9,000 cases in the United States.

Dr. Benjamin Purcell has seen the numbers rise and fall like waves throughout his twenty-year practice. He fears we are in the middle of an upswing in the number of cases. His advice for parents is four-fold.

Keep children from becoming overtired and rest every afternoon.

Ensure children do not touch the spout of public drinking fountains with their mouths.

Keep children from any body of water or even pools.

Avoid crowded public places.

Akron Beacon Journal, June 30, 1931, Section b, p. 2.

Chapter 19

<Sarah Jane and Isaac Guymon
<Betsey and John Hussong
Marie & Louise

"Look at the magic cane Poppa gave me last night," Marie said to Bridget as soon as the hired girl walked in with the breakfast tray.

"Aye, that's a fine looking cane for sure. Will you be wanting to try it out today?"

"Yes. Will you help me?"

"After you eat breakfast, I'll come and help you get ready. You be thinking about which dress you want to wear."

When a little later Marie put on her favorite yellow dress, the color of daffodils, it was too big. Bridget tied a ribbon around her waist to give the dress a snugger fit. With her hair neatly combed and held back with another yellow ribbon, Marie put on her shoes and reached for her cane.

"I'll be a brave little girl, won't I? For Momma and Poppa and Louise." Marie stood the cane on the floor a little in front of her right strong leg and with a hesitant step, put her weight on it and her right foot. It was her left foot that gave her trouble when she tried to move. She dragged it forward. Next she moved her right foot and repeated the movements. It took her about five minutes to reach the door of her bedroom. Out in the hallway Bridget's footsteps behind her meant she was not alone in the dark hall. After what seemed forever, she was at the end and looked down the stairs. Her legs wobbled. "I can't do it."

"That's enough for today, little one. It's back to bed with you."

"Did I do good?"

"Yes, just like Niamh. Remember how brave she was when she rode Embarr on the waves like it was grass?"

"She wasn't scared, just like me."

Every day Marie walked a few more minutes with her cane. Bridget stood beside her and gave encouragement. On the fourth day Marie pestered Bridget about going downstairs. "Look how strong I am. I know I can go make it all the way down."

Bridget stopped to consider. Her mouth clamped shut in a funny way. She looked like she was going to say no. Then, at once, her mouth eased. "Why don't we try two steps down and two steps up?"

"Four down and four up cause I'm eight?"

"What would we do if you were already nine?"

"That's funny, Bridget. You can't go down four and up five." Marie laughed.

They made a game of the stairs and added three steps down and up every day until only three steps remained. "Tomorrow I'll be downstairs," Marie said.

"What dress do you want to wear for your grand occasion?"

"I think the blue one. And a picnic on the front porch with King. Can I do that?"

"With a nap or two on the front swing, yes, you can."

"And I can surprise Momma and Poppa at lunch."

Marie didn't know how she was going to keep her secret that long, especially when Poppa came in to say good night.

The next morning, Marie bolted down the oatmeal as soon as Bridget put the tray by the bed. Within minutes she was dressed and ready for her trip to the porch and King.

Bridget insisted that she be presentable. "Hold still. Your part's not straight. You don't want to look like you slept on the top of your head, do you?"

"Hurry up. King's waiting on me."

"I know, after you have your hair brushed."

Finally, she passed muster. Bridget gave her a kiss on the forehead and said, "You look like an Irish princess. Be strong, you can do this."

It took a while. When Marie arrived at the foot of the steps, she turned around and looked up the staircase. She was so brave and proud.

"I did it, Bridget, I did it."

"On to the porch?"

Marie nodded and started toward the screen door.

Bridget placed a hand on her shoulder. "Let's be quiet when we go past the sitting room. That's where your momma's at rest. You'll see her

132

for lunch."

After Marie settled into a wicker chair, King sat by her feet, his nose resting on her lap and his tail thumping on the wood floor. Bridget took one long look at her and said in her no-nonsense voice, "You sit here while I fetch a glass of lemonade. You're as limp as an old dish rag."

Marie did not put up any fight. Her legs trembled. She hooked her cane over the chair arm and remembered to sit with her spine straight. Her mother had told her many times that a true lady never touched the back of a chair. Marie leaned down to inhale King's doggy smell and petted him in his favorite spot, the soft brown fur right between his eyes.

She decided that she was the happiest girl ever because she was downstairs again. Then a sense that part of herself was gone blanketed her delight. Marie thought about it and realized that Louise had taken part of her away when she died.

Marie had felt the loss of Louise ever since that horrible night. Yet it was strange how the sounds of ticking from the big clock in the hallway comforted her. Maybe because the steady beat was something Louise used to hear.

Bridget returned with a glass of lemonade. "I'm going to hang out the wash. Will you be a good girl while I'm in the backyard?"

Marie promised and sipped from the glass. Her strength returned after she drank the lemonade and rested for a few minutes. It was time to find her mother.

Every night when she had asked Poppa where Momma was, he answered that she was resting. To her why question, he said Dr. Purcell wanted her mother to get better. Soon she would be stronger, and they'd all be together again.

"Momma will be happy that I'm back downstairs, won't she, King?" Marie rose from the chair and left the dog on the porch. Her goal was her mother's sitting room, a room little girls were never allowed in unless they had been invited. This day was different. She needed her mother.

Marie found the door closed. When she tested the doorknob, she rejoiced that the door came ajar. She leaned on her cane and knocked lightly on the door. "Momma, Momma, may I come in?" she called. Her mother spoke some words she didn't understand.

"Momma, did you say come in?" Marie knocked again. The door creaked and opened. Her mother lay on a daybed with pillows behind her head and her eyes closed. The drawn window shades dimmed the room to twilight. Marie went to her mother and touched her hand. "Momma, it's Marie. I've come all the way downstairs to see you. Can you hear me?"

"Louise? Oh, Louise," Momma opened her eyes and locked onto her visitor's face. Marie saw the hope in her mother's expression die and disappointment take its place. "It's you, Marie. Why are you still alive? Why you? Why did God let you live and take my lovely Louise?"

Her mother's raving words stunned Marie. The next thing she felt was Bridget's hands on her shoulders.

"Why are you here, little one?" Bridget said. "Your momma needs her rest."

Marie heard the young woman's warm lilt and backed away.

Momma sat straight up, raised her arm, and pointed her finger. "Get out of here. I never want to see you again."

"Come," Bridget said quietly and led Marie from the room. "She doesn't know what she's saying. Dr. Purcell gave her some medicine to calm her. She talks nonsense all day. Forget what she's said. It's the grief. She'll be better soon. You'll see. She loves you. She truly does."

"The wrong one died. Should have been you." The shouts came to Marie in a fog. Her happy day was in ruins. She could hear her mother's words long after Bridget closed the door behind them.

In October, Dr. Purcell pronounced Marie healthy enough to go to school for half a day. At first, she didn't want to take her cane. But when Poppa reminded her how the magic cane helped that other little girl named Marie, he looked so worried that she changed her mind. She found she didn't need the cane as much on her morning walk to school as she did when she returned home for her lunch and afternoon rest.

By the first of November, Dr. Purcell gave her permission to attend school the whole day. Her spirits lifted when she spent more time among her friends.

The evening meal made Marie a nervous wreck since it was the only time she and her mother were together. Anxiety swept over her each time she felt her mother's eyes fall on her. She didn't want to hear those numbing words again. When she returned the look, Momma had her attention on her plate or focused on the darkening garden outside the dining room window.

Marie struggled to find the rhythm of the family as it had been before she and Louise had become ill. When Momma returned to work afternoons in the bakery the week before Thanksgiving, Marie hoped joining her parents might help things get back to normal. However, only the occasional customer broke her mother's shrouded silence draining energy from the very air, and her father had so little time to talk with her. The time together in the bakery left Marie with a sense of loneliness while she sat behind the counter and decorated cookies.

The second week of December, Grandmother Hussong moved into the front parlor, remade into her bedroom. The older woman gave warm smiles and hugs in the morning and welcoming conversation along with cookies and milk when Marie came home from school at three. When her grandmother told her she was needed at home to help her and Bridget, Marie gave up her afternoons in the bakery. She was happier at home, yet she missed the aroma of fresh bread and cookies in the ovens next door at the bakery.

Fortunately, Marie soon realized Poppa's clothes carried a fresh baked bread scent on them for a few minutes after he walked through the back door. Every day she watched for his return. Then she'd throw herself into his arms and inhale the comforting yeasty smell.

On Christmas Eve morning, Marie caught her grandmother's festive air, and together they kept the family traditions. She put all her favorite ornaments on the small tree first. Then she found the ones Louise usually hung.

"Grandmother, do you think Louise is looking down at us?"

"I certainly do, child. Just ask her to come into your heart. That's what I do with Grandfather Hussong. He's been with me ever since I hung that first angel hair bulb on the tree."

After they finished the Christmas tree, they arranged some greenery on the dining room mantle with Grandmother's old-fashioned village and her father's childhood train set. When they finished their cocoa break, they baked and decorated gingerbread men. Marie wanted to finish before the holiday morning rush at the bakery ended.

Marie asked her grandmother, "Do you think Poppa will like his cookie? I made this one specially for him. See all the red hots on it?"

"I'm sure he will. He always did as a boy." Grandmother Hussong smiled at her.

"Can I give it to him tonight at supper?"

"Yes, and make one for your momma and another one for Bridget."

"Are you going to ask me about my Christmas wish at supper?" Marie remembered last Christmas Eve when Grandfather Hussong, the oldest person in the family, asked her, the youngest person, what her wish was. She had answered more snow and in turn asked her father what he wanted. One by one everyone had shared. Waiting for her grandfather's question was hard to do, and all day she had changed her mind off and on about what to answer.

This year was different. She already knew.

"At the right time. You'll just have to be patient," her grandmother said.

The early supper at five o'clock brought all four together for their only family time. Although the adults had quickly developed the custom of simple meals and no long conversations after Louise's passing, Marie hoped their meal would be different that evening. But it remained much the same. In the silent dining room, splendid in its gold-flocked wallpaper, Poppa sat at the head of the table, Momma at the end, Marie to the left of her father, and Grandmother where Louise used to sit.

At the close of the meal, Marie showed off her gingerbread men. "Poppa, would you like this one for dessert? I put extra red hots on it for you."

"Thank you, Miss Marie. This is a lovely cookie. I don't think I've ever seen a nicer one. Have you, Betsey?"

Momma didn't respond. She sat there, as still as a mountain.

"Momma, I made one for you too," Marie offered. Her mother reached out her hand and took the cookie though she did not meet her daughter's eyes. Momma's behavior left Marie disappointed, and only her grandmother's touch on her hand stopped the tears.

"What is your Christmas wish, Marie?" Grandmother asked. Marie didn't answer. She struggled to keep her pain clamped way down inside. Grandmother asked again in a warm, patient tone, "Marie, did you hear me? What is it you want more than anything?"

"Louise. I want Louise back, and she's all I want." Silence reigned around the table. "I want Louise back. You told me God wanted her in heaven. He can return her to me now. He has had her long enough. I need her here with me."

Marie noticed her grandmother and father struggled to fight back their sobs and was about to apologize for making them sad when she heard a chair crash on the floor.

Momma stood, quivering with fury, her mouth turned down in anger, "How dare you say such things? You're so ungrateful. God in his mercy has allowed you to live. Now I know why. Your shriveled leg is his mark of displeasure. It's your fault Louise died. If you had come to us sooner, she'd still be with us. You killed your sister. I wish God had given me a choice. I'd have told him to take you."

Marie sat frozen with fear. Would God strike her dead at any moment? Her heart pounded as if she had run a mile, and her mind raced to find a way to please God. At last, Marie found she was wrapped in her grandmother's embrace. Out of the corner of her eye, she saw her father start toward Momma and Bridget rush into the dining room with the laudanum bottle.

"Marie." Grandmother held her safe. "Your momma didn't mean it. She loves you, we all do. We thank God every day he spared you. You are our blessed sunshine."

Across the room, Poppa stood behind Momma to hold her in place while Bridget filled a serving spoon with medicine. "Give her a large dose," he instructed. "Enough to put her to sleep. Yes, another spoonful." Poppa walked Momma out of the dining room to put her to bed. Bridget righted the chair and began to clear the table.

"Marie, come help me to my room," Grandmother said. The two each took their canes and moved haltingly out of the dining room and down the hallway. "Marie, do you know how some days you feel good and other days sad?" Marie nodded. "Like you, your momma has good days and bad days. Today has not been a good day for her."

"Will she have a good day tomorrow?"

"I don't know. But you can help me have one."

"Because it's Christmas?"

"Partly. I've been thinking how I'd like some company. My room is too large for one person. Would you like to share it with me?"

"Move in here with you?"

"Yes, I need someone to help me at night, someone to read to me and to talk to me. Would you leave your upstairs room for me, Marie? That is my Christmas wish."

Chapter 20

Mr. and Mrs. John Hussong are proud to announce their daughter Marie Hannah Hussong is a member of the 1943 graduating class of Ohio State University. Miss Hussong earned a Bachelor's of Arts degree in Fine Arts and will soon move to Winter Haven, Florida where she has accepted a teaching position. An open house celebration for Miss Hussong will be held at her parents' residence, 305 Claremont Street, 6:30-9:00 p.m. June 15th

Akron Beacon Journal, June 11, 1943, Section C, p. 3.

Chapter 21

Part 3

Sabina, Ohio, June 1926

<Esther Thompson
<Sarah Jane and Isaac Guymon
<Betsey and John Hussong
Marie & Louise

Last Will and Testament of Esther Mercy Thompson

I, Esther Mercy Thompson, lately of Sabina, Clinton County, Ohio, being of sound mind and under no duress, hereby set down the terms of my wishes on the 14th day of March, 1922.

1. I direct my son, Jeremiah Thompson of Sabina, Ohio to pay my funeral and doctor expenses first.

2. I bequeath to my granddaughter, Mollie Elizabeth Hussong, of Akron, Ohio, my Havilland china set.

3. My daughter, Sarah Jane Guymon, of Sabina, Ohio, is left the garnet brooch and paisley shawl I inherited from my mother on the condition that she promises to pass them on to her daughter, Mollie Elizabeth Hussong. Sarah Jane Guymon is to inherit nothing else from my estate since she has taken her share during my lifetime. I also forgive all debts she owes me.

4. The family Bible and its contents are to be included in the share belonging to my son, Jeremiah Thompson.

5. The balance of my other assets, real and otherwise, are left to my son, Jeremiah Thompson, after he pays all outstanding valid debts and claims to my estate.

Signed on the 14th day of March, 1922

Witnessed by:
Ambrose Reed of Sabina, Ohio
Cornelius Garrett of College Corner, Ohio

Probated June 7, 1926

Esther Thompson

Chapter 22

Sabina, Ohio, September 1929

<Esther Thompson
<Sarah Jane and Isaac Guymon
Betsey and John Hussong

Startled by the knock on the door at seven o'clock in the evening, forty-eight-year-old Sarah Jane Guymon opened the door part way. Her heart danced at the sight of her visitor holding a basket of apples in his hand. Richard Steele gave her a nervous smile, but she thought he did look nice in his dark suit and white shirt and deep blue tie. She especially liked the golden mum in his lapel. To a casual passerby on Main Street, it might appear he had called to deliver the fruit from his trees.

"Richard, how nice of you to stop by. Those apples look delicious. Jonathans, aren't they?" She smiled and bid him to come inside her tiny two-room apartment above Jamison's Dress Shop where she altered dresses.

"Yes, from my orchard," her visitor managed to say and offered the basket to her before he was over the threshold.

"Please have a seat," she indicated the battered dark leather sofa her brother Jeremiah had allowed her to take from their mother's home and put the apples on the small kitchen table in the opposite corner.

"Sarah Jane, I've something to say. I'm going to ask you to listen and please don't interrupt me, I might not finish," he said with another weak smile as she sat down beside him.

"I've been thinking about us. It's been two years since Eleanor's passed and much longer since Isaac left. It's time for us to move on."

He hesitated, cleared his throat, and loosened the knot in his tie a bit. "I want to marry you. I think I fell in love with you when you marked the anniversary of Eleanor's passing with yellow mums. You didn't notice me, but I saw you kneel down and put the vase beside her headstone. That is the kindest thing anyone has ever done for me."

As if he could sense her refusal, he rushed on. "We can be happy on the farm. I know you won't be living close to your brother and his family. I hope that's not a problem. However, it wouldn't take long to get here to Sabina from our home place. Or on Sundays after church. This isn't very romantic, not like in the movies, but how do you feel about marrying me?

Sarah Jane gazed at the man she had known about ten years. The man she had watched care for his wife during her long illness and grieve after her death. The man who was polite and tipped his hat when he saw her in town. More importantly, he was the man who all of a sudden a year ago started wearing a few new dress shirts and macassar oil on his light brown hair when he showed up at the church socials and picnics. Though he was very tone deaf, he even joined the choir and walked her home after the weekly practice. She had sensed from the second time he attended church in new clothes what his intentions were. His pursuit brought her ambivalence. She alternated between feeling terrified and unsure or honored.

That evening was the first time he had been inside her apartment. After the church events, he usually dropped her at the door because he respected her reputation. Some of the old bluenoses in town made it their business to be the morals monitors and keep an eye on every unmarried woman. Although she was in fact married, Isaac was nowhere in sight, and her every move had become common gossip. It wouldn't take long for all of Sabina to know that he had been inside her apartment. Someone was sure to notice and comment on how long to the minute he had stayed.

"Richard, I can't. I'm already married."

He took her hand in his and continued his wooing. "I've pondered that dilemma. I guess I've a lot of time to think out in the fields. You can get a divorce."

Shocked, Sarah Jane removed her hand from his. "I couldn't. No lady ever divorces. Mother and Father would roll over in their graves if they knew, and Jeremiah would disown me."

"It's the only way we can marry, dearest."

"How can I explain that to Mollie and go to court and tell everybody about my personal affairs? Mother always stressed that you don't wash your dirty laundry in public. Family business is family business and not for the whole town to talk about."

"You are entitled to some happiness." He gave her hand a gentle squeeze to emphasize his point and let go.

"Even if I wanted to, I can't. I have no idea where he is."

"You don't have to know. You go to court and tell the judge how he ran out on you. It's called desertion. You told me you've haven't heard anything from him for over ten years. He may be dead, and how would you know?"

"Divorce," she said more slowly and tumbled the word around in her mouth as she considered the chance of happiness at long last.

Richard's excitement grew contagious. "I talked to a lawyer friend in Lebanon. His name's Waite Tryon, and he's willing to help us. We can go see him next week. If we file at his courthouse and not here, that should keep some of the old busybodies away. But it's no secret that Isaac has left." He reclaimed her hand and promised, "You don't have to do this alone. I'll help, and you'll never have to be alone again."

"I don't know."

"Say yes. Please say yes. We'll marry the same day the divorce is final." Richard enclosed her hand between his. "I'll pay for the lawyer and the court fees. I want you to be my wife. Please say yes."

She did. Richard kissed her, their first real kiss.

The next morning when Sarah Jane brushed her hair, her thoughts focused on how fortunate she was. She had trouble believing her future had changed that quickly. Imagine a grandmother marrying for love. How strange love felt since she was long past the age when a woman followed her heart and married. A woman her age might choose a man because he could support her. Lord knows she did need help, but she shook her head no. She was sure she and Richard had a love match.

During the few minutes it took to brush and arrange her hair in its tidy bun, she wondered what Richard Steele saw when he looked at her. It wasn't vanity but curiosity that drove her to examine her reflection. Did he see a woman who looked every bit of her forty-eight years? Medium height, medium brown hair, medium build. Nothing special about her except for her green eyes. Cat's eyes her mother always said. She touched the wrinkles that edged those eyes. Some people called those laugh lines, but she knew better. Her lines had not come from laughter. There had not been any reason to laugh for some time.

She prodded herself away from sad thoughts. Enough of this melancholy, it was a day to enjoy her new happiness. The only other recent joyful times she remembered were when Mollie gave birth to Louise and

Marie. Among her few blessings, she counted how Mollie had sailed through her pregnancies. No trouble at all. So much better than when she had been with child. Part of the trouble had to rest upon Isaac.

Life with her parents also had its own worries and in the end had not helped her marriage. Every time she wanted to move out and have their own little house, he'd say, "Hold on darlin', it's going to get better. My ship's ready to come in any day. I can feel it. We'll show the whole town what a smart man you married."

However, the talk about success vanished a few years before he did. He'd missed seeing his granddaughters grow. Sarah Jane sighed and slid in the last pin.

Next, she moved to her small closet where the items Jamison's couldn't sell hung. The storeowners didn't give her the same clothing allowance the two clerks got, but they did want her to be dressed to step away from her sewing in the back room and on to the sales floor at a moment's notice. The choices before her were a dark green silk dress with a dropped bodice and knee length hem from last year's selections and a lightweight bright orange jersey tunic dress from three years ago. In a celebratory mood, she chose the silk.

The next Monday, she and Richard traveled to Lebanon to see his lawyer friend. No one in Sabina knew where she was going. The story she told her brother was that she had to go to Cincinnati to buy some dress material. To Mrs. Jamison, she said she had to visit her brother's family.

She insisted that Richard pick her up in his truck by the Greenlawn Cemetery on the edge of town. He hadn't been pleased with her request but seemed to understand how people in town loved to gossip.

"I was expecting you in your customary brown hat," he said after he helped her in. "The one with feathers and flowers."

"I don't wear my black one very often."

"Well, it looks good on you," he said and put the truck in gear. "Goes with your black dress and church gloves, but I guess I'm used to you in more colorful clothes."

She rolled the veil over the hat and tried to give him a reassuring smile. "I didn't want anyone to recognize me. I'm hoping to cover my tracks."

"Are you ashamed of me?" he teased.

"No, Richard, it's nothing like that. Please understand. I just hate giving the townspeople a free dogfight. They aren't interested in me, only the excitement a scandal brings. The men at their card games are every bit as bad as the women at their quilting bees."

"Now I'm a scandal?" He winked.

"I apologize, I'm putting this all wrong. You know how small towns are. I feel I lived all my life with people watching and talking about me and my personal business."

"Soon you'll be a safely married woman without any gossip attached to you." He moved the truck into a higher gear before he held her hand tight.

The visit to the lawyer started off as frightening as she had feared. Her heart was in her throat when Richard opened the door for her and they entered the office. She looked back to see if she recognized anyone passing by. Thank goodness only strangers hurried on their way to and from the courthouse.

After they were inside, Mr. Tryon warmly greeted Richard and gave her a professional smile designed to put her at ease. He was movie star handsome, just like that new British actor Ronald Coleman, with his slicked-back dark hair, and pencil-thin moustache and well-cut business suit. Yet his manner was friendly which helped because he began with some very personal questions about her life with Isaac. She knew she blushed several times when she stammered out her answers.

Richard took her gloved hand. His slight squeeze reassured her that the ordeal would soon be over. "I'm going out to smoke. Don't worry. I'll be in the alley and not out on Main Street for all to see."

When he closed the door, the lawyer resumed his interview. "Mrs. Guymon, I'm sure you realize how important these questions and your answers are. You are petitioning the court to declare your marriage null and void. The court considers divorce a serious matter and one that it does not like to act upon unless there are extraordinary circumstances. However, Mr. Steele has explained a few things about your case to me, and everything he said to me is confidential as is everything you say."

"Does that mean you won't have to tell the judge my personal business?"

"No, not exactly. What I mean is I have to present a strong enough case to the judge for the court to grant you a divorce. I can only determine the strength of your suit from your information." He smiled at her. "We have to convince the judge to say yes."

"Is his decision also confidential?"

"No, but we don't have to put all of the information you give me in the printed plea. We use a standard format and fill in what is needed. That also becomes public record. What doesn't become public are any statements I make to the judge and any questions or comments he makes before he rules on your case."

"Will I have to go to court?"

"Probably not. We try to keep you ladies out of the courtroom if at all possible. It's not a proper place for the fairer sex. However, if you do have to go, the judge shouldn't ask you too many questions," he said, and his answer reassured her. "Now, am I correct that your one child is married and no longer lives with you?"

"That's right. Why?"

"It's in your favor that there are no minor children in your household."

"Thank you for taking the time to explain. No one in my family has ever divorced. I don't even know one person who has."

"Let's finish up before Mr. Steele returns from his cigarette."

After five minutes, Mr. Tryon distilled her situation, and Sarah Jane thought she saw how he would persuade the judge to rule in her favor.

"From 1899-1910, you and Mr. Guymon had to live with your parents most of the time. He was never steadily employed except in 1911 when he rented a house for you and your daughter Mollie. He lost his job as a deliveryman later that year, and the three of you moved back in with your parents. Thereafter, you, he, and your daughter continued to reside in your parental abode. He would periodically disappear for long periods of time, and you did not know where he was or when he would return. This behavior continued until the last time he left you and your daughter in 1919. You have not received any word on his whereabouts or even if he is alive or dead."

He stopped and wrote a note on the paper, then went on. "Your occupation has always been a seamstress. Your earnings supported you and your daughter. What money he earned he spent on gambling. He even borrowed against your inheritance from your parents. Those advanced loans caused an estrangement from them due to his nonpayment of the principal as well as interest. For this reason you inherited only some personal items of sentimental value from your mother's estate."

He turned the page of his legal pad. "After your mother's death you moved out of your parents' house and into your own apartment where you lived for one year. Financial straits forced you to move to a smaller apartment. Your current residence is where you have lived alone chastely for over ten years. You attend the Central Methodist Church and sing in the choir. Any errors or omissions?"

"No," Sarah Jane whispered. She had never before thought about her life in such stark terms. All she could be proud of was Mollie and her two granddaughters.

"Good," Mr. Tryon said. "I think we have a viable case. I'll put it on the docket and notify you, no, don't worry. I won't mail anything to your apartment. Instead, I'll notify Mr. Steele, and he'll let you know the court date. Any other questions?"

"No, I don't think so. Thank you Mr. Tryon."

Richard returned to the inner office and gave her an encouraging smile. He shook hands and thanked his friend. After she replaced the veil over her face, he escorted her out the door and to his truck.

"Are you all right?" he asked once they were clear of the courthouse traffic.

"Yes, why?"

"I've known you long enough to tell when you're angry. Your eyes give you away. They're usually calm, but now they're flashing. What did Waite say to upset you?"

She paused to gather her thoughts and figure out how to phrase them. "I am so angry at myself. This is the angriest I've ever been in my life. Until Mr. Tryon summarized my life, I didn't realize how Isaac had misled me. He waltzed into my life, all smiles and a smooth line of promises. He sweet-talked me into marriage when he knew he'd never support me." She looked at him. "Does it vex you to hear about him?"

He parked the truck under a glorious yellow maple and turned to face her. "I'm not a jealous man. I realized some time ago that Isaac Guymon did me the biggest favor when he walked out of your life. I'm sorry he brought you such pain. However, if he had been a true husband to you, you would not be marrying me. What I don't understand is why you're so mad at yourself."

"I let him take advantage of me. I never lived anywhere else but in Sabina, and everyone knows everyone else. But no one knew anything about him when he came to town on his sales route."

He leaned closer and said in a low voice that contained traces of anger. "You were still an innocent. He was a grown man. He took advantage of you."

"That he did. When he called at my father's shop, he gave me little gifts of ribbons and told me stories of all he'd seen on his travels through Ohio and Indiana." Sarah Jane laughed in a rueful tone. "Can you believe he made Cincinnati sound exciting? The hustle of the people and the speed of streetcars. I enjoyed how he described the latest fashions the smart women wore and what hemlines and sleeves were fashionable. He did open my eyes to what was outside of Sabina and enticed me with the larger world."

A crisp fall breeze caught a strand of her hair. She poked it back in place and shrugged. "I wanted to believe all the things he told me," she continued. "He painted such pretty pictures of our life together. I began to dream I'd leave Sabina and see cities like Cincinnati and travel all over the United States. He promised we'd go to Florida, swim in the ocean, and eat oranges. But they were just pipe dreams."

Richard pulled her to him and said, "I'm not real long on talking, but I do listen."

Sarah Jane sank into him and said. "Thank you, I haven't been able to tell anyone about Isaac. Maybe if I had a sister, I'd have someone to talk to."

A few minutes later, she pulled back so she could look directly at him. "When I knew you were in love with me, I was scared. I didn't know if I wanted to trust and love another man or risk marrying again. The one thing I did know was I couldn't live through another bad marriage. I have no such fears now." She touched his arm and kissed his cheek.

He blushed, and his voice choked when he said, "I promise you I will never make you unhappy, dearest."

Sarah Jane rested her head on his shoulder as he drove closer to Sabina. A few miles from the edge of town, he broke their companionable silence. "Maybe you would like to come out and look over the house to see if you would like new curtains or things? My mother reminded me this week that's important to women." He looked at her. "She's heard me talk about you. I'd like for you to meet her. Maybe next week after church?"

She told herself again how fortunate she was to have this man. "Thank you and please thank your mother for her kindness. Next week after church is fine."

At her request, Richard left her at the cemetery where he kissed her good-bye. "This is our second kiss," he said. "Soon there will be so many you'll never be able to keep count."

Sarah Jane was not surprised when her absent husband did not respond to any of the notices put in the newspapers of the surrounding counties during October. No one at work even mentioned they had read the legal notices. Nevertheless, she knew. The locals always gossiped about the latest news on farm foreclosures and estate settlements. She appreciated their tactfulness.

In late December, Sarah Jane gave her one week notice, and Mrs. Jamison and the staff at the dress shop didn't act surprised. On her last day, they closed the shop early and gave her a bridal shower. She had to stop them from sending a write-up to the paper. It wasn't done for second weddings.

On January 10th, Sarah Jane waited with Richard outside the Superior Court on the second floor of the Warren County Courthouse. Inside the courtroom, Waite Tryon argued before the judge that her marriage to Isaac Guymon should be dissolved. After forty-five long, tense minutes, she drew her first deep breath all morning after he came out through the large doors and told her she was now a free woman.

"Everything went the way we thought. Since Mr. Guymon did not come forward to contest the divorce, the judge ruled very quickly. The clerk has to make a copy of the divorce decree. It should be ready sometime next week. I'll mail you a copy, Richard. Any questions, Mrs. Guymon?"

"No sir. Thank you again."

Richard shook his friend's hand and thanked him again for the help. Waite Tryon wished them well and returned to the courtroom for his next appearance. Sarah Jane put her arm through Richard's, and he proudly escorted her down one flight to the County Clerk's office where they filled out the forms for their marriage license. He listed himself as a widower. She wrote spinster. A white lie, but she felt it was necessary.

While they waited for the clerk to seal and stamp the license, he held her hand and said, "You have made me the happiest man in the world today. Are you all set to get married?"

"Oh yes, but first I need to freshen up. I'll join you back here in a few minutes."

She went into the Ladies' Room, straightened her bun, and checked to see if her mother's garnet brooch was still centered on the cowl neckline of her green silk dress. A quick repetition of the timeless bridal tradition followed. The something old was the garnet brooch. The something new was a lace handkerchief. The borrowed item was the bracelet Richard's mother had worn when she had married. The paisley shawl provided a touch of blue. She reached into her purse and took out a dime to put in her shoe. "You would approve of this man. We will be happy," she offered to her mother.

"I'm ready to marry you, Richard Steele," she said when she rejoined him. "For better or worse until death do us part."

He gave her a kiss on the cheek, and they left the courthouse and walked the next block to the office of the Justice of the Peace who married them.

What came to be known as the "Great Depression" devastated Sabina's business district, and Jamison's had to close its doors later that winter. Sarah Jane lost her income from taking clothing home to the farm to alter and return the next week. For the first time in many years, she found herself unemployed.

"Look at it this way," Richard said one morning in March over breakfast. "Instead of stewing about how much money we don't have, tell me what you would want to do if suddenly you had a big pot of gold?"

"That's easy. I'd travel to Akron and see Mollie and the girls."

"Great idea. Let's do it. Write them a letter and tell them we're on our way."

"Can you just leave the farm?"

"Better now than in April when I have to get ready for spring planting. Old Man Fleming owes me some favors. He and his sons will feed the cattle and chickens, but I can't be gone much longer than a week to ten days."

"A vacation? I've never had one. Are you sure we can afford it?"

"It won't be fancy, but yes, we can."

One week later Sarah Jane introduced her new husband to Mollie. The scene was not quite what she had anticipated. Mollie was civil but aloof towards her new stepfather. She never quite met his eye or asked him a question, let alone smile. The girls must have noticed their mother's feelings. Louise and Marie were overjoyed to see their grandmother again but kept their distance from Richard.

At the dinner table, Louise and Marie sat their grandmother between them. Mollie's coldness toward Richard embarrassed Sarah Jane, and John tried to make up for it. He pointed out the place next to him and asked Richard to sit there. Sarah Jane looked frequently at her new husband while she found out about her granddaughters' new dog King and their best friends at school. After a few attempts to interact with Mollie, Richard gave up, turned all his attention to John, and discussed how Babe Ruth made more money than Herbert Hoover.

As soon as the girls finished eating, Mollie made a reluctant Louise and Marie get ready for bed and left her mother to go upstairs with the children. A few minutes later John excused himself to go next door and check on the bakery.

Sarah Jane seized the opportunity to whisper to Richard across the dining room table, "I'm so ashamed. I can't believe how rude Mollie was. She didn't even give you a chance."

"Give her time, sweetie, she'll come around. I'm sure I'm a surprise. But those girls, aren't they something else? They're just as cute as June bugs. Maybe Mollie will let them come visit us on the farm this summer."

Sarah Jane loved how Richard could make a bad situation better and touched his arm. "I'd like that. It'd be a blessing to have some time to be a grandma. We could do all those wonderful things I used to do with my grandparents, make homemade ice cream, ride horses, and play with the cats in the barn."

Memories of her summer visits with her McConkey great-grandparents on their farm gave Sarah Jane hope that she could do the same for her granddaughters. Any future visits with the girls, though, would have to wait until she had shared some painful incidents from her past with Richard. It was only fair that she tell him, and the sooner the better. Mollie's actions convinced her. She should have done so earlier, but she had miscalculated her daughter's ability to hold onto the past.

The first chance Sarah Jane had was after they were in bed and the rest of the house had settled into quiet. Sarah Jane waited until Richard had turned out the light. Moment by moment, the dread had built layer upon layer while he prepared for bed. The weight of her guilt almost kept her from breathing as he removed his reading glasses and marked the place in his library book. After he gave her a goodnight kiss, she realized she could not put off what she had to say any longer.

"Richard, I need to tell you something about me and Mollie from when she was younger. It's not easy, and I hope you won't judge me too harshly. When I look back at it now, I realize I might have been wrong, but at the time, I felt as if I were a lightening rod for all the family arguments. I was trapped between my mother, my daughter, and my husband. I won't go into the harsh words that my mother and I flung at each other, or for that matter, how Isaac and I exchanged such bitter accusations. While all three of us were so good about not arguing in front of Mollie, I now imagine that she overheard many of our altercations."

Remorse swept over her, along with tears, and Richard, bless his heart, silently passed his handkerchief and waited for her to continue.

"I am not excusing her bad manners toward you," her voice faltered. "I hoped her anger would melt once she had children of her own, but I can no longer ignore that she's still angry with me."

Richard took her hand and said, "Remember when I told you I was a good listener? You can tell me anything." His gentle squeeze gave her the courage to continue.

"When Mollie was a young girl, I would send her to visit her cousins in College Corner during the summers. Jeremiah was closer in age than Havilla, about three years older. Havilla was more like a toy for Mollie since he was seven years younger. At first Mollie wanted to go spend the summer with Havilla and help Aunt Catherine, but as she grew into a young woman, Jeremiah became more important in her conversations about summer. I thought it was an innocent, passing fancy and Jeremiah would soon grow bored with her attentions."

As Sarah Jane said these words, she remembered the flush that would come to Mollie's cheeks each time she or anyone else spoke the young man's name. Maybe one reason Jeremiah was so important to her then was his kindness. But that was Jeremiah. Ever since he could walk, he would notice what people needed and go help them. She had thought Mollie had taken his native kindness and overblown its importance.

"The summer Mollie turned fourteen, Uncle Cornelius became very concerned about the closeness that was developing between them. He'd find them engaged in secret conversations and unaware of anyone around them. He sent me a letter asking me to come and take her back to Sabina. I got there a day too late. Jeremiah had taken Mollie to a barn dance, unchaperoned, the night before. His parents knew nothing about it until Cornelius caught them sneaking in early in the morning. The dog barked and woke him. That's when Cornelius put the pieces together. Earlier, he was puzzled why he could not find the dog to chain to the front porch when he made his nightly rounds before turning in. He was even more puzzled when he found the dog in bed with Havilla. He decided not to wake the boy, but he promised himself as he led the dog to the porch that it would be a topic of conversation in the morning."

The arguments she and Mollie had over the next month loomed large in her memory, and she felt too tired to go into all the details with Richard. He had never experienced the bittersweetness of rearing children.

"Evidently, well, nothing untoward happened," Richard's words called her back. Sarah Jane chose the next words carefully.

"No, seemed it was an innocent, uh, adventure. However, Cornelius didn't want to provide another opportunity for them. He kept them apart and busy until I arrived. Then Mollie returned with me. I thought that would be the end of the matter. I knew Jeremiah had enlisted. Catherine wrote that after Mollie left, Jeremiah stormed out of the house and enlisted. He stayed in Eaton until he shipped out to Mississippi."

Sarah Jane considered stopping the story. She was not proud of her actions even though she was convinced they were still the correct ones. However, she also had to look Richard in the face tomorrow, and she wanted to do that as an honest woman.

"Then a letter came. I remembered putting it in my pocket when I collected the mail after work. I wasn't in any hurry to give it to Mollie. She had stopped crying herself to sleep and seemed resigned to accepting Cornelius' and my decision. But later in the week, the next one arrived while she was at school. Since she was smiling and I had my happy daughter back, I decided I was not going to give her the letters. I realized that I could never explain to her why I had kept the letters from her, but I hoped Jeremiah would also accept his father's decision and the letters would soon stop. But just the opposite happened. By fall, there was a flood of them. Some days two or three would be in the mailbox. They haunted me. After all, Jeremiah was most certainly homesick, scared, and wanting comfort. I wrote to him and asked him to desist. I explained how he should let Mollie alone."

Sarah Jane coughed as her throat closed. Richard got out of bed and returned a few minutes later with a glass of water. He gave her hand a gentle squeeze and a kiss on the forehead. She hoped he would still love her when she finished.

"Jeremiah continued to send letters. For some reason I cannot explain, I kept them. I was feeling so guilty. I had watched him grow up. I loved him so much. But I had to protect my daughter. I forced Mollie to write him and say she had fallen in love. I told her it was only fair that there was no chance of a misunderstanding. I had expected a battle royal. However, she was strangely compliant.

After the good-bye letter, his came less frequently and finally stopped. My nightmares also stopped, and by the end of the war, I had a small cardboard box full of unopened letters. I never had the courage to give them to her, and when she married John, I burnt them." She paused. Something felt unrecognized and unspoken. She had left out how she had kept Mollie's letters to Jeremiah. She lacked the courage since that act seemed more horrid than hiding Jeremiah's letters. Richard waited patiently in the dark as if he also sensed the story was unfinished. Suddenly, she realized something else was out of balance, Jeremiah's life.

"He never married after he returned from the war. I have seen him only two times since that summer day. One was for his homecoming celebration. The last time was at Mollie's wedding, and he looked so sad each time."

The next morning as she sat with Mollie and Richard over breakfast, Sarah Jane appreciated her husband's tact when he announced, "I think I'll walk downtown to get a newspaper and some cigarettes. Be back soon, sweetie."

He got up from the dining room table, left the women seated across from each other, and nodded good-bye to Mollie.

 They were alone since Louise and Marie were at school and John had been next door at the bakery since before dawn.

Suppressed rage radiated from Mollie, and Sarah Jane found herself tongue-tied in front of her daughter. She was uncertain how to broach the subject of her marriage to Richard.

However, she didn't have to since Mollie surprised her with her words. "Feeling happy, are you?"

"Yes, I am." Sarah Jane tried a smile, but it died, stillborn.

"Do you find being married to a man you love brings you happiness?" Mollie said.

"What did you say?" Sarah Jane asked as a headache throbbed at her temples.

"Why don't you tell me what it's like, since you've married twice for love?"

"Mollie Elizabeth, what are you talking about?"

"Surely you remember how you made sure I'd never marry Jeremiah and know true love. You forced me to abandon the only love I will ever have. Now you've come all the way up here from Sabina to show off your new husband. How could you be so mean and thoughtless?"

"How dare you talk to me like that. I'm your mother." Sarah Jane folded her arms and put some anger in her answer. She could not show any weakness.

"You're the woman who drove off my father. I loved him and you made him go away. He loved me, not you, and he didn't leave me. Instead he left you."

Where did her daughter get such addled ideas? "That's not how it was. You don't understand everything that was going on."

"I understand all right. You're the woman who made sure I didn't marry Jeremiah. We loved each other and would've been happy together. But something inside of you had to rob me of my one chance of happiness. You didn't let me have Papa, and you didn't let me have Jeremiah."

Mollie stopped to draw a breath and learned forward to continue her invective. "Now you show up with Richard. Am I supposed to welcome him into the family and around my daughters? You expect too much. You always have."

A fleck of spittle fell from Mollie's mouth onto the tablecloth. "Do you have any idea of what's it like to be married to a man you don't love? Louise and Marie are the only good things out of my marriage. They are my sunshine, but my children should have had Jeremiah as a father, not John."

"How can you think such things? You know the family would never have allowed you to marry a close cousin. Remember the Lines and what happened with their children?"

"I'll expect you to leave as soon as he returns." Mollie stood up and glared down at her mother. "I'll make your good-byes to Louise and Marie."

With this last statement, Mollie turned and left Sarah Jane in the sunlit dining room that overlooked the frozen remains of the extensive flower gardens.

Sarah Jane was still stunned as she sat in the dining room when Richard returned. "Did you girls…" His voice trailed off.

"We're leaving, Richard. Please help me pack." As Sarah Jane rose from her place, she felt fifty years older. Mollie's rage and unsettled mind had aged her.

On the trip back home, they discussed how disturbed and unhappy Mollie seemed to be. Sarah Jane couldn't remember her daughter ever sinking to that level of misery. "I feel so helpless. I've lost her, forever."

"Maybe not."

"You should've seen the look in her eyes. I was terrified. I didn't even recognize her."

After Sarah Jane sent a few letters and they returned unopened, she let Richard persuade her that time would heal their breach. It was her first harvest on the farm, and she kept busy canning and preserving fruits and vegetables for the winter. In the evenings, she worked on new holiday dresses for her granddaughters and hoped Mollie would allow the girls to wear them.

In early November, the influenza swept through the county. Richard nursed Sarah Jane, but she quickly succumbed. Driven by grief, he went to his work shed after the undertaker came to take her away. He took the planed wood down from the loft where he had placed it after he had harvested the old black walnut trees on his farm earlier in the fall. His plans to make a dining room table for their first Christmas together changed, and he toiled over the unfinished boards to make her casket. As his tears fell, they mixed with the beeswax and seasoned the wood while he finished the casket. After his all-night carpentry work, his hands swelled and bruised, but the pain in his heart overrode what he felt in his hands.

Dry-eyed and with a firm step Betsey, dressed in a stylishly belted black crepe dress and matching toque hat trimmed with a decorative veil, entered the parlor of the Steele farmhouse.

"That's Mollie Elizabeth, the daughter who moved up north," she heard the town gossip say as her gaze took in the old and plain furnishings before she glanced at Richard. He stood by the front windows and next to the black walnut casket, which was by far the most elegant piece of furniture in the house.

With one curt nod, Betsey dismissed Richard, his status as her mother's husband, and his newly born sorrow. She then walked in triumph toward her mother. Without thinking, she reached out her black-gloved hand, and let her fingers lightly caress the highly polished wood.

"Your happiness didn't last very long, did it? Perhaps there is justice after all," she uttered in a low voice as she leaned over Sarah Jane. "Girls, come say good-bye to your grandma," she said in a louder voice after she straightened and turned to her children.

Louise and Marie, with their father John between them, broke away and stepped forward to see their grandmother for the final time. Betsey turned and curtailed her husband's condolences to Richard.

"John, I see Uncle Jeremiah and Aunt Nila. Come girls, I want you to meet your grandmother's brother. He's never seen you before." Louise and Marie took her hands, and Richard renewed his attention to John.

Betsey made sure her family did not linger after the funeral. By four o'clock, they were on the train, and the daughters were soon asleep. When Betsey smoothed her skirt, her foot hit something under the seat.

She bent down and pulled a small traveling trunk into the open space. "What's this, John?"

"Richard gave it to me. He said to tell you the only thing of your mother's he kept was the lace handkerchief she bought for their wedding. Everything else she owned, except her clothes, is in that trunk."

"Must be Grandma's brooch and shawl. I already have her china."

"He did mention something about family heirlooms, some personal items, pictures, and such."

Betsey smiled at Louise and imagined telling her the story of the brooch and shawl. However, she felt her smile vanish as the heat of victory grew within. She knew the trunk promised no letters written so long ago by a handsome soldier and a love-sick girl. She had only the few that had escaped her mother's burning, and they were hidden deep in her closet where no one else would ever find them.

Chapter 23

SUMMONS IN DIVORCE

The State of Ohio

Warren County, ss to the Sheriff of Hamilton County,

Greeting:

You are commanded to notify Isaac Guymon that Sarah Jane Guymon, has filed in the office of the Clerk of the Court of Common Pleas of Warren County, and State of Ohio, a petition, (a copy of which accompanies this summons) charging him with gross neglect of duty and asking that she be divorced from him and for other proper relief. Said petition will stand hearing during the term of said Court next ensuing, and six weeks from and after the service of this writ. You will make due return of this summons on the 15th day of November A. D. 1929.

Witness my signature and the seal of said Court, at Lebanon Ohio, this fourth day of October A.D. 1929

Augustine Fish Clerk

Common Pleas Court of Warren County, Ohio

Sarah Jane Guymon, Plaintiff

vs

Isaac Guymon, Defendant

PETITION

The plaintiff, Sarah Jane Guymon, says that she is a bona-fide resident of Clinton County, Ohio, and has been a resident of the State of Ohio for more than one year last past, that she and the defendant, Isaac Guymon, were married on the first day of June, 1899, and that one child has been born to them.

That she has always conducted herself toward the defendant as an affectionate and dutiful wife, but that the defendant in total disregard of his marital duties has been guilty of gross neglect of duty toward the plaintiff in this: that by reason of his idleness and dissipation, he has willfully failed and neglected to provide this plaintiff with food, clothing, and the common necessities of life so that she has been compelled to live by her own exertions and labor, and on the assistance and charity rendered her by relatives and friends, although he was, and is fully able to properly support her.

That immediately after their marriage they went to live with her mother, where they continued to live there until September 25, 1919, and her mother not being able to keep and support them, and the defendant being well able to work, and support plaintiff, and fully neglected and refused to do so plaintiff was compelled to and did go to work and support herself, and on or about November 1, 1919, plaintiff became very sick, and defendant failed, neglected and refused to provide any medical aid, nurse, or any common comforts of life.

Defendant would frequently obtain money from plaintiff and her mother upon pretense that he wanted to go and hunt work, and would then spend the money in slot-machines and other worthless amusements, and would refuse to work when offered positions.

Defendant has two good trades and has refused to take them up. He has been offered employments numerous times, but would refuse to work at them. He never furnished plaintiff with a home or any of the common necessaries of life, and had not lived or co-habited with plaintiff since December 30, 1919. He has also abandoned his residence at Horndale's Rooming House.

Wherefore, plaintiff prays for a divorce, and all proper relief and that the defendant pay the costs herein taxed at $7.94.

Sarah Jane Guymon Plaintiff
Wm Wrenn Her Atty.

Sarah Jane Guymon being duly sworn says that the several matters and facts set forth in the foregoing Petition are true to the best of her knowledge and belief.

Subscribed by the said Sarah Jane Guymon in my presence, and by her sworn to before me this 22nd day of November, 1929.

> Wm Wrenn
> Notary Public in and for
> Warren County, Ohio

Certified Copy of Court Journal Entry
Common Pleas Court of Warren County, Ohio

At the January 1930 Term of said court, the following proceedings were held on the 10th day of January 1930, to wit:

Sarah Jane Guymon, Plaintiff

vs   No. 16535

Isaac Guymon, Defendant

This day this cause came on to be heard upon the petitioner and the evidence, the defendant not appearing.

On consideration whereof, and the Court being fully advised in the premises, finds that the defendant has been duly and legally served with summons and process, and that he has failed to appear, and is in default for answer or demurrer, that at the time of the filing of the petition herein, plaintiff was a resident of the State of Ohio, for more than a year, and was a bona-fide resident of the County of Clinton.

It is therefore ordered, adjudged and decreed that the said marriage relations now existing between the said parties be, and the same are hereby dissolved, and the said parties are hereby released there from, and that the said defendant be ordered to provide all proper relief.

It is further ordered, adjudged and decreed that the defendant pay the costs herein taxed at $7.94.

The Honorable Roderick Pullen

Chapter 24

Sabina, Ohio, 1930

<Thomas and Naomi Clopton
<Agnes and Matthew McConkey
<Hannah and Jeremiah Garrett
<Esther Garrett and Harry Thompson
Jeremiah Thompson

<Thomas and Naomi Clopton
<Agnes and Matthew McConkey
<Samuel McConkey and Lavinia Yeargin
<Abel Edwards and Betsey McConkey
Lydia Edwards Grooms

Dear Cousin Lydia,

I certainly enjoyed your letter and certainly will share what family information I have in my possession.

I can make a fair copy of the pages if you wish. However, since the family register contains a great deal on the births, deaths, and marriages from both sides of my family, I have included only the McConkeys. I didn't want to bore you with the other family information.

We have in common our Great-Grandfather Matthew McConkey and his wife, our Great-Grandmother Agnes nee Clopton, daughter of Thomas and Naomi Clopton according to the Bible record. Naomi's maiden name is so far unknown. Agnes and Matthew were married June 12, 1838, in New Kent County, Virginia at the same church where George Washington married Martha Custis.

Matthew was born on May 21, 1818 on the family plantation called Fairlawn, in New Kent County, Virginia, while Agnes Clopton was born February 24, 1820 at her family's estate called River Front, also in New Kent County. Matthew passed first on November 14, 1905, and she went almost a year later, November 7, 1906.

One of the most interesting passages written in the Bible is the one where Agnes explains their reasons for coming to Ohio. I have copied it verbatim.

We, Matthew and Agnes McConkey with our daughter Hannah and son Samuel, left our family home Fairlawn Plantation on the north branch of the Pamunkey River in New Kent County, Virginia in the spring of 1855 and set out for Sabina, Ohio. As advocates for the abolitionist cause, we could no longer abide with slavery so we joined with the Yergans and other members of their Friends church on their northbound wagon train.

Agnes McConkey

The fourth day of July in the year one thousand eight hundred fifty-five A.D.

I've transcribed the Bible entries for your grandfather, Samuel McConkey, who married Lavinia Yergain. His birth date is March 15, 1846, and hers, June 7, 1847. They were married here in Sabina August 12, 1865.

The other information you asked about follows. I have always been curious about it. If you have any light to throw on the subject, please do so. On the back cover of the Bible, our Great-Grandmother Agnes had penned the following.

I am writing this at the request of Patience McConkey, one of our former slaves named Agrippina who ran away from Virginia with her husband to join us in the free state of Ohio. She requests that I record her sons' birth in our family Bible.

Born in freedom to Jacob and Patience McConkey a son named Noah on the third day of August in the year of our Lord one thousand eight hundred and sixty-three.

Born in freedom to Jacob and Patience McConkey a son named Josiah on the eighteenth day of December in the year of our Lord one thousand eight hundred and sixty-four.

Your new cousin,

Jeremiah Thompson

Chapter 25

Salt Lake City, Utah, 1930

Dear Cousin Jeremiah,

The Bible information was very helpful. It added depth to the story of my grandparents and great-grandparents.

I might be able to help you with the entry that Patience McConkey asked our Great-Grandmother Agnes to write into the family Bible.

The Yeargins were Friends or as they were sometimes called, Quakers, and they decided to leave Virginia and join other Friends who established the Underground Railroad around Sabina. Matthew and Agnes McConkey decided to go with them for safety's sake. It took almost six weeks to reach Ohio. They had to walk along side their wagons because there was no room for all the adults to ride. Their son Samuel, my grandfather, rode in the wagon a few hours each day since he was so young. Once they crossed the Ohio River, they stopped to sing and rejoice that they were on free soil at last.

A few years after the family arrived, an escaped house slave from Fairlawn Plantation by the name of Caesar showed up at the McConkey place. He had his wife Agrippina with him.

I will always remember their names because I had to take Latin in school. Caesar had heard his master's table talk about our Great-Grandfather Matthew's leaving for Ohio. Somehow, Caesar taught himself to read and write although it was against the law. Part of his duties was to bring the mail into the dining room on a silver tray. He read the return addresses on the envelopes and committed to memory the

McConkey address. That was where Agrippina and he planned to run away to when they escaped. They did not have an easy trip even with the help from the Quakers and other abolitionists along the way.

Our ancestors gave them shelter and helped them settle into living as freed people. Your Grandfather Jeremiah Garrett was a shoemaker and hired Caesar as an apprentice at his shop. Caesar changed his name to Jacob McConkey. Agrippina changed hers to Patience. Their sons, born after they came to Ohio and were free, were Noah and Josiah. Noah died early as a young man, but Josiah went on to be a teacher at the Negro School in town.

I remember my grandfather telling me that Uncle Jeremiah left money to the Negro School to establish an apprentice program for the young men to learn how to make shoes. Aunt Hannah also left money to the school. She funded book purchases for the library.

Your cousin,
Lydia Grooms

Chapter 26

Sabina, June 1881

<Thomas and Naomi Clopton
<Agnes and Matthew McConkey
<Hannah and Jeremiah Garrett
Esther

There it was, on the dining room table, at her father's place, the letter from Oberlin College. Esther stared at it for a few minutes before she took it over to the window and tried to read what was inside. The slender envelope contained her whole future. Since it was addressed to her and her parents, her mother said they'd open it when her father came home from the shoe shop for lunch. Only a few more minutes more until she knew if she would matriculate in the fall or stay here in Sabina and do nothing exciting for the rest of her life.

Doubts struck her. Was there something else she should have accomplished before she applied? She had no idea. Her grades were the highest in the class. Her teachers wrote letters to convince the admission director that she was an exceptional young woman. No, she decided, she had done all she could have.

At last, her father, in his usual white shirt and dark pants and straw hat, came up the front walk at his customary slow pace. He never seemed to hurry. It didn't matter if it was winter, summer, rain, or snow. She was poised to rush out the front screen door when she heard her mother's voice from the top of the stairwell.

"Let your father enter in peace and give him time to wash up. Take the bread and butter to the table and sit down. I'll be down as soon as I put the twins to bed for their nap."

Obediently Esther did as told, took her seat next to her father's place, and planned the promised shopping trip to Cincinnati. If she was admitted to Oberlin, her parents had agreed on a few new clothes. Finally, she'd leave behind the schoolgirl dresses and begin to look like a grown-up woman. No more demure, pastel cotton prints and calicos. She'd choose serious dark skirts and matching blouses. Her mother had given permission for her to restyle her chestnut-colored braids into a more mature sedate bun at the back of her neck. She had her eye on a new brown felt hat to sit snugly on top of the new hairstyle and held in place with a small yet decorative jeweled hatpin. No more girlish hats frilled with bows for her. Come fall, she'd look like an actual college woman.

Her brother Cornelius rushed into the dining room, and she saw that his hands were still damp. Although he was now as tall as she was and looked more like their father every day with his wavy dark hair, he was still childish. She knew he'd do it. Self-control seemed beyond him. He flicked water on her as he began filling the glasses with water. She'd not miss his teasing when she left.

Her mother, still dressed in her dark blue laundry dress but now without the apron, carried roast chicken and vegetables, and her father brought in the gravy boat. A happy smile took over his face.

"We'll open your letter right now. I imagine you won't be able to swallow a bit of food until you know. Right?"

"Yes, Papa, thank you."

He took his butter knife and slit the envelope. When he had the letter unfolded, he read.

> Dear Miss Garrett,
> It is with great pleasure we accept your application to attend the 1881 Fall Term and pursue studies…

Esther let out a very unladylike "Hurrah," and her father stopped reading. As he handed the letter to her, he said, "Your mother and I are very proud of you. We know you'll be a fine student. You've also been offered a scholarship with the understanding you will read the fifteen books listed in the letter. Seems you'll have to write some essays when you go to class."

He handed over the letter with the widest smile she had ever seen him make.

She borrowed the titles from the public library and shared them with her childhood friend Noah. Esther enthusiastically and cheerfully planned their reading schedule, and together they worked through the books. Since his formal education had ended when he graduated from the Harriet Tubman School and went to work for his father, he had not read much. He told her over and over how he missed the discovery reading brought.

They read and discussed as she carefully took notes for her future essays. One of her recent books was *Uncle Tom's Cabin*. This powerful story brought Esther to tears while she read Mrs. Stowe's masterpiece. It was all the more personal because Noah's parents had also escaped from slavery in Virginia.

She could hardly wait to discuss her ideas about *Uncle Tom's Cabin* with him and find out his reactions to Mrs. Stowe's novel since he surely had stories to share. She got her chance after the 4th of July fireworks. Noah walked her home. They stood near the grape arbor in her parents' backyard, and she broke into tears when she asked him about his parents' escape. He put his arms around her to comfort her, and somehow they kissed and not as friends. She at last stopped the battle against the unacknowledged desire that had smoldered through her teenaged years.

At first, the kisses and embraces felt strange because Esther had never kissed anyone except family. But as the passion increased, her soul told her that Noah was the special one for her. Happiness filled her heart, and Esther realized she loved Noah with all of her being. That was the same feeling she had read about in novels her friend Joan from school had given her, books her mother didn't know she read, books Joan told her would open her eyes to the way of the world.

In the next few minutes, as their bodies met, waves of joy rushed over her. She felt his hands first tenderly, then with increasing fervor, caress her arms and move over her body. Esther had never experienced those sweeping emotions that followed the hot trails of exquisite tingling his hands marked on her body, and she touched him in places she had never before touched a man. In her mind, a warning bell that sounded like her mother said, "Stop, stop before it's too late."

Noah unbuttoned his trousers, and she bunched her skirt up around her hips and stepped out of her underwear. When he lifted her up and entered her, Esther gasped softly. Soon the pain receded as they rocked back and forth together. She had never felt so loved and happy. Full of love, she gazed up at him.

The guilty look on Noah's face chilled her before he shattered her happiness with his words. "I am so sorry, Esther. I shoulda stopped."

Her feet settled on the ground, but he still held her close and whispered. "I love you. I have wanted you, it seems forever, but I never wanted to take you like this."

"Noah, I've always loved you. You feel it, don't you? Our love is so special. We're like Romeo and Juliet. We were meant to be together."

"That can't happen. We can never be together like this again. Our parents will not approve." She shook her head in protest to his next words. "We can't even marry. It's against the law. You know white people and Negroes can't marry."

"We'll run away, maybe to Canada. We don't have to marry to be happy."

"Girl, you have to grow up." He put his hands on her shoulders and gently gripped her. "That's not how the world is. Wanting something doesn't make it so."

"If you loved me enough, Noah, you'd make it so," she replied and shook his hands off her shoulders.

"Look at me. I love you and always will. But we cannot be together ever again."

"What are we going to do?" She looked into his eyes filling with tears, and inside she felt a newly grown-up woman struggle to replace a romantic schoolgirl.

"We'll pretend this never happened. We'll be friends. You'll go off to Oberlin in the fall, and I'll stay here."

"How can I leave you now? I love you."

"I wish it didn't have to be this way. But I can't make the world the way you want it. It is what it is."

The next morning she sat in the grape arbor, with an unread book open on her lap. Her mind had wandered once again back to last night when the sound of the back door screen screeching open registered. She glanced up and saw her mother hurry down the wooden steps and dab a white handkerchief to her eyes. Esther slowly rose from her chair and watched Momma close the distance. Her red, tear-filled eyes made Esther tremble with fear over what catastrophe had just exploded in their lives.

"Your father came home a few minutes ago with the most terrible news. Noah McConkey is dead."

Esther sat back in the chair and tightly clutched her book to her chest. "No, that can't be true. I saw him last night. He can't be dead."

Esther keened and crumbled forward in her chair. In her heart, she cried out that he loved her and wouldn't leave her.

Momma knelt down, and Esther fell into her arms. "What happened?"

"He and his horse were found on the Sabina Road at daybreak. He must have fallen from the horse and broke his neck. His poor parents." Momma pulled back and looked at her. "His saddle bags were packed with clothes and food. It appears he was running away. Did you know what he was planning?"

"No." The rest of Momma's words were unheard as Esther's thoughts raced. Had he run away because of their lovemaking? Why didn't he take her with him? How could he leave without saying good-bye.

Her mother's touch on her shoulder brought her back. "Get up now. I want you to go with me to pay our respects. It's part of being a lady. Our families go back a long way. I'll get some food ready to take, and we'll leave. Esther, Esther, do you hear me?"

"Yes, Momma, I'll go with you." Esther unsteadily regained her feet, but she felt cold, numb, and suddenly much older. She couldn't look her mother in the eye and gazed down at the ground until she heard her walk away. Her knees wobbled, and she sat down again. Had God punished Noah for what they did last night? Was she next? What did God have planned for her? To die tonight in her sleep or be run over by a carriage? Would God be so cruel to leave her to live on without Noah?

Momma soon returned and upbraided Esther since she had not stirred. "Esther, you have to get moving. Cornelius has the horse harnessed to the cart. Go grab your hat."

Esther dreaded seeing Miss Patience and Mr. Jacob in their grief.

In silence, Momma guided the horse cart to Jacob and Patience McConkey's small, neat shotgun house. Reverend Eads showed them into the house and led the way into the kitchen where Noah's parents and brother Josiah sat. Esther stood close to her mother and watched as she gathered the somber-clad, thin form of Miss Patience to her and whispered how sorry she was for their loss. Tears gushed down their faces.

"Miss Hannah," Patience said as she broke the embrace, "We can't figure out why he'd run away. Josiah found his note right here, on the kitchen table. All it said was he had to leave, right away. He'd send word when he got work someplace. He must've snuck out the back door." Patience dissolved in grief.

Her husband Jacob put his arms around her and turned to their visitors. "Mr. Stratton was on his milk run when he found Noah around six this morning."

"Mr. Jacob and Miss Patience, I am so sorry. Noah was very special." Esther's words ceased because she could find no more to console his parents.

"Why'd he want to run away?" Patience asked. "I won't rest easy til I know why."

Esther was torn. She knew the reason, and it was not hers to share. Noah had made that clear when he packed his belongings and got on that horse.

A few minutes after she and Momma settled in their cart, Esther could not think of one thing about Noah that was safe to say out loud.

Momma broke the silence. "Do you remember how you and Noah played together as children?"

"Noah was always there, he'd explain the world, play games with me. He even read to me. I'm going to miss him so much." Esther's voice faltered. Blotting her tears, she attempted to find some comfort in her old memories.

"You were so jealous that he could read and you couldn't that you made me teach you. I think you were almost five."

"I didn't want to go to school after I found we wouldn't be together."

"You didn't like it when I said it was because Noah was a Negro. You kept asking why Negroes went to their school, and you had to go to yours." Esther nodded. She remembered. "I finally told you that was the way things were. Negroes lived in their own part of town. They went to their own churches, and they had their own schools."

"When I was eight, Noah looked at my schoolbooks and said he'd never seen a new one. Josiah even told me he saw my name in one of his."

"I was surprised too," her mother agreed. "I didn't know the white school gave their old textbooks to the Negro schools. I thought they got new books when you did."

Esther wanted to talk about Noah. She wanted to keep all her memories alive and never forget. "When it got cold, their school never heated up. He had to keep his coat and gloves on."

"And again I had to explain that's the way things were, not fair, but better than they were, especially on the plantation." Momma flicked the harness to urge the horse across the railroad crossing and asked, "How old were you when you learned about their escape from Fairlawn?"

"Noah and his mother told me bits of the story. Noah's eyes lit with pride. He bragged about how smart his father was. But Mr. Jacob never talked about it much with me." Esther removed her straw hat and used it as a fan. The morning breeze had stilled, and against the background sound of the sawmill, she listened to her mother's fuller account of Noah's parents' escape from the family plantation.

"Did you know he learned to write with pieces of charcoal left over from the fireplace? He'd rise real early in the morning to get the fires going and practiced on the hearth. He'd read the books in the schoolroom when he cleaned upstairs. Later on he'd sneak reading a few chapters in Great-Grandfather's library."

They passed their church and turned homeward, Momma continued. "He listened to the table talk about your grandfather here in Sabina and memorized his address when he'd carry the mail to the dining room. However, he had to be careful. Most whites didn't want Negroes to learn how to read and write. Virginia law even said it was legal to beat any slave who knew how." Momma shook her head.

"He was brave, wasn't he?" Esther said.

"He had to be. The trip here was long and hard," Momma said. "We didn't have an easy journey in the wagon train. It was much worse for Jacob and Patience. They had to be so scared. They were almost caught many times. They looked half-starved, Grandmama said, when they knocked on her back door and asked if they could come in. They most certainly would have died if they had tried to run away in the winter."

Esther tried to picture a younger Mr. Jacob and Miss Patience, hungry and in rags, at her grandmother's back door. "They had help though, didn't they, from the Underground Railroad?"

"Yes, and unlike most of the other runaway slaves that went on up to Canada, Jacob and Patience decided to stay here in Sabina. They wanted to live free and safe with people they knew."

The irony that Noah had not lived safe and free shook her composure, but she couldn't let her mother see. So Esther decided to tell another story. "Miss Patience was brave too. She told me about the time an abolitionist came to the plantation summer kitchen. He explained to all the house slaves how they could escape and go up north to freedom. That's what started her dream about raising her unborn children as free."

"Yes, she was very courageous. Now she and Jacob will need all their strength to survive the loss of Noah," Momma said as they reached their house.

Esther panicked when her womanlies did not come on time. She thought she might be with child and yet hoped against hope that it was not true. When her mother wanted to know why her monthly linen was not in the wash, Esther somehow had the fortitude to look into her mother's eyes without a flinch and lie. "It has to be the shock over Noah's death."

Momma seemed to believe her. "You're such a tender-hearted soul to grieve this much over a childhood friend. You do look a little peaked. Better keep your strength up. I'll start a dose of castor oil if you aren't better soon. College will be strenuous, and you need to be strong and not get sick when you go to Oberlin."

"Everything will be fine next month," Esther said to convince herself as much as her mother.

"I'm sure it will be. But if not, there's always castor oil."

In August, she counted back on the calendar from the day's date of August 18th to July 4th. There was no doubt. She flung the undeniable proof she was pregnant down on her bed.

Just one time. Momma was right. All it took was one time. Esther couldn't get the refrain out of her head.

Esther sobbed in her pillow and struggled to accept she was with child. Her symptoms matched her mother's when she didn't know whether she was going through the change early or was pregnant. Esther remembered those afternoons her mother and Grandmamma Agnes sat at the table with the calendar and discussed the early signs of pregnancy, an uneasy stomach, a swollen uncomfortable bosom, and delayed monthly flow. Two months went by before Doctor Davis had confirmed what Momma and her mother already knew. Momma was pregnant.

The very word pregnant caused Esther's mind to stumble. Nice girls didn't say that word, but then, nice girls didn't get pregnant. And nice girls certainly didn't get pregnant by a young man who came from slavery.

Esther returned her face to her pillow and cried until fatigue crept over her. The tiredness gave more credence to her fate. Momma had also been exhausted when she was expecting Charles and Hattie.

An overwhelming sense of desolation grew within her. She had never felt so alone. Who could she turn to? Not her parents or grandparents. Or her friends either, especially Joan who never kept a secret. Esther would have to face her situation without help from anyone.

Her brain raced to find a solution as she rejected each plan, one by one. Stop eating, go to college and have the baby there. But Mrs. Porter, the woman she was to live with, would certainly write her parents and inform them she had given birth.

Runaway. She had no money to take care of the baby and no chance to earn any. No one would hire her.

Rid herself of the baby. No money to buy the potion from Old Grace. Besides, the older girls said it didn't always work and women could die in agony.

She would be disgraced. Her parents might turn her out, but worse was her child's future. She knew that just the rumor of being touched with the brush was enough to doom a white person in polite society. She had absorbed that ugly fact through the years of gossip and discussion around her grandparents' table. The adults had repeated many stories about how the amount of white blood a slave had determined his worth within the plantation society. The lighter-skinned slaves worked in the main house and not in the fields.

Esther never heard how some slaves were lighter than others. Later she was shocked when she realized the white blood had come from her great-grandfather and his male relatives, past and present. They had impregnated their female slaves.

To the best of her knowledge, she would be the first woman in her family to bring Negro blood into the family. Even though her own grandpapa was unable to tolerate the cruelty he had seen his parents and relatives inflict on the slaves, she knew he'd never welcome a grandchild with slave blood. She was not fooled by his lofty statements when talk turned to the plantation life he and her grandmother had left.

Esther didn't want her child to be an outcast and placed her hand to her stomach. "As far as anyone else is concerned, you'll be white. I promise you that. There just has to be a way to make this better," She bargained under her breath as she looked out her bedroom window for inspiration.

Out of the corner of her eye, she saw the solution to all her problems, Harry Thompson. He slowed as he neared her house. Exactly the same time every evening, Monday through Friday, after he left his job at Poppa's shop. He had to walk three blocks out of his way to pass by her house. Harry liked her. She knew by the way his face reddened whenever she smiled at him and his voice stammered a "Hello, Miss Garrett" during her visits to the shoe shop.

Harry strolled by her house, and there was a flicker of hope followed by a sickening sense of disgust and dishonesty. Her moral compass jumped to hard cold practicality and remained on that point the few minutes it took for Harry to pass on by the house and unsuspectingly walk to his parents' house.

Esther paced back and forth in her bedroom and schemed for her child's future. They could elope. That's what the women in the novels did when they wanted to marry in a hurry. Elope to Kentucky.

Esther's plan took form. A note for Momma and Poppa explaining how much in love they were. After they spent the night in Kentucky, they'd live with Momma and Poppa. Everything could work out.

However, she soon realized there was a chance she might not succeed. The baby might be too dark.

Since Harry was not light, he would never know the baby was not his if it was white enough. Noah and his parents were also light, just a little dusky.

Her practical side took over, and her mind gave reassurance. It might work, but she could never ever tell a soul.

Her conscience briefly rose and warned that Harry would be the only one who was cheated. She made another promise. Every day for the rest of her life, she would pray to God and beg forgiveness. However, she would have the baby and a husband and Momma and Poppa.

Esther shoved her conscience aside. Harry would also have what he wanted, her. Could she marry a man she didn't love? She didn't really have any other choice.

"I'm damned if I do and also if I don't. There's no other way. I have to do it," she whispered and made a third promise. She'd be the best wife ever to Harry.

Early on Thursday, the next day, the campaign to ensnare Harry began. First Esther washed her hair in rainwater and rinsed it with vinegar. Next, she curled it in rags and waited for it to dry. Thirty minutes before Harry was due to walk past her house, she dressed carefully in her best church dress, blue and white gingham which fit a little snugger than usual in the bodice and waist. Her final step was a pinch to pink her cheeks and to bite her lips until they reddened. At last armed with her book, lemonade, and cookies, she sat on the front porch and resembled a female spider lying in wait for her chosen mate to come calling. If Harry was on schedule, he'd be by in seven minutes.

"Good evening, Miss Garrett. Nice weather we're having tonight, isn't it?" Harry said and tipped his bowler hat.

"We certainly are. Why Mr. Thompson, are you a little overcome by the heat? Would you like some lemonade?"

Harry looked stunned and could not speak. He mutely inclined his head, walked onto the Garrett front porch, and sat in a wicker rocker opposite her in the swing. "Yes, Miss Garrett," Harry croaked and removed his hat.

"Won't you visit a while and let the lemonade refresh you?" Esther forced herself to smile at him. Harry unsteadily reached out for the offered lemonade and cookies. "How has your day been, Mr. Thompson? I hope it went well at the shop?"

The idea of batting her eyelashes briefly flashed in her mind, but she reconsidered. Too much, too fast. It'd not do to scare him off. She heard again her grandfather's advice on how to land a largemouth bass when they had spent afternoons at the creek. "Set the hook before you pull, Esther girl, and you'll have a big fish to eat tonight for supper," her grandfather said when she had jerked too soon on the fishing line. She eyed Harry and realized she had to dangle the bait and set the hook today in order to land him by next week.

Pity sprang within her. Poor Harry, he was so unaware. Yet Esther remembered Joan saying that every woman had to trick her man because otherwise men would never get married. "Chase him until he catches you" was her advice. Besides the most important consideration was her baby. She swallowed a sip of lemonade and bit into a gingersnap cookie in hopes of settling her stomach.

Harry devoured the offered lemonade and several more cookies. He looked like a young man who had won a horse race. To Esther he resembled Proserpine, the ill-fated daughter of Ceres. Pluto had abducted and taken the young woman to his underworld kingdom where she ate his pomegranates and therefore had to stay six months of each year. It was the same for Harry. His future might be determined by the food just eaten.

"Today was rather slow," he spoke after he took a big gulp of lemonade, "Must be the heat. People are not downtown when it's this hot."

"Why I imagine you'd appreciate a slow day every once in a while. You work so hard. Poppa says all the time how you help with the books and orders. You pay such close attention to detail. I know he depends upon you."

Harry puffed out his chest a bit and said, "That's right, how clever you are, Miss Garrett. Not everyone understands business. Balancing the books is a big responsibility."

Responsibility was exactly what she needed Esther thought. She smiled at him and tilted her head coquettishly as she raised her eyes to look up at him. "You explain the business so well. Every time I'm in Poppa's shop, you always tell me about the ledgers. I do so enjoy our talks, don't you Mr. Thompson?"

He looked dumbstruck. Esther inwardly prayed for God to please forgive her deceit. She vowed again to make it up to Harry and be the best wife she could be. She knew she'd forever thank God for delivering this young man to her.

Harry opened his mouth. Nothing came out. He closed it, swallowed, and cleared his throat. Esther patiently waited for him to take the next step. Harry tried again. "Miss Garrett, I have enjoyed every one of our talks." He gulped again. "Will you walk out with me tomorrow to go to Hamilton's Soda Shoppe?"

Esther tried to give him her best smile while she told herself to be brave and think of all the people who'd see her with Harry. The old gossips in town would soon tattle about the new couple. She needed to be seen with him. Set the hook, she thought again.

Harry frowned. "Don't you like ice cream sodas, Miss Garrett?"

"Yes, Mr. Thompson, I do. I'd enjoy a walk tomorrow, with you. And please call me Esther," she said and tried her smile again.

"Thank you, Esther. Is four o'clock a good time for you? And call me Harry."

"I'll meet you here on the porch at four tomorrow, Harry."

Later after supper, Esther found traces of blood in her underwear and quickly got her monthly linen from her clothes press. That night she thanked God for her deliverance and planned how she'd let Harry off the hook.

She woke early and soon realized her monthly flow had stopped. In reality, it hadn't even started. Despair deeper than before made her climb back into bed, and she wept.

"Esther, time to get up." Her mother's words words startled her. The sunlight told her it was past eight o'clock.

"I think my womanlies have started," Esther began but stopped after she saw her mother frown. Momma didn't believe in coddling. "I'll be down in a few minutes."

"See that you are. I'll have some nice chamomile tea ready for you."

Esther rose and rechecked her linen. No more blood. She sat back down and chewed on her fingernails. When the first drop soaked into her nightgown, she knew she'd found her answer. A few minutes with her embroidery scissors, and she'd have enough blood to satisfy her mother. After a quick recovery from her menstrual discomfort, she'd keep her appointment with Harry.

When they walked down her street toward the ice cream shop, Esther sensed old, bony hands pulling back the lace curtains in every front parlor. Her neighbors would get a better look at them, the new couple in town. She told herself to be brave and remember she was doing this for her baby and her parents. But by the time they reached the town square, Esther did not feel awkward anymore. At first, Harry talked about the shop's ledgers, which was so boring, but fortunately he soon changed the subject.

"How are you spending your summer?" he asked.

"I've been doing a great deal of reading. Do you like to read?"

"My favorite books are *Ben-Hur* and *Tom Sawyer*. When I read them, I was in the Holy Land and Hannibal Missouri. Have you read them?"

Esther was surprised to learn he enjoyed books and wanted to discuss them. She drew hope from the fact that he could talk about more than numbers and shoes. It might be possible that after they knew each other, one day she might love him, maybe.

On their return trip back to her house, Esther no longer thought about what the neighbors might say. When they turned onto her front walk, she noticed that her parents sat on the porch next to the lattice woven with roses. Poppa had on a clean shirt, and Momma had removed her apron. They were dressed for company.

"Hello Mr. and Mrs. Garrett, nice weather we're having, isn't it?"

"Hello Harry," her father said. Won't you visit for a while? Esther, come and give your poppa a kiss on the cheek and go in with Momma to help with dinner."

Esther turned to her new beau, "Thank you, Harry for a pleasant afternoon."

"It was my pleasure, Esther. May I bring by some of the books we talked about?"

"Yes, especially *Ben-Hur.* Good-bye."

"Good-bye, Esther until I see you again," Harry managed to say without blushing.

Esther went inside with her mother. She wanted to lurk in the front hall and listen to the conversation on the porch. But Momma said no, it was time for the men to talk.

At dinner Poppa said, "Harry is a nice young man, Esther."

"Yes sir."

"He knows you are to attend Oberlin in the fall."

"He's a friend. I told him about all the books I have to read."

"You may walk out with him, but you must remember at all times how fortunate you are to be going to college. Very few girls will have the opportunity you have. Make sure you remember that, Esther."

"I'll remember about college," she answered and put down her fork. Her stomach turned over, and she knew it would be impossible to eat any more. Her parents would be heartbroken when they found out about Oberlin and the baby.

On Friday and Saturday afternoons, Harry and Esther walked again to Hamilton's Ice Cream Shoppe. Harry was becoming a friend, and Esther's conscience ambushed her. How could she do this to him?

Her guilt brought on terrible nightmares in which different scenes played out. Harry changed his mind because he fell in love with another woman. Or her father fired him, and Harry couldn't marry her because he didn't have a job. Her most terrifying dream was she was lying in bed after giving birth, and Harry walked in, crying with happiness. After he kissed her on the cheek, he unwrapped the blanket and saw the baby didn't have the face of a newborn baby, but Noah's face on July 4th, the one she had last seen in her grape arbor. Harry looked at the baby and at her. His face changed to disgust and rage. The fear she felt after seeing his reaction was so overwhelming that she woke up and found sleep was gone for the rest of the night.

Esther invited Harry to Sunday dinner. She sat and watched him talk with her parents. Harry even said a few things to Cornelius about baseball. They talked, and she accepted her future. No Oberlin. A new baby in the house. Harry, sweet unknowing Harry, across the dinner table from her for the rest of her life. She felt a sob spring up and quickly silenced it as she remembered what she had to do.

Harry came to dinner on Monday and Wednesday. Wednesday was the day she had determined he must ask her to elope. Certain of success, Esther didn't doubt her plan since the borrowed novels had provided a map on how to make a man propose and run away with the girl he loved. An uneasy conscience still ate away at her spirit. But no other suitors appeared in her sights, and time was running out.

After dinner on Wednesday evening, they sat in the swing alone on the front porch. The first step was to place her hand on the cushion between them and will Harry to touch it. He did, and at very moment, she hoped he had set his life's course on the pivotal point of no return. Esther bit the inside of her cheek until tears came to her eyes.

"Harry, I am going to miss you so much when I go away," she half-whispered, holding his gaze.

"I am going to miss you something awful," he groaned. "I think about you every moment. But I promised your father I would not interfere with your education."

His honest declaration made her wish that her intentions were as honorable. She moved to the next step and said a little louder, "I don't think I can leave you. Oberlin is so far away. I won't see you until the first term ends. That's too many days of not being with you." She looked far away and sighed, "I just can't imagine it."

"I can't either. I love you so much. I've already counted the days until you return. It's going to be a long time."

The next few minutes were crucial. If she played Harry right, her baby had a father. If not, she didn't know what she was going to do or where she was going to go. She looked away from him and at the lavender in bloom by the front walk. She paused before she continued. "What are we going to do?" she sobbed.

"We can write letters. I might get some time off to come up and see you. Don't worry. I'll figure something out," he said and drew her close.

Inside the house, she heard familiar sounds. Her mother was putting Charles and Hattie to bed. Her father snored in his chair. Cornelius had yet to return from his bicycle ride around town. The coast was clear. Esther nudged her intended to the next stage. Her breast brushed against his arm. "Do you love me Harry? Really love me?" she said in his ear, and allowed her voice to stutter with tears.

"I do, Esther, with my whole heart and soul." His declaration of love was rewarded when Esther took his hand and placed it on her breast.

"If only we could marry right away and Momma and Poppa not stop us," she whispered again into his ear. He nodded. "There has to be a way. We love each other too much to be apart," she continued and kissed his neck.

Esther sensed Harry's resolve was wavering. He caught his breath, and his pulse increased under her lips. Her strategy called for him to be the next to speak. She withdrew from his embrace and forced a tender look into her eyes by thinking of Noah. More little tears came to her eyes and ran down her cheeks. Her lower lip quivered, and she propelled Harry forward toward her goal.

"There is a way," Harry stammered. "Sometimes, when people find they are in love, they run away and get married. Nice girls like you don't know these things, but we could elope."

Esther sensed it was better to stay quiet and let Harry rush through his ideas.

"We'll run away and get married in Kentucky. I'll borrow my father's carriage and meet you someplace. It'd have to be where no one could see. We don't want anyone to stop us."

Esther snuggled her body closer to him. Harry's parents hadn't even come into her mind before this. Panic hit, but she considered what they might voice about their son's marriage. What would she do if they didn't accept her or the baby? She couldn't think that far in the future. She had no other choice.

Through the cloud of her thoughts, she heard Harry natter on. "I'll tell him I have to go to Cincinnati for the baseball team. It's about time to get some new bats and gloves. I've done it before, and I spent most of the weekend coming and going. We'll be gone hours before anyone will suspect what we've done."

Exuberance rushed through Esther. She had done it, hooked Harry. "I'm so glad you've planned all this out," she kissed his cheek. "I'll tell Momma and Poppa I'm going to Joan's house."

"You know, don't you, that they will be angry?"

"I don't care, Harry. I want to marry you as soon as possible," and she sat back and let a few more tears trail down her face.

"We have to elope before you leave for college. My next payday's in two weeks."

Two weeks, Esther thought, she couldn't wait that long. So she leaned forward and kissed him softly. When he kissed her back, she increased the pressure of her lips on his and felt him tremble. She pulled away.

"Harry, when we're married, we can kiss all day, and," she hesitated and hoped she was blushing, "and we can kiss all night. I want to marry you tomorrow. Tomorrow night can be our first time together."

"Esther, my love," Harry sputtered out the fateful words. "Can you meet me at Greenlawn Cemetery at nine o'clock in the morning?"

"Yes, oh yes, Harry, I'll be there." Esther snuggled up to him and spoke into his ear. "Eloping is so romantic. I'll leave a note for Momma and Poppa telling them we are so much in love that we decided to elope." She straightened up and reeled him in as she looked into his eyes. "I'm so happy you thought of this," Esther said. She embraced and kissed him. Relief flowed over her that she'd landed him. Soon sadness touched her conscience. Even so, she congratulated herself.

Chapter 28

Mr. and Mrs. Jeremiah Garrett are pleased to announce the marriage of their daughter Esther to Mr. Harry Thompson, son of Mr. and Mrs. Harry Thompson, also of Sabina, on August 25, 1881. The bride and groom will reside with her parents.

Sabina News, September 2, 1881, p. 2.

Chapter 28

Sabina, March 1882

<Agnes and Matthew McConkey
<Hannah and Jeremiah Garrett
<Esther Thompson
<Sarah Jane Guymon

Hannah gazed in wonder at her first grandchild and recalled her friend Dicey Burrow's words from last December. "The first time you lay your hands upon that child, Hannah, all your anger, disappointment, and hurt will evaporate. You'll be filled with love," Dicey had promised in response to Hannah's ire over Esther's pregnancy. Hannah didn't believe her friend's wisdom at the time and told her so as they stood on the corner of Grand and Center before they shopped for the holidays.

Dicey shook her head and went on. "It's the most moving experience you'll ever have. You can't imagine how it feels to look at your grandchild's features and see traces of your parents and your husband and your children all wrapped up in this new person."

"Dicey was certainly correct, yes she was," Hannah cooed to Sarah Jane as they rocked. Across the room, Esther, exhausted, slept soundly under the multi-colored crazy quilt Harry had brought from his home. While Hannah cradled the newborn for the first time, the silence of the house soothed her.

The frantic pace that started when Esther's birth pangs intensified around three o'clock in the morning was over at last. The whole household hadn't calmed down until two hours after the baby's safe arrival. Finally the midwife went home, the men had their breakfast and left for the shoe shop several hours late, and Hannah took time to dress properly in her old dark blue cotton day dress and switched to a clean apron. However, she had not yet had time to recapture the gray-streaked hair that tumbled from her braid and to change out of the carpet slippers that warmed her toes.

Grandmother and granddaughter rocked back and forth in the old Shaker rocker on the early spring day, and Hannah, tired and exhilarated, let her long-held anger and disappointment lift. Sarah Jane, dressed for warmth in a long white cotton sack and, wrapped loosely in a crocheted blanket, had only her face visible to Hannah.

"I can see you wrinkle your forehead just like your Grandfather Jeremiah. Your little mouth is like your mother's, and I believe you have my chin." Sarah Jane squirmed and worked an arm loose from the folds of the blanket. The sleeve fell back.

Suddenly Hannah's head swam and a roar rushed in her ears as she moved Sarah Jane closer to her eyes for a more careful examination. At once the reason for her shock fell into place.

"This is no early baby. I know early babies. The twins were early. They looked unfinished and had no eyelashes and no fingernails," she whispered and gently brought the newborn's other arm out and examined it. Hannah became even more convinced that this baby was late. The peeling and cracked skin, especially in the elbow crease, proved it. Only late babies had skin this dry.

Sarah Jane was small, but she was not an eight-month baby. The midwife thought she weighed close to six pounds. Old Grace would know. She had cared for hundreds. Probably even "early ones" weighing in at nine or ten pounds. She knew all kinds of secrets about most families in town. Yet Hannah had never heard that any gossip pointed back to the midwife who must keep her own counsel.

Hannah rocked and counted back. She tried to remember when Harry started to show up on the front porch. August, mid-August. Was that when Esther became pregnant? No, not unless she and Harry were together in July. What was going on in that month?

All she remembered was Noah McConkey had been killed right after the Fourth of July celebration when he ran away. She continued to rock and think. When did Esther have her last monthly flow? She was still irregular. Sometimes up to two months went by without any substantial bleeding. June? Yes, June. Nothing in July. A little in August.

Her rocking motion stopped, and nausea spilled throughout her stomach. No. It can't be. But Noah was the only boy around. "No one else," she said out loud with a heavy heart.

Hannah rose, and with slow, measured steps out of the bedroom, she moved toward the front hallway window to look at her granddaughter in the spring sunshine. It seemed to be the longest walk she had ever taken.

"Do I really want to know? No, but I have to. I need to look her over in the direct light," she muttered. "Please God, don't let it be so."

Through her mind raced all those stories she'd overheard as a girl on the plantation. The time-tested wisdom of both the black and white old women predicted how dark a baby would turn out to be. The baby was never darker than the darker parent nor lighter than the lighter parent. There was also that quick peek behind the new baby girl's ear or a boy's groin. However dark that spot was would indicate how dark the baby would end up. Another old wives' tale was it took ten days for the color to set in, and a child's fate was thus determined.

While the late morning sunlight warmed them, Hannah slowly undressed Sarah Jane with her right hand and snuggled the infant in her left arm. She looked closely at the sleeping baby. Her examination revealed the newborn was not as light as Cornelius and the twins. But Harry's people were not blond with fair skin. They had dark hair. They also had blue and green eyes. Though Jeremiah and his people had dark hair and eyes, it was still very possible Noah was really the father of her grandchild.

"How could I have not seen what was really before me? Oh, it's going to be a long ten days," she sobbed as her eyes filled with tears. "I'll just have to wait and see."

But wait for what she realized with a jolt, and her knees weakened. What would happen if Sarah Jane darkened? She was still their grandchild. Nothing would ever change that. She had already loved her from the moment Esther had taken her hand and placed it so she could the little legs kick. Hannah redressed her granddaughter and returned to Esther's room.

While the rocker creaked, she put herself in her daughter's place and tried to imagine what Esther's life had really been during her pregnancy but failed. She must have been terrified. To endure that fear all alone? Hannah was so ashamed and wondered why Esther didn't come to her. Where did the girl get her strength?

By the end of her conversation with herself, Hannah had decided to do nothing for the moment. She continued to rock the baby and thought about the turmoil in their lives since Esther's August elopement. It had taken most of the pregnancy, but she had just about accepted Harry as her son-in-law after Esther's actions had shattered her long-held dream of her first daughter's wedding.

The pain over the elopement hadn't even begun to heal when Esther announced she was with child. Every mother must have envisioned when her little girl would become a bride and a mother. That day was one of those special times she'd looked forward to when she watched Esther play with her dolls and help with Cornelius and the twins. Her dream had also dimmed. She had no strength left to revisit the weight of rage that had overwhelmed her months ago. The depth of her anger had been a new experience, even more intense than the betrayal she had felt when Jeremiah told her about enlisting all those years ago.

The path away from her anger opened up when Hannah heard her mother's voice in her head repeat the same advice given so long before. "Put your hot temper to good work, daughter. Many times you're going to be so angry you could spit. Don't. Remember you are a lady. A lady does not lose her temper. Make bread and beat carpets. At least you'll have something good to show for all that emotion. If you're still out of sorts, take down the curtains and wash and starch them. Eventually, you'll work off your anger when you wear yourself out."

For days, after Esther came home with Harry and their marriage license, Hannah made bread in the kitchen early in the morning and beat carpets on the clothesline in the afternoon. She found herself arguing in a low cadence as she worked the carpets and bread dough.

"Had herself a wonderful future. Going to Oberlin. Destined for great things. Now all gone, gone, gone. No college. Her fate is sealed. No education." Esther's choice of husband also displeased Hannah. "Harry of all people. Works for Jeremiah. It'll be years before he's on his own. Still can't believe it. She ran off and married him. I didn't even know she loved him. He's so dull. How could I not know what was going on?"

Jeremiah had been more angry and disappointed than she was when Esther and Harry returned as a married couple. During that frantic August night when Esther said she would be at Joan's house and didn't return home on time, Jeremiah was first a loving father convinced his daughter was in trouble and needed him to rescue her. He became the picture of paternal dark displeasure when he read her note explaining she had eloped with Harry and not to worry.

The uproar that had taken place in their parlor the next evening was horrific. Jeremiah shouted, she cried, Harry stood with his arm around Esther, and their daughter leaned against her new husband. After Jeremiah had exhausted himself and collapsed into his chair, Esther asked if she and Harry could live with them, in her bedroom. Hannah remembered how Jeremiah jumped out of his chair and stalked from the room. His parting words were they could do whatever they damn well wanted since that's what they already had chosen to do.

From that night until early in October when Esther told them they would be grandparents, Jeremiah would leave the room whenever Harry entered without Esther. How they worked together in the shoe shop when Jeremiah was so angry she could not imagine.

As Esther's pregnancy became more evident, he softened toward Harry, and the two men sat in the front parlor after dinner to smoke and discuss world events. Hannah admired how Jeremiah changed his attitude. Her anger and disappointment however did not abate. She tried to explain it to Jeremiah. "Something's not right about this marriage."

"It's legal, Hannah, and it's a fact you can't change."

"I know I can't change it," she snapped. "I'm telling you something's wrong. Her face doesn't glow when Harry walks into a room. She doesn't light up when he talks."

"He'll be good to her, Hannah. He loves her."

"That's easy to see. He sits at the dinner table and looks at her like the besotted fool he is."

Jeremiah tired of her rages and didn't want to hear them. In her heart she knew she was fortunate her daughter lived in her house where she could care for her. Even her own ears and mind grew weary of her ongoing vent about Esther's ruined life. She switched to new verses, "the best laid plans of mice and men" and "unto all a little rain must fall." Those words did not assuage her anger either.

When Hannah glanced again at her granddaughter, tears of remorse crept down her cheeks. All the pieces had fallen into place. She thought of how unflinching Esther had been in her pregnancy and delivery. Her daughter had kept her secret. Guilt grew from Hannah's center and spread through all of her being. Pride and anger had blinded her. When Esther needed her the most, she failed her. Choking back a sob, she admitted Esther was the bravest woman she knew.

Hannah cuddled her granddaughter and vowed to her daughter and granddaughter that she would guard them from all the hate and ugliness in the world. If it was up to her, Esther's secret would be safe.

Sarah Jane was a quiet baby, and they catnapped together. A short time later Hannah rose from the chair and placed Sarah Jane in her bassinet by Esther. After she contemplated her daughter with new respect, the older woman straightened her back and left the room.

Hannah carried her burden while she went about her daily chores. She hung up the birth linen she earlier had put to soak in salt and considered Jeremiah. Should she tell him? Would he even want to hear about her suspicions? They never kept any secrets from each other, at least not from the moment they had first declared their love for each other, and this was not the time to start. The day he gave her the brooch, he promised his love and respect. The two had lived side by side and shared everything that happened. Never had there been the need to lie to him she thought as her fingers brushed the brooch at her neck.

She kept up her deliberation as she bent down to take the laundry basket back in the house. Should she stay silent? The memory of how Jeremiah gazed at Sarah Jane only a few hours before came to her. He looked so lovingly at his granddaughter, at Esther, and then at her. His expression was one of wonderment and joy. The awe of the moment had melted her heart.

While the iron heated on the wood stove, indecision overwhelmed Hannah. What was the right thing to do? Betray Jeremiah by not telling him what must have happened to Esther and Noah? For Jeremiah also grieved when Noah died. He was the boy they'd watch grow up. Often they had shared their concern how Noah's death had aged his parents overnight. The question was could she burden him with the knowledge. Not yet was her answer.

The afternoon brought her parents, Matthew and Agnes McConkey, to the house. Sarah Jane was their first great-grandchild, and they came loaded with baskets and gifts. Her father came in and kissed Hannah on the cheek and called her grandma as he chuckled. He placed his basket on the kitchen table and said he would go have a little peek at Sarah Jane and sit by the fire in the parlor.

"I don't like being around babies. Never did. Mother, you come find me when you're ready to leave."

"I will, Father," her mother promised.

"Wake me up if I'm asleep," he asked his wife who tried to shoo him on his way.

"Hannah, your mother worked hours getting her baskets filled with food to bring. I'm surprised she let me wait until two o'clock to come over."

"I'm sure Esther would love to see you, Papa." Hannah patted her father's arm.

"Go on upstairs and take a gander at your new grandbaby, you old man," her mother said over her shoulder before she reached for one of

Hannah's clean aprons in the pantry and placed it over her dark brown work dress.

Undeterred, he still talked on. "You women and your babies. You'd think they were fixing to disappear or something the way you rush around after they get here. I told her you all needed your sleep." With those words, he grinned and left to go upstairs.

"Hannah, you look a little tired," her mother said.

"A bit." Hannah hoped her mother did not read what else was in her heart. "I'm happy you're here today. I might have a lie-down in a little while if you can stay that long." She raised her right hand to cover a yawn.

"Let me put this food away in the pantry," her mother said. "I brought Esther's favorites, pickled beets and strawberry jam. Then we'll go upstairs to see Sarah Jane. I can stay most of the evening, if you need me." Mama arranged her offerings from her kitchen on her daughter's shelves. "Do you need help with the ironing? I saw the birthing linen on the line. I'll go take it down after I see the baby."

Mama moved to the sink and started to wash her hands with lye soap and hot water from the kettle. "I always like to have clean hands when I hold babies. Just feels right."

Hannah heard her father's footsteps come down the stairs and go into the front parlor. She turned to her mother and said, "I know Esther wants to see you. Go on upstairs. Jeremiah moved the old rocker from the twins' room to Esther's."

"Your father's right. I've been ready to come here and hold this new baby since Jeremiah came over with the news she was finally here," her mother laughed and dried her hands on a clean tea towel.

"You can sit up there and rock Sarah Jane and visit with Esther. After I start dinner, I'll join you in a few minutes," Hannah turned back to her stove and listened for her mother's steps and wondered if her mother would notice the peeling skin? How good were her eyes now? Esther's room got the morning sun. Maybe the light would not be strong enough for her mother to notice Hannah considered as she chopped vegetables for the family's dinner. She heard the rocker's gentle creak and a low murmur of voices but couldn't understand what was said.

Hannah was arranging the potatoes around the beef roast when she heard Mama come down the stairs. Was she overreacting, or were her mother's steps slower than when she climbed the stairs? Hannah let her breath out after she realized she was not breathing as she waited for Mama's return to the kitchen. The steps went toward the front parlor.

She's gone to look in on Papa, Hannah thought and straightened up to close the oven door. Footsteps from the parlor reached her, and she wondered if her parents were leaving. However, only her mother's came toward the kitchen. Hannah turned to the kitchen door and waited with a dishtowel in her hands.

Mama entered with a heavy step and did not quite meet Hannah's eyes. She sank slowly into a chair at the kitchen table. "Father's sound asleep in the front parlor. He was in as big a hurry as me to come and visit." She hesitated for a few seconds. "I must be getting old, Hannah, now that I am now a great-grandmother. Could I have a cup of tea?"

Hannah put the kettle on to boil and busied herself with the cups and saucers while she listened to her mother's words. "Sarah Jane is sure a pretty baby. All that long straight dark hair. She has the same delicate features in her face you had when you were born. I think she will be fine-boned like our side of the family. Harry's people lack our family's short stature. Maybe the next baby will take after their side of the family and be a big strapping boy. It is always better if the girl is small and not the other way around."

Hannah nodded, and Mama went on. "Esther says she is feeling good. I warned her not to put her feet on the floor until the ninth day. It's probably an old wives' tale. But that is what my mother told me and her mother told her. She said Old Grace gave her the same advice."

When Hannah gave her mother a cup and saucer, Mama touched her hand and looked her meaningfully in the eye. "It is a blessing she is a good size baby coming early as she did. Remember early babies don't need a lot of company. Best keep the visitors away for a few weeks until Sarah Jane gets a good start. In this family we protect our babies, Hannah, above all else. We keep them safe and out of harm's way."

Hannah returned her mother's look and took up the older woman's carefully worded suggestion. "Yes, Sarah Jane can be christened a few weeks from now if the weather's good. We do not want to take an early baby out if it is raining. The kettle's ready, Mama. I think I'll have a cup of tea too." The two women sat across from each other and drank their tea in silence. Hannah noticed her hand shook as she raised the teacup to her lips.

Mama sighed after a few minutes. "I can help you with the chores now. What do you need?"

They planned their work for the rest of the day. By example, her mother guided Hannah. Some things were better not said aloud. Hannah managed to keep busy enough during the rest of the day and most of the evening. When she thought of Sarah Jane, she forced her mind to think of how healthy she was. When she thought of Esther, she made herself think of how grateful she was that Esther had not come down with childbed fever. Throughout the rest of the day, she repeated she had many blessings and turned back to her tasks. Yet her heart refused to lift.

That night, however, as the house settled down and quieted, Hannah's thoughts spun through her head. While she lay in bed and listened to Jeremiah snore and sleep soundly, she debated yet again about sharing her suspicions. Their commitment so long ago to each other demanded loyalty and honesty. Hannah resolved to share what she thought with Jeremiah the next day.

The newborn's fussing came through the wall. Esther must have gathered the baby to her breast to feed because the cries ceased. The image of her daughter and granddaughter made tears stream down Hannah's face. The noise from the next room combined with her sniffling awoke Jeremiah.

He must have seen her tears glisten in the moonlight from the bedroom window. He mover closer and asked, "Why are you crying?"

"It's Esther." She could not look at him.

"I thought she was all right."

"That's not it." She gathered her strength, put a pillow behind her back for support, and voiced her fears. "Jeremiah, I feel so guilty. I've broken our pledge we made to always tell each other the truth. I have been wrestling with this ever since I first held Sarah Jane."

He rearranged his pillow and demanded, "Woman, you're not making any sense. Come out with it."

"Sarah Jane is not an early baby."

"What do you mean?"

"Do you remember how the twins looked when they were born? No fingernails or eyelashes?" Stunned, Jeremiah motioned with his hands for her to go on. "I can't carry this burden alone anymore. I thought I could, but I'm not strong enough. I don't want to betray Esther and Sarah Jane. And I don't want to betray you."

"Tell me." Jeremiah took Hannah's hands in his. "You know it always seems worse at night. Come on, we can face any trouble, together."

"I don't think Harry is Sarah Jane's father. He wasn't around here in July."

"July? What's so important about that month?"

"That had to be when Esther became pregnant. The only boy hanging around here in July was Noah McConkey."

The look on his face was as stricken as she predicted it would be.

He sputtered a few words before he managed to say, "You think Esther and Noah? No. I can't even say it."

"I think Esther and Noah made a mistake. I think that is why Noah ran away." Hannah let that settle in before she resumed. "She has already paid a heavy price. She gave up college and married a man she most certainly doesn't love."

"That means our grandchild is part Negro." Jeremiah struggled out of bed and paced angrily on the floor. "Is that what you're saying?" he hissed.

"Yes, and I am not alone in my suspicions about Sarah Jane being a late baby either."

"Who else?" He stopped and looked at her.

"Mama, she knows what an early baby looks like, too."

"And Old Grace?" Jeremiah sat heavily back down on the bed.

"Yes, Old Grace. She's never said anything about the secrets she must know about every family in town." Hannah waited until Jeremiah stilled. "We have to consider what is best for them. Esther grieved alone and in secret when Noah died. She has had to carry her guilty secret along with carrying this child. I know people say you make your bed and you have to lie in it, but she is so young to have to pay this price."

"My little girl. Are you sure?"

"Yes." There was a pause.

"You've asked her?"

"I can't. I have to respect how she's handled this by herself. She didn't come to either one of us."

Sadness marched over his face when he said, "And if there's even a hint of suspicion about Sarah Jane, she will never be able to marry a white man." Jeremiah put his head down in his hands.

"I know. Our grandchild and her children will be labeled Negro. They won't be part of white society." Hannah's tears started again. "Why is the world such an ugly place for our innocent children? Why does it matter who your parents and grandparents were?"

"I agree. That's one of the reason we left Virginia. So we wouldn't be hobbled by the past, the past we had nothing to do with," Jeremiah angrily said and stared at her. "Harry can never suspect," he added.

"Harry?" Hannah's conscience began to torment her over her behavior toward him. "I have been so mean to him. I didn't want him in our family. How can I ever make it up to him?"

"Does he know enough about babies and slavery to figure it out?"

"Maybe he doesn't, but what about his parents?" She looked at husband. "I feel like a conspirator."

He nodded his understanding. "They moved here to Sabina when Harry and his brother John were small, didn't they?"

"Yes, where did they come from? From back east someplace, New York was it?"

"No, Vermont, some small town where the winters were so cold Mrs. Thompson had to leave for her health," Jeremiah said.

"So they're not from the south. They probably don't have any experience with how people look over babies for any hints of mixed blood."

The clock chimed three times. Hannah spoke in the stillness of the house. "When I was little, I heard the old saying you don't wash your dirty laundry in public. I remember how puzzled I was by the old women's words."

"I suppose every family has secrets."

Hannah heard defeat in his words and said, "Ones they do not even talk about with each other."

"But it's difficult to keep them hidden in a small town."

"Mama always says the only way to keep a secret is to keep it to yourself. That's what Esther did."

"You're right. She kept the truth to herself," Jeremiah sighed.

"Come, let's get some sleep," Hannah said and reached for her husband. They settled back under the covers and lay side by side. She tried to absorb the reality of how their life had changed.

Until Esther could get out of bed, Hannah took the baby and changed her clothes from the skin out. On the tenth day, Esther got out of bed and took over the care. Hannah planned her work so she was present when Esther dressed Sarah Jane. Her explanation to her daughter was it had become her favorite part of the day. Esther said she was glad for her mother's help since the baby was strong and squirmed. To Hannah's eye and relief, the newborn did not seem to darken.

Sarah Jane's christening day was set for her third Sunday. She wore the same lace christening-gown her mother and grandmother had worn at their ceremonies. Esther, attired in a butterscotch striped dress and yellow straw hat, sat in the family pew with her parents and grandparents. Reverend William Cockrell performed the ceremony at the altar of the Central Methodist Church during the morning service. Cornelius stood beside Harry and promised to be his niece's godfather. Great-Aunt Lavinia McConkey, dressed in her dove gray linen dress and matron's cap, stood on the other side and vowed to be the godmother.

The minister ended the baptism with the announcement that there was a reception at the family home that afternoon and all were invited to attend. Following the town custom, Harry had also put an announcement in *The Tribune*. The new father proudly boasted he wanted every one to see how beautiful Sarah Jane was.

Hannah, however, was very nervous at she nudged a teacake into better alignment next to the sandwiches on the dining room table. The old busybodies in town, who resembled black crows in their old-fashioned dresses and veiled hats, would come as a flock and cackle. They'd stare at Sarah Jane and decide if she was too little or too large, if her head was shaped nicely or still deformed from the birth canal, and if she looked like her mother's or father's side of the family.

Not having a reception would be worse. No reception meant grist for the gossip mill, and it needed very little to keep it turning. Hannah realized that spreading rumors was a barter system. The only way to find out what others said was to offer up some tale to exchange. It seemed tittle-tattle was the fuel that kept some of these people in Sabina alive.

She shuddered and remembered again how the old plantation gossips waited until the tenth day to bind a child's fate with a whisper of scandal that may or may not be true. She wondered if those blabbermouths ever stopped to consider that a child's parentage and ancestry were in no way its doing or fault.

She forced herself to put those thoughts aside because she had only moments to spare before the guests were due to arrive and turned her attention to her appearance. After she removed the large apron, she tidied her hair, smoothed the skirt of the garnet red linen dress, and straightened the brooch on her bodice before she gave the twins and Cornelius one last inspection. Somehow, all three had remained presentable from the time they arrived home after church until that moment.

During the reception, Hannah was making the rounds in the front parlor when she noticed Noah's parents' arrival. She stood frozen in place for a few seconds before her innate good manners and training took over and compelled her forward to greet her new guests dressed in their Sunday best. Jacob wore his somber dark suit, but at his neck was a cheerful red and blue paisley cravat while Patience wore a two-tone green silk day dress with matching bonnet set off by a white egret feather. Hannah approached Patience with her arms stretched out in greeting.

"Patience and Jacob, thank you for coming to share Sarah Jane's celebration with us," she warmly greeted them. "Can you believe how the little one is asleep in her cradle with all of these people talking and laughing around her?" Hannah guided them to the corner of the parlor where Esther was seated next to the cradle.

"We read the notice in the paper about your get-together," Patience said to Hannah before they reached the baby. Hannah stood beside Esther who was seated between Agnes and Harry's mother Sallie.

Jacob and Patience went to the foot of the cradle. He bid the women hello and said to Esther, "That's a fine looking baby girl, Miss Esther." He nodded his head once more and left to join the men standing in the hallway.

Patience placed her gloved hands on the top of the cradle's footboard and gazed at the baby stretch in her sleep. Sarah Jane wrinkled her forehead and blew bubbles in her sleep. Hannah watched in apprehension when her visitor's hands tensed and gripped the wood. Patience raised her eyes and looked at Esther and down again at Sarah Jane and back at Esther. Tears were in her eyes when she said, "Miss Esther, you've got a pretty baby girl there. You sure do."

"Thank you, Miss Patience," Esther said in a low voice.

"She's going to be a real pretty girl. I hope she's smart like her mama." Hannah felt her gaze. The two grandmothers stood there and with a look from each other's eyes communicated wordlessly their understanding that they'd protect this innocent child. Esther, Hannah, Agnes, and Patience would be lionesses fearlessly guarding Sarah Jane. Hannah slowly let out her breath, unaware she had been holding it. Patience also released her held breath and loosened her grip on the cradle.

"You know, Miss Esther, my people have been making things for your people's children for years. I'd like to keep up that tradition."

Hannah could not speak because her throat was so tight, but she inclined her head and heard Esther reply, "Didn't you make some booties and caps for me?"

"That's right, I did. I've been working on some things for your baby and have almost finished them. Is it all right to bring my gifts by next week?"

"I would be proud, Miss Patience."

Hannah recovered enough to say, "Patience, you are welcome here anytime, both you and Jacob."

Sarah Jane Thompson
1881

Chapter 29

An Old Friend Is Called Home to His Maker

Mr. Jeremiah Garrett, age forty-three, died unexpectedly May 3rd instant at his residence on Center Street. He had returned home from his cobbler shop for dinner and suddenly clutched his chest and fell forward. The only word he spoke was Hannah before he died. Mrs. Hannah Garrett told the neighbors that she had noticed how pale he had become as they discussed the unusually hot weather.

Mr. Garrett, an early settler in Sabina, left his parents Jeremiah and Mercy Garrett in New Kent County, Virginia and traveled here as a young man. He disagreed with the issue of slavery and joined the Yeargains as they along with other members of the Society of Friends came north. He enlisted in the Ohio's 90th Volunteer Infantry and served with distinction until discharged at the end of the war.

After his return home, he married Hannah McConkey, and together they reared a family of four children. His cobbler shop was on Main Street, and there he worked until the day he died. Every citizen of Sabina has walked in shoes he repaired. Mr. Garrett will be remembered for his craftsmanship and his charitable gift of shoes to the Children of Soldiers Home and the Harriet Tubman Negro School.

Mr. Garrett leaves his wife Hannah, daughter Mrs. Esther (Harry) Thompson of Sabina, and his young children Cornelius, Charles, and Hattie, and a granddaughter.

Services are at the Central Methodist Church May 5th at 2:00 p.m. followed by interment, Greenlawn Cemetery. The Reverend William Cockrell will officiate.

Sabina News, May 4, 1883, page 2.

Chapter 30

Mrs. Hannah Garrett Joins Husband in Heavenly Reward

Mrs. Garrett, nee McConkey, age 70, gently passed on to her reward while surrounded by her family members. At her bedside were her daughters Mrs. Esther (Harry) Thompson of Sabina, Mrs. Hattie (Robert) Brown of Richmond, Indiana, and son Cornelius of College Corner, Ohio. She had been living with her daughter Mrs. Thompson since she fell and broke her hip at the Garrett home place. She called all of her children and grandchildren together to say farewell and bid them not to grieve. With a smile, she said it was time for her to join her husband Jeremiah and their children, Charley, Emma, Lida, and Minnie.

Mrs. Garrett was one of Sabina's early settlers. She accompanied her parents, Mr. Mathew McConkey and his wife Agnes on their long trip from New Kent County, Virginia to homestead in Sabina.

Mrs. Garrett will be remembered for her good works in the community. She was an active participant in the Central Methodist Ladies' Guild and the Clinton County Orphanage.

Two daughters, one son, and various grandchildren survive Mrs. Hannah Garrett.

The Rev. Walter Butler will officiate the 2:00 p.m. services on the 26th of November at the Central Methodist Church. Internment is at Greenlawn Cemetery.

Sabina News, November 22, 1915, page 5.

Civil War Railroad Depot

Chapter 31

Sabina, Ohio, August 1862

<Agnes and Matthew McConkey
Hannah

Time was running out for Jeremiah to propose. He had enlisted on July 21st and had only two weeks left until he and Samuel had to return to muster in.

"It has to be today. I can't put it off any longer," he tried to convince himself as he followed Hannah and the family out of the Methodist church. "Whatever made me believe I could stand up to the Rebs? It's all I can do not to cut and run before I ask her to marry me, and I've known her most of my life. She's the only woman I've ever wanted. I want to come back and marry her. I want her in my bed and in no one else's."

When he saw Hannah glance over her shoulder and search for him, Jeremiah straightened his tie and willed his feet forward. "Hannah, will you walk with me a bit," Jeremiah said and held out his arm for her to take as she stepped onto the wooden sidewalk.

Hannah's heart galloped and she ordered it not to give her away while she nodded with her warmest smile.

"Of course, Jeremiah," she answered, anticipating the most important question a man ever asks a woman and slipped her arm through his.

They had gone only a few steps when Jeremiah said, "Hannah, I'm not a fancy man. I've don't have a pretty speech ready."

Hannah stopped and gave him her most fetching looks. Hours of practice in front of the hall mirror had led to the perfect angle to tilt her head under her new blue parasol.

"Dearest," he said.

With bowed head and raised eyes, she waited for him to say his heartfelt words. Instead she heard, "I love you, but I can't ask you to marry me yet. I don't have any right. I've enlisted. Me and Samuel have, together," Jeremiah stopped mid-sentence as Hannah abruptly withdrew her hand.

"How could you?" she blurted.

"Do what?"

"Enlist. You didn't even talk to me about it, and you kept it a secret. That's lying. You lied to me," she fumed. Turning on her heel, she stomped off.

Jeremiah's spirits sank farther with each bounce of her dark brown-coiled curls keeping time with her angry steps.

For three days, she refused to see him or talk with her brother Samuel. Finally, her mother sat her down in the kitchen. Hannah knew she was in for a scolding.

"Hannah, I had hoped you'd work all your anger out after thumping the bread dough and scrubbing floors. Yet not even beating carpets got it out of you, and you're just as sullen today as before. The only thing I have to say to you today is you're too proud and selfish for your own good."

"He lied to me. He didn't tell me about enlisting," the girl said.

"I admit he should've talked it over with you first, and Samuel should've said something to us too. However, you don't see your Papa and me refusing to talk to him, do you?"

"No." Hannah knew her mother had a good point, but she wasn't ready to let her sulk go. She kept her face lowered and her arms crossed.

"No matter what happens, Samuel is our son. We love him, and he loves us."

Hannah sensed her mother's eyes had not moved off of her. "Remember, Jeremiah loves you."

"Mama, if he loved me, he wouldn't leave me."

"Pay close attention to what I'm telling you. Jeremiah doesn't want to leave you. Consider how he feels. He is going to war and fight for an ideal we all believe in, freeing the slaves. He wants to go off knowing you will wait for him. You know you love him. You have ever since he joined us on the trip out of Virginia."

The memory of how she had settled on him for her husband when she was only eight softened her inner fire, and she raised her head.

"I don't want him to go."

"Of course not, no one does. However, men have their duty to fight. We women have our duty to be brave and encourage them when they do go off to battle."

Shaken by her mother's words, Hannah left the kitchen to seek comfort in her "thinking spot" by the welcoming willow on the riverbank. Hannah almost turned back into the house when she entered the road and saw Jeremiah by the side yard gate.

"Dearest," he pleaded, "Don't turn away. For God's sake, please hear me out."

She paused, took a steadying breath, and walked toward him. "I'm listening."

As she stood next to him, she realized how much his appearance had changed in three days. He was haggard and pale. His eyes had lost their usual good humor. Pride and anger left her, replaced by a commitment to him and whatever path their future took.

"Please don't be angry with me," he hurried his words. "But this war is about everything we believe in. It is worth fighting for. I've got to go."

Hannah reached up and gently touching his cheek, whispered, "Please forgive me. I've been childish. I wanted to keep you safe."

"Will you wait for me until I return?"

"Yes, however long it takes."

Taking her hand, Jeremiah bent down to kiss it, and slowly his lips brushed her cheek salty with tears. "I'll come back to you, I swear. This is a token of my promise."

Jeremiah reached into his vest pocket and brought out a small cloth bag. Hannah waited as he untied the drawstring and reached for her hand. He then emptied the contents on to her palm.

He leaned closer. "I want to give this to you because garnets mean faith and loyalty. With this brooch, I promise I'll love you all the rest of my days. I'll let nothing come between us, nothing. I will always tell you the truth, please believe me, even if it is painful. Dearest, we'll give this brooch to our first-born daughter. She'll pass it down to her daughter so they will always know how much I have loved you."

After church the next Sunday, Hannah gave Jeremiah her betrothal gift, a green garnet stickpin she had purchased mid-week in Wilmington. "Please stay safe and come back to me," she begged.

"I'll do my best. I promise."

"Do you swear you will wear this every day? I pray it will keep you safe and return you to me at the end of the war. I love you, Jeremiah. I always will. I pledge my love to you. Our marriage will be one of love and honor. I also vow I will never keep secrets from you."

"Yes, I promise," Jeremiah's love showed in his eyes and voice.

When Hannah looked at the calendar each morning, she saw her days with Jeremiah and Samuel melting away. Finally, the day arrived for their planned trip to take the new recruits to Circleville. Well before dawn on the following day, Hannah and her family traveled by train and wagon and reached the Ohio 90th's campground around noon. The camp, three miles outside of the town railroad depot, was a farm transformed from a quiet rustic scene to a bustling place of smoke, noise, and smells swirling in the August humid heat. Wagons unloaded soldiers and their loved ones and enough supplies to provision the men and the army animals before the August 29th pullout date. Over one thousand men were expected to muster in during the next three days.

Her father commented that no order was evident in the whole camp. It was confusion in all corners. Sabina had never been this busy, not even when the revivalists came to town for their yearly tent meetings.

Too soon, it was time to say good-bye. The young men escorted their loved ones to the camp gate so they could catch their ride back to the depot. Hannah first bid her brother Samuel good-bye. "Be careful, keep your head down," Hannah whispered in his ear as she gave him her parting hug.

Telling herself to be brave and smiling so the last picture he'd have of her would not be one of tears and a red runny nose, she turned next to him. "Jeremiah," was all she managed before her lower lip began to tremble.

"I'll be back for you. You have to believe that. Me and Samuel will watch out for each other," Jeremiah spoke his tender farewell and with a kiss lifted her into the wagon.

On the other side, Samuel had helped his mother climb aboard and shook hands with his father before the older man climbed into the wagon.

Once the three were settled in, the driver snapped the reins, and the wagon started off down the dusty country road back to the town. Hannah turned around in her seat to wave good-bye and saw their men pull their hats and wave them in the air. A feeling of success started through her. She had been the brave woman Jeremiah wanted.

Hannah and her family followed the war through *The Tribune* and the letters Jeremiah and Samuel sent home. The newspaper accounts brought the war into the house where it sat as a presence by the hearth. Their words frequently differed from Jeremiah's letters. She suspected the newspaper, unlike his stories, was closer to the unvarnished truth of the war.

The Tribune led off on August 31st with the headline "Union Forces Buckle and War Front Moves Closer to Ohio." The front-page story detailed a disastrous Union defeat in Kentucky. The Confederate forces overran six thousand inexperienced Union soldiers and had taken over four thousand men prisoner. When the battle ended, only one thousand Federal soldiers were left battle ready.

In her mind, Hannah pictured Jeremiah and Samuel ordered to march south into Kentucky to pursue the rebel forces and rescue the prisoners of war. The fear of their newly formed regiment engaging in battle so soon took over her thoughts. No amount of work or prayer drove her panic into silence.

Jeremiah's first letter didn't arrive home until mid-September and contained no hint of any battle or complaint about army life. Instead, he chose to tell her how much he loved her and to regale her with interesting tidbits of him and Samuel becoming soldiers.

My dearest Hannah,

I miss you so much. Every night I go to sleep and recall your gentle face and loving voice. Please try not to worry about us. We are having such an adventure. Our regiment's finally capable of marching together. It took a might of practice.

We haven't gone hungry yet. Every place our train has stopped, mothers of Union soldiers pass some home cooking through the windows. At one little town, they handed me and Samuel two apple pies and a lemon cake. Sometimes bonfires marked our arrival late at night, and the town's people cheered and ran over the tracks to greet us.

Across from Cincinnati, we even saw General Grant's father. We stopped to give his son a round of hurrah, and he came out on the front porch to wave at us.

I'll write another letter when I can. Please remember, dearest, that you mean so much to me.

The Tribune's September headlines, "Bragg in Kentucky," "Harper's Ferry Scene of Slaughter," and "Bloody Antietam" haunted her and spilled out in her next letter to Jeremiah.

> I miss you so very much. I try not to worry about you and Samuel, but at times, I do become so very frightened. Your letters always brighten my mood. I know you can't write as often as you wish, but I walk every day to the post office to see if any of your letters have arrived. My heart jumps so when Mr. Nelson hands over your latest letter.
>
> I stop outside the newspaper office to sit and read it. Mama is aghast at my bad manners. She lectures me that a true lady reads her personal correspondence in her house, not on the street like some common ill-bred person. I think I'll go into the church to read your next letter. I cannot wait until I walk the mile back home.
>
> Every day I miss you more. Yet I rejoice that you and Samuel are well. Mama and Papa are very impatient to hear from him. Tell my brother he must write to them soon.
>
> Papa says I shouldn't trouble you with my worries, but the newspapers have such awful stories about places like Antietam and Harper's Ferry. Please write back and tell me if the battles are as horrific as the Tribune says.

Jeremiah pleaded in his next letter that their correspondence was his only chance to escape the talk of war and the hardships of the army life.

> Please indulge me, my love. When I return home, we'll sit down together, and I'll take your hand in mine and answer all your questions. But for now, your letters provide me with the only respite I have from the war. Please let me tell you instead about the amusing side of our life in the camp.
>
> Just this past week I was reminded of how my Grandfather Cornelius used to say that trying to get the Scot-Irish to obey was like trying to herd squirrels. I see how hard it is for our captains to control our regiment. Most of us are those Scot-

Irish Grandfather muttered about.

Jeremiah's next letter almost made her believe her loved ones were playing at being soldiers and were enjoying a camping trip through Kentucky.

That all changed in late October with *The Tribune's* headline, "Barefooted Soldiers Leave Bloody Footprints in Snow." Since the town's own young men were involved, the newspaper focused on the storm and reported that an early snow had caught the 90th Ohio unaware while they were capturing a salt works in the Cumberland Gap. The men had worn through their shoes. They had to walk barefooted in up to six inches of snow. Their tents were lost, and they slept without any cover.

Jeremiah stuck to his resolve and kept his letter on the topic of the soldier's life.

> I know, dearest, that the newspaper accounts about the snowstorm have caused you concern. But we all survived and were thankful the snow melted as quickly as it did.
>
> I want to learn how to be a shoemaker when I come back to Sabina. I got my hands on some leather scraps and have fashioned, in a very rough manner, passable shoes for a few boys from town. They tell me they are the best footwear they've ever worn.
>
> We have marked two months of army duty and are quite fit from covering six hundred miles, mostly on foot. Samuel says I must reduce my grand total because some of the miles were not walked since we did ride the train.
>
> Please keep your letters coming. Their arrival gives us a reason to celebrate.

Hannah wrote that her last two months had been nowhere near as adventurous as theirs. Like all good storytellers, she exaggerated the details.

> My darling, our chickens are becoming quite astute. I believe they communicate with each other when I come out the back door with the egg basket on my arm. I've even tried to hide it behind my back. But they must know I'm coming to liberate their eggs. Several of the young ones rush toward me

when I open the gate. I've tried bringing some corn and other scraps to entice them away from the chicken coop. But they insist on squawking around my ankles. I don't dare show any fear for I know they will certainly attack.

The billy goat has learned from them because he now glares at me when I cross the barn lot. He doesn't even obey Papa. Maybe when you return home, you can teach that animal some manners.

Christmas arrived with Jeremiah and Samuel still safe and untested in battle. Hannah had no way of knowing if the gloves she knitted had reached them for the holidays. On Christmas Eve, following their family tradition, Hannah sat between her parents and joining hands led off with her Christmas wish that their men were safe and warm and would soon be home. Agnes and Matthew's wishes echoed hers.

January brought Hannah reports of the Stone River Battle. "Brave Soldiers of the 90th Engage in their First Bloody Battle" was the headline. Hannah devoured the newspaper stories. Almost 80,000 men waged a battle stretching over several days of fighting under fog-ridden gray skies and tormented by freezing cold and sleet. Finally, the battle's tide changed from a Union defeat to victory as reinforcements arrived to chase the enemy further south.

She tried to make sense of the battle statistics. Some reported soldiers lay on the cold battlefield for up to seven days before they received any assistance at all. Hannah knew the odds were not favorable that Jeremiah and Samuel had escaped harm. She and all of Sabina waited for letters and telegrams to learn the fate of their soldiers. Every day Hannah stopped to read the casualty list posted outside the Tribune before collecting the mail at the post office, and every day familiar names leapt out at her. One in particular pained her, James Parris. He was close to her age. They had shared a bench in school since their last names were in alphabetical order.

A few weeks after his death, his mother stood during the church services and read the letter sent by one of his friends. Hannah wanted to remember the important parts to tell Jeremiah.

Mrs. Parris,

Well you might wish to know how your son was beliked by the boys in camp. I can say that he was loved by all. Jimmy was a favorite, and as regards his bravery, there was none to excel him. It was through one of his bold attempts that he was shot. He stood up to the battle like a man until he was killed dead. He died without a groan. Poor boy, his death was regretted by all his brave fellow soldiers.

You can say to all who knew him that you have lost your son to an honorable cause and his spirit has gone from this to another world.

Yours respectfully,
Thomas Nevitt

The next day a short letter that Jeremiah wrote after the Battle of Stone River arrived and told her that he and Samuel were unharmed. She could not shake a nightmare image of her and her mother sometime in the future. They were standing in front of the church members as Mrs. Parris had stood. Her beloved's words could not drive her fears away even though she was offering up prayers of thanksgiving.

He wrote,

My dearest, I have seen many strange things during this war, dear one. The strangest so far happened on the eve of the battle. Remember how I wrote before that both the Rebs and us like listening to the music our bands play. Sometimes our boys try to out perform theirs. When that happens, even the best song can sound out of tune.

At dusk, one band began playing "Home, Sweet Home." Slowly the jumble of music stopped. One by one, the bands joined in playing. Soon we were all sharing the same music while knowing that in a few hours we'd be killing each other.

Hannah, after the battle and the noise from the guns ceased, the music from a few hours before still haunted me.

Take care, my dearest. Keep safe for me. Know that you have all my love always.

In their home, Hannah's family quietly rejoiced over Jeremiah and Samuel's escape from harm and paid their respects to families, including the Parris family, who had received notice that their sons and husbands were not as fortunate. Disease and battlefield injuries and deaths continued to claim their neighbors' loved ones. Agnes and Hannah made extra portions when they prepared their meals so they could take food on their sympathy calls. Hannah did not mention the visits in her letters to Jeremiah. Instead, she focused on how busy they were getting ready for the spring planting.

The spring turned out to be a very rainy one for the 90th camped in Tennessee, and the dull tedium of drilling, foraging, and picket duty occupied Jeremiah's life. His letters gave Hannah some needed laughs when she read his stories.

> Dear One, you will probably not be surprised to find out that me and Samuel are in trouble. Do you remember Tim Ramsey, the biggest weakling in Sabina? Somehow, he was promoted to sergeant. Samuel got angry and told him that he'd never salute him or follow his orders. I tried to pull your brother away from the argument but in vain. So I earned the same punishment as him, three extra days of guard duty. The worst part was listening to your brother complain the whole time.
>
> The rumor mill is very busy. One week the Army gossip carries tales that we're going to ship out west to join with another regiment. The next week they say we're to move into Georgia. Now the boys are taking bets and gambling on their next orders.

The front-page news of the Union victories at Vicksburg and Gettysburg on July 5th gave Hannah some hope that the war might soon be over. It was as if Jeremiah knew what she was thinking. The last week of July, Hannah received his own hopeful letter written after the Union victories.

> My most dear one, please pray that the fighting me and Samuel did in these mountains of Tennessee shortens the war. General Rosencrans claims it is so. The boys sit around the campfires at night and brag that Gettysburg and Vicksburg will get us all home by Christmas.

Hannah had her own worries with war hysteria and Morgan's Raiders. The governor declared a state of emergency, and the whole town seemed to live in panic. But by this time, Hannah had begun to distrust all the details reported in news stories. But one story spoke of Morgan as a gallant gentleman, and she shared it in her next letter.

We are all safe my dearest. Morgan did not come that close to us. Did you hear about his adventure in some town in Indiana? He went to the courthouse and demanded all of the money locked in the safe. The county clerk had anticipated the rebels' arrival and buried most of the county's money outside of town. So when Morgan and his men forced the county officials by gunpoint to open the safe, all Morgan saw was $5,000 and the reticules local widows had deposited with the county treasurer. Their intent had been to keep them safe from the very man now standing before the opened safe. Morgan took the money but refused the ladies' belongings, claiming that he didn't rob widows.

Hannah was disappointed when Jeremiah no longer hinted about the war ending early.

We are still hunkered down outside of Chattanooga. I miss you very, very much. Please tell me more about what's going on back home. I need to know that you're safe and the crops are good. Our sutler left for home yesterday, and I gave him three long letters to pass on to you. He promised to make sure you'd receive them. I picture you wearing the brooch and sitting in the church reading all three letters, and I have great hopes of rejoining you as soon as this war is over. I think of you all the time and long to be with you once more.

Hannah was in tears after she read the opening sentences in Jeremiah's next letter.

I wish I was back home with you. The memory of your eyes and good-bye kiss come to me every night before I fall asleep. I am thankful that at present we are out of the fighting even though time passes very slowly. Some of the boys are disgruntled they aren't part of the nearby action.

I am watching the leaves on the trees turn and remember the sugar maple in the front yard and the many hours the three of us filled with climbing its branches and raking its leaves.

Every fall the sunlight from its golden leaves brightened the front parlor. I am even more homesick than last Christmas.

I want to end this letter with some good news. Do you remember Adam Nichols from Wilmington? He found his way back to our camp yesterday, and did he have quite a story to tell. He's been missing since summer. We all thought he'd lit out for home. He claims he was out foraging and filling his haversack with ripe apples when five Confederate scouts stopped at the same tree and captured him. After two months, he managed to escape, and it took him all this time to rejoin us. He also swears that he has had enough of the Tennessee mountains.

It was difficult to think of another Christmas without their young men, but the family prepared their Christmas packages early. On November 23rd, Hannah took them to the post office. After Mr. Nelson handed her a letter, Hannah thanked him and retreated to the choir pew to read her letter.

Have you made your Christmas wish yet, my love? I have. I'm confident ours are similar. I wish I was home again with you. Me and Samuel are still well. I miss seeing your smiles and hearing your laughter. When I return, we must laugh and smile every day to celebrate we are together again.

"Jeremiah, I pray every hour for your safe return," Hannah sighed before she gathered her father's old brown overcoat around her for the walk back to the farm. Once outside, she stuck her hands in the coat's large pockets and put her head down to escape the cold air that blasted ice into her face. Another winter storm was marching through the town and fields and made it difficult to see much more than a few yards ahead. She wasn't worried. The road back to the farm was so familiar. Every bare tree and fence post along the way guided her home.

Soon her usual daydreams of planning her wedding and the war's end took over. She imagined Samuel and Jeremiah upon their return, her intended looking ever bit as handsome in his uniform as the day he left.

At the second crossroad outside of town, the sight of two figures ahead on the road made her stop. Not many neighbors lived between where she stood and the farm a quarter mile ahead. Her parents' often spoken words of caution sprang into her mind, and she considered retreating to the Carson house back on the last crossroad.

After a more careful inspection of the strangers, Hannah decided they didn't look dangerous. They moved slowly, side by side, and hunched over to protect themselves from the northerly wind blowing across the open fields.

Hannah thought she'd invite them in to eat and warm up. She liked to think someone might take a notion to do likewise for Jeremiah and Samuel.

It didn't take long to reach them. "Pardon me," she said, "Would you like to come by our farm for some hot food? We…" Hannah stopped.

The two men had straightened up and turned to face her. "Hannah? Is it really you?" they said at the sound of her voice.

"Jeremiah? Samuel?"

All three embraced and kissed. Samuel let go first. However, Hannah would not let Jeremiah go, and she reclaimed Samuel. "You're home? For good? The war's over?"

"Dearest one, we're on Christmas furlough until the new year. Now, don't look so sad. We have over a month."

"Let's get on home, little sister. It's cold out here, and we're hungry."

Samuel flung open the back door, and Hannah noticed alarm flicker in her mother's face as the woman froze in the act of rolling out dough on the kitchen table. When three people instead of one entered the kitchen, Momma's right hand rested on her heart, and she let out a gasp of surprise. Tears brimmed before they fell down her cheeks.

"My boys, my boys are back," she sobbed, and Samuel and Jeremiah gathered her to them.

Over Jeremiah's shoulder, Hannah saw her father enter from the hallway at almost a run. Joyful tears came to him also, and he moved to join his family.

After Jeremiah and Samuel praised every bite of the first homemade meal they had eaten since they left for the army, the family gathered in the parlor. Soon all three men snored in their chairs. Jeremiah had dozed off with a firm grasp on Hannah's hand. Momma, closest to the fireplace, tatted lace around a handkerchief. The two women looked at each other and exchanged smiles.

"Is that for my trousseau?"

"Yes, I have to make every minute count before your wedding."

"Wedding?"

Momma didn't look up. Instead, she rounded a corner and continued the tatting up the other side. "Yes, I don't think Jeremiah will leave here before he's married you. He seems very determined when he looks at you. Do you still want to marry him?"

"Yes, more than anything. But what if he doesn't ask?"

"He'll ask. I recognize that possessive air he has. Trust me, he will. I think tomorrow I'll need Samuel and Papa's help in the kitchen. We'll leave you two alone here in the parlor for a few minutes."

A little while later, Momma bit the thread in two and tied off the last stitch.

The next afternoon Jeremiah found Hannah knitting in the parlor and sat down beside her on the settee. The sunlight from the window enveloped Hannah, and the flames from the fireplace reflected in her eyes as she smiled up at him. Jeremiah knew she was the most beautiful woman he had ever known. The frayed edges of her cuffs and the small patched worn spots on her dark green woolen skirt didn't really register.

"Hannah, my dearest," he said after he took her hand and kissed her cheek. "You make such a pretty picture."

"I am so happy you are back with me. I feel my prayers have been answered."

"It's selfish, I know, but I don't think I can leave you again until I know you are mine, truly mine," Jeremiah said. He leaned forward, kissed her lips, and brought her close to him.

When Hannah felt the tenderness in his kiss and embrace, she promised herself that moment would be one she'd remember forever as she returned the kiss.

The next day, Hannah slid her arm through Jeremiah's and entered the county clerk's office in the Wilmington courthouse. A few minutes later, she signed her name and listed herself as a spinster in the large marriage bond book. Jeremiah's signature followed on the next line as surety that Hannah could lawfully marry him. Her father signed as the bondsman who would guarantee the bond fee if the marriage was unlawful.

She and her mother didn't have much to plan, just a small wedding in the home with the friends and neighbors to witness the vows. Since the war had curtailed many traditional bridal luxuries such as orange blossoms and imported Belgian lace, the recent weddings Hannah and her parents had attended were very simple events.

Hannah chose to redo one of her best day dresses, a blue and green tartan plaid silk dress. The narrow shoulders and flowing sleeves accentuated her slender figure. Momma rooted around her sewing basket and found a few yards of lace saved back from an earlier project. She attached it to the collar where Hannah planned to wear the garnet brooch. More lace went over the worn edges of the sleeves. When Hannah tried on the remade dress complete with its hoop skirt, she felt like a princess. Her mother's delicate filigreed gold bracelet completed her bridal ensemble.

She kept the tradition that their ceremony should begin on the half-hour to ensure good luck, and they were named man and wife as the minute hand swept toward 3:00 p.m. Jeremiah whispered that she was the loveliest bride he had ever seen and vowed he would tell her the same on every anniversary, December 5th at 2: 55 p.m.

The honeymoon was also another wedding tradition that the war had put an end to. She and Jeremiah spent their first married night in her bedroom. Samuel slept the night on a pallet in the parlor so the newlyweds would have the whole upstairs to themselves. Hannah found breakfast the next morning a little awkward, but within a week, she was relieved that the family had returned to their prewar routine.

When Hannah had marked their departure date on the calendar that first evening they returned, she didn't realize how soon it would come. January 4th was their last night together. The men would leave at dawn the next morning. The soldiers had one week to travel to their regiment. In November, their trip from Alabama to Louisville was five days by train, a day to reach Cincinnati by boat, and another half-day to get home to Sabina on the connecting train route. The only change on their return trip would be a walk across the frozen Ohio River and catch a westbound wagon to Louisville. If the weather held, Samuel and Jeremiah would be guarding the railroad yard again by the twelfth.

"My love, promise me again you will come back safe to me," Hannah spoke into his ear when they lay wrapped in each other's arms in bed that night.

"My dearest, I swear I will return to you as soon as I can. The war should soon be over. Pray for the end in your prayers for me and Samuel."

"I'll go with you to the station tomorrow."

"Hannah, the memory I want to take with me is you lying in this bed." He glided his fingers through her unbound hair. "I want to remember your curls flowing around your head and your eyes shining with your love for me. That is what I need to carry in my mind."

Hannah felt a blush come over her. Newly awakened to the power of lovemaking, she thrilled over the effect it had on both of them. She giggled and touched his chin. "Let's practice that memory. I want to remember this moment forever."

Jeremiah's next letter reported in his letters that their army life remained the same and thanked Hannah for her tender and loving letters. They made camp life bearable.

Hannah's letters showed how thrilled she was with her new status of wife.

> My dearest husband, please don't worry about the tears you will see on this letter. They were truly tears of joy. I wept when I saw the word husband and realized it was the first time I have written this word and it meant you, my love. I am still the happiest person here in town though I miss you and long for you to return to me and our bed. Please keep yourself safe.

Jeremiah's letters also showed how his love had grown since their marriage.

> My lovely and loving wife, I sometimes feel I dreamt the month we spent together, but I realize it could not be because I have such vivid memories of our time together. We are very safe and well out of the action. Imagine us in a single file march up and down railroad track with only a few foxes and ground hogs to keep us company.

By March, Hannah knew for sure she was going to have a baby.

> My love, our month together was no dream. I have the best news to tell you. You are going to be a father. Mama thinks

the baby will come by August 15th. Don't worry about us. I am feeling quite well and happy. Think of me in the parlor much as you saw me when you proposed. I am still knitting, this time for our baby.

Hannah's news of their baby terrified Jeremiah. He knew giving birth was dangerous. He added his unborn child to his nightly prayers and thanked God that his wife was in the care of her mother. While he patrolled the railroad tracks, he knew there was no one he could tell about his fears that he might leave Hannah behind as a young widowed mother. He railed at himself for selfishly marrying her before the war ended. But his letters home indicated none of those fears. The news of his unborn child matured him more than anything else in his life had.

My dearest wife, your news about our baby filled me with joy. Are you truly feeling well? You are resting, aren't you? I am sure your mother takes good care of you. Now when I picture you, I will think of you and our child as he grows and you both stay healthy and strong. How I long for this war to be over before our child is born so I can return to both of you.

As Hannah's pregnancy advanced, Jeremiah's regiment had the good luck to remain behind the front. It wasn't until the siege of Atlanta that the 90th Ohio left their guard duty and moved into action. At last, the birth announcement arrived just before his regiment broke camp and followed Sherman to the sea.

My dearest husband, our healthy daughter, Esther Mercy Garrett was born August 6th at ten o'clock in the morning. We are all very well. She is the prettiest baby ever born. Jeremiah, I wish you could see her head full of glorious brown curls. Mama says she will lose them so I have cut a few curls to save back. Did you find the one I put in the letter? Isn't it silky? I love touching her hair.

Her eyes are blue, but Mama says they will change also. She is the most perfect baby. I have tried to draw her likeness for you. When you look at my drawing, remember it doesn't capture her essence, but don't you see how much she looks like you?

We miss you. I tell Esther about her brave and handsome

father every time I rock her to sleep. Take care, my love, and hurry home to us.

The birth of his daughter tormented Jeremiah with longing. He missed Hannah more than ever and read that letter every night before sleep.

In Ohio, Hannah read aloud the first letter Jeremiah had written to Esther every day and vowed she would until he returned.

To my dearest wife and little daughter,

Hannah, your letter filled me with love. I thank you for our daughter Esther and naming her after my mother. My nightly prayers are filled with pleas that this war will end soon and I can come back to both of you. Your drawing was wonderful, my love.

Esther, I traced your face with my finger and told myself this would have to do until I can hold you for the first time. When I return home, I will tell you every day how brave your mother was and how much I love both of you.

All my love,
Your Jeremiah

Chapter 32

Sabina, Ohio, November, 1858

<Thomas and Naomi Clopton
<Agnes and Matthew McConkey
Hannah

"Hannah, let your father get in the house," Agnes said to the gangly thirteen-year-old bolting out the door. Sometimes she despaired that her daughter would ever develop the poise that had been expected from her own generation. But then, she had to remember that girls had been reared differently in her time. Back in the Tidewater area of Virginia, cotillions and lessons from a dance teacher were customary. He traveled from one plantation to another so the planters' children would acquire the expected social graces. However, since she and Matthew had moved to the wilds of Ohio, Agnes had never seen a dancing teacher of any kind.

Hannah's words were indistinct, but her complaints filtered through the door left open in her rush. When Agnes closed the door, she heard the indignant tone that revealed her daughter's mood and could provide the subject matter. No amount of tears would move her to allow Hannah to read the letter from her Uncle Walter.

When they came through the kitchen door, Matthew was explaining that the letter was probably about boring legal matters having to do with settling her grandfather's estate. Hannah's expression remained sulky.

Agnes feared his reasoning would only fuel their daughter's imagination about how elegant plantation life was. The Clopton and McConkey costly silk and rich dark mahogany furnishings, carted overland from Virginia, certainly looked out of place in the farmhouse. However, she couldn't bear to part with the soft pillows and expertly carved wood although they betrayed their previous use in far more refined drawing rooms and boudoirs. Hannah's questions about growing up in Virginia had been easy to answer at first, but lately the questions had become more penetrating. The answers led to more questions, and Agnes recognized that her daughter was finding it difficult at times to reconcile her romantic ideas of beautiful dresses and manners with the enforced labor of others.

The tricky part was how to couch the truth and not be blunt. Hannah, at her age, did not need to learn the raw details that ruled both the courtly, graceful life in the big house and the ugly existence in the fields and slave quarters.

Agnes was all set to speak her piece when a miraculous transformation occurred. Her sullen daughter had become a smiling angel the moment Jeremiah walked into the kitchen from the mudroom, his face and hands freshly washed and a clean shirt exchanged for the one he wore for work in the fields.

It was plain as day that they were both quite taken with each other. Agnes hoped they still felt that way in a few years when Hannah would be old enough to be courted and marry.

The arrival of twelve-year-old Samuel broke the spell as he barged in the door, pulled his sister's braids, and made kissing noises to Jeremiah.

However, mercifully, Hannah had dropped the subject of the letter, at least for now.

After the kitchen had been put to rights from the evening meal, Agnes at last had the chance to share her brother's letter. She took advantage of a sudden change in the weather, and wrapped in her grandmother's shawl, she invited Matthew to join her on the veranda. They would be alone for a few minutes while the young ones checked the animals in the barn for the night and brought up more firewood.

As the quarter moon peeked through the leafless trees by the front pastureland, she said, "You were right, Matthew, Walter's letter is about Father's estate. It seems he's going to come visit us as soon as the harvest is in."

"Then why do you look so worried?"

Agnes realized she should not have been surprised that her husband knew her so well. She could never hide her feelings from him.

"He's not coming alone. He's bringing at least seven slaves with him."

232

The concern on Matthew's face changed to disapproval. "That doesn't make sense. Seven men. There's no need for even one. This is not Fairlawn or River Front. We don't live like that any longer."

Agnes glanced to see where Hannah and the boys were. The light from the lantern showed they were at the pump, still quite a way from the house. Nevertheless, Agnes lowered her voice. "He's bringing two families, including children. One is Patience's brother Cicero, his wife, and two boys. The other is Jacob's sister Portia, her husband, and infant girl."

"You think he's going to attempt what young Tallmadge did last spring?"

"Yes, why else tell me the number and their ages?"

"Clever." Matthew stroked his forehead in thought. "That way we would have enough clothes and shoes at hand."

"By my reckoning," Hannah said, "We have about two weeks to gather supplies and make arrangements with Coffin and Stanley."

"That's about right." Matthew took a few moments to mull over something weighty. "We'll have to bring Jeremiah into the plans. He's very levelheaded for being only sixteen. What about Hannah? Do you think she's old enough?" He leaned his head toward the trio walking single file to the kitchen door. Their arms were loaded with firewood, and Hannah led the way, swinging the lantern from side to side. Rex barked and chased the moving light, which provided very little help for staying on the path. She knew that fortunately, they could walk the well-worn path with their eyes closed.

"Maybe not, but with the way she's become so aware lately, I think we have to."

"And Samuel?" Matthew asked.

Agnes was torn. It would be difficult keeping anything secret from their son, but she felt he lacked the maturity to fully appreciate how grave the situation was for all involved. If her brother had waited a year or two, then yes, Samuel would probably be ready to participate.

She shook her head. "Let's tell them after Samuel goes to bed."

Later that evening, Agnes fought against sleep and tried to outlast her son as she sat in her rocking chair by the open fireplace. The only good thing about mending socks that night was she was so accustomed to the task her mind could roam through all types of mental mazes. Some plans she kept. Others she rejected as impossible. She glanced at her daughter who was content to read on the low bench in front of the fire and hoped

Hannah would be responsible enough to participate in their plot. Matthew's nearby snores comforted and reminded her how blessed she was to have a husband whose beliefs so closely dovetailed with hers. Not so for every family in their small town.

At last, Samuel shook his hands and flexed his fingers. Agnes knew it wouldn't be long before he and Jeremiah would sweep the shavings from their woodworking into the fire. They kept reassuring her that Matthew's chess set would be finished in time for Christmas.

After some stalling and another reminder from her, Samuel woke his father to bid him good night, took his candle, and went upstairs. He wasn't happy, and Agnes understood. She, like Samuel, had possessed an uncanny and unerring childhood sense whenever she was about to miss something important. She had learned to trust that feeling and hide around corners and in hallways. However, the farmhouse didn't have any of those convenient hiding places she had found at River Front, and she could tell by the creaking sounds overhead that her son was in bed. She gave Matthew the nod to begin.

"Hannah, your mother and I agree that you are old enough to know the true import of your uncle's letter. Jeremiah, we want you to read it also."

Agnes pulled the folded paper from the mending basket and watched Jeremiah join Hannah on the low bench. As they held the letter closer to the fire in order to read it, their shoulders and heads almost touched. They looked so young and innocent that she renewed her hope she and Matthew were doing the proper thing by including them. After all, Jeremiah wasn't kin. He was a boy who had lived close to Fair Lawn and had what her father would have called itchy feet. His parents considered it was safer for him to accompany them on their trip west than light out on his own, and so he had joined them on the trip. Then her next thought sent her heart racing. Where did Jeremiah stand on the slavery issue? His family were shopkeepers and didn't own any slaves. In addition, he was a taciturn young man who preferred to watch and listen to the men talk about politics. Agnes had never heard him express an opinion.

When Jeremiah finished reading, he drummed his fingers on the bench and waited, silent as a sphinx. Agnes feared that they had just given away the whole plot. Nevertheless, it was too late to retreat.

Hannah, however, flushed with anger and narrowed her eyes. "Why is Uncle Walter bringing all these slaves with him? To sell along the way? Why tell us? Momma, the three children are younger than Samuel."

Agnes's arms encircled Hannah, and she said, "Hannah, the letter is written in a code. He's helping these families get to freedom. He's bringing them to us so we can help. They are kin to Jacob and Patience."

Hannah's eyes danced with excitement. "I'm sure Mr. Jacob and Miss Patience will be happy beyond belief to see them. What are we going to do to help?"

Matthew must not have shared her concerns about Jeremiah since he answered, "First, you all must swear on the Bible that you will not divulge the contents of Walter's letter. He could be imprisoned or worse if the true nature of his visit becomes known."

"Sir," Jeremiah said, "Though we are not in the south and slavery is illegal here, the law changed. They will not be free as soon as they cross the Ohio. In all respect, Aunt Agnes, your brother will make those poor slaves' lives worse if the hunters catch up with them."

Agnes' knees started to go weak with relief while Matthew answered him, "So true, son, there are southern sympathizers all through this part of Ohio. Even some of the Quakers believe that the fact their fellow church members are breaking the law supersedes the evil of slavery. We cannot be sure of anyone outside of our house."

"So will I get to carry a gun?" a voice asked from the dark.

Agnes's heart beat so fast she put her hand to her chest. She didn't know how much more she could take in one night. "No," she answered the same time as Matthew who looked just as startled as she felt.

"Young man," Matthew said in the sternest tone Agnes had ever heard him use. "Come over here." Samuel walked to face his father, and Agnes noticed that he still had on his shoes. "I am mightily displeased with you." Samuel hung his head. "This is not a schoolyard game, son. We are talking about the lives of innocent families who want to be free, and don't forget your uncle. All are in danger. Do you understand?"

Samuel said, "Yes, sir, I do, and I promise to keep what I hear secret, forever." He completed his pledge with crossed fingers and heart.

The mixture of the schoolboy promise and Samuel's earnest look made Agnes' own heart melt with pride and apprehension. They were all now in her brother's scheme, for better or worse.

She looked at the three young people and said, "Our job will be to gather supplies for the families and hide them after they arrive. Tomorrow Hannah and I will visit Mrs. Coffin and Mrs. Stanley so their husbands can contact the abolitionists while you men folk make a trap door to the root cellar and close part of it off from prying eyes. No outsider knows how large it is supposed to be."

"I, ah, can reach the conductors tonight," Jeremiah said.

Agnes stared at him. How did he know anyone or anything about the underground railroad?

Matthew gave him a solemn nod of approval while Hannah and Samuel looked at Jeremiah as if he were King Arthur.

Two weeks after, Agnes paced the front porch and looked out over the valley for any sign of her brother and the soon-to-be-free slaves. The talk of marauding groups of slave hunters made her very nervous. More bands of men seeking runaway slaves had snaked their way through the county last year after the Dred Scott decision. Jeremiah was correct. Once the slaves were out of her brother's care, anything could happen.

Her fears had been compounded over the past two weeks. Matthew had cornered Jeremiah to find out what the boy had been up to. Her husband gave her no deep details, just an outline that the young man was a runner who delivered messages and served as lookout on occasion. He also kept the trails freshly marked so the runaways knew which fork of the road or river to take.

When Agnes asked for more whos, whens, whats, and hows, Matthew just winked and urged her to not get all bothered about something she had no control over. Yet that did not take away any concern for Jeremiah's safety. Nor did Matthew's remark that they should be thankful the young man was helping the underground railroad instead of getting into trouble gambling and drinking. He said there were worse things than getting involved with abolitionists. Her mind agreed, yet each beat of her heart thrummed from the unknown dangers she imagined.

Patience unwittingly added to Agnes' nightmares though the former slave's words were most likely intended to sooth her concerns. As Agnes turned and worked her way north along the veranda, she replayed the scene from her kitchen a week ago when Patience had come to work on a dress and she had shown the former slave woman the letter.

"They're doing things right. Leaving after the quail sings, taking the National Road here. They don't hafta run through the woods and hide, Miss Agnes. It's gonna be just fine. Now calm yourself."

Patience had to explain the significance of the quail. "That's from a song I grew up with. It means wait until the first frost. Then it'll be cold enough to walk across iced rivers."

Agnes figured that must mean the waterways closer to Canada than Ohio. It had frosted last week, but the rivers weren't frozen over yet. The mention of the National Road meant that her brother and the families would travel with more comfort and safety, but the route also meant the trip wasn't secret. That was the part of the whole scheme that bothered her the most. Seven slaves couldn't come through town unnoticed, let alone just disappear. She debated about asking Patience, but her friend must have read her mind. She reached over and covered Agnes' hand.

"Don't you go and borrow trouble. That's what Jacob told me when I asked how seven of our family was just gonna up and disappear. He's got something up his sleeve."

Agnes had to be content with that since Matthew had told her not to worry either. According to him, only two people knew the whole plan. Safer that way he said before he turned over and went to sleep as if nothing unusual was about to happen to them.

However, she wouldn't be at peace until she knew everyone in her family and Patience's was safe.

Some motion caught her eye, and when Agnes squinted to bring it into focus, she saw Rex charge off the veranda and zip toward a large covered wagon drawn by a pair of mules and a stranger snapping the reins. Disappointment welled from deep inside until she realized the dog was wagging his tail and she recognized the other man sitting beside the stranger. What was Jeremiah doing up there? The question went unanswered until the stranger shouted her name, her childhood name, Nessie. Only one person left alive knew that name. Her brother. Her elegantly mannered and clothed brother was a bedraggled ruffian in coarse clothing, with a long beard, and driving the worst-looking farm wagon she had ever seen. Her heart sank when she realized there was no one except the two men in sight. What had happened to the slaves?

Once the two families came out from hiding under the blankets and supplies in the wagon, Agnes had only one answer to her many questions. She was too busy helping with the children and making sure everyone had eaten their fill to ask for other answers. It was past twilight when Patience and Jacob arrived unseen after taking the path through the woods, and she couldn't take it anymore. She had to know the plan first and then the details of their journey.

Matthew, Walter, and Jacob smoked their pipes and took turns. Their eyes snapped, and their faces almost never stopped grinning as they told the story.

Matthew started with the most recent events first. "Those poor mules. They no sooner pulled that wagon into the barn, but Coffin's boys had them unhitched and on the way to their house. Those mules will be lucky to rest more than a few days before they see service again. Coffin says the number of underground passengers has taken a big jump lately."

Jacob took those last words as his cue and said, "That wagon's now filled to the brim with all kinds of bales and stuff you had in the back stalls of your barn, Miss Agnes. We plain cleaned up your barn and moved the wagon to the back and then scattered other stuff in front. It won't see daylight until we need it."

"What happens then?" Hannah asked.

Walter laughed and said, "That's the best part, Nessie, and I've been sworn to secrecy."

Agnes gave the three men a look that dared them to keep the plan a secret from her one more moment. Matthew intervened. "We don't know all the details yet either, dearest. You can trust me, I'll let you know as soon as I find out myself."

"Any trouble on your trip, Walter?" Agnes asked. She wasn't content but decided to practice some of that very same patience she kept urging Hannah to have. By God, the girl did come by it honest.

"No encounters with danger on the boat ride to Maryland. We kept the children hidden in the cabins. As you saw, even our women were dressed as men. However, I thought I saw the same handful of ill-bred men looking curiously at me after we landed that day. So I took the first wagon I could find, and once we were provisioned, left around two in the morning." He stopped to refill his pipe. After he got it going to his satisfaction, he continued. "I thought I had evaded them until a messenger from a relative of one of your neighbors joined us one night after we had made camp."

"Who was it, Uncle Walter?" Samuel asked.

"I've promised not to reveal names, young sir, but he warned us that we were being tracked. So, after he gave the proper password and showed me the letter, he advised that we split the group. Therefore, he took Cicero and his family another route. We met up with them at

Wheeling. Don't you worry, Nessie, we exercised the utmost caution. But it would be prudent to move the families soon."

The next day Samuel returned from school with a black eye and no note from Mr. Fowler to explain events. He refused to tell Agnes and Matthew about it. All he said was that it had been taken care of but would not say how. It saddened Agnes that her son had to go through such a rite of childhood, but Matthew assured her it was necessary. According to him, every boy worth his salt had to prove himself to his peers.

She and Matthew were on their way to bed when Rex started barking outside. Matthew took the gun from the rack by the door and motioned for Agnes to move into the far corner. Her heart was beating at such a pace she thought it was going to come up and right out her mouth. She had never been so scared, not only for herself, but also for all the souls sleeping under her protection.

Then the dog stopped barking, no yelp, no whimper, no other sound until someone knocked on the door.

"Matthew, it's me, Elias Fowler."

Agnes wondered why the schoolmaster was at their house so late. If it was about Samuel fighting, he would have written a note or come sooner. For a moment, she considered that Samuel had badly injured the other boy, but she could not picture her son doing harm to another.

When Matthew unlocked and opened the door, Rex came in with Elias who was scratching the fur behind the dog's left ear. After declining anything to eat or drink, the schoolmaster told them the purpose of his visit.

"I thought you would want to know what was behind Samuel's altercation today. At recess I overheard Oliver Acton tell the other boys that he had slaves chained up in his barn, for safekeeping until the slave hunters finish rounding up a few more runaways."

"His old man is about as rabid a copperhead as they come. I'm not at all surprised he'd work in tandem with the slave hunters, but how did that lead to a fight?" Matthew said.

"He dared Samuel to tell him what was in his barn. Your son denied there was anything unusual going on, only that some peddler had come by, sold some stuff to you, Mrs. McConkey, and then moved on. One thing led to another, and before I could stop it, they were rolling around on the ground." Fowler stopped and gave Matthew a meaningful look that made the hair on Agnes' neck stand up. "So, I'd guess," he continued, "that if your peddler left anything behind, it should get going soon."

Before she or Matthew could answer, he got up, and with the dog at his heels, closed the door behind him.

Agnes could not make her feet move quickly enough as she headed to the kitchen to wake her brother. However, he met her at the door.

"I heard. Is your visitor trustworthy?" he asked Matthew.

"I have no way of knowing. He's not been part of any discussion or meeting I've been to. But then again, he would probably lose his position if he openly declared one way or the other," Matthew said.

Jeremiah spoke from the stairs. "He's run the signs with me before. You can trust him."

"So," Agnes said, "our guests will have to leave sooner than we planned. Though I hate to wake the children. This is probably the first good night's sleep they've had for sometime."

"We've got it all taken care of," Cicero said. He and his family stood fully dressed with jackets buttoned and shoes laced. Maecenas, with his wife Portia and daughter, joined them. "Mr. Stanley's told me he'd be here by midnight. Maecenas is set to leave with the Coffin boys before dawn. We'll say our good-byes now and go down into the cellar so you good folks can snuff your candles and go to bed."

Once the runaways were safely down below, Agnes moved to the kitchen to bundle food for them to carry on their next journey. The men soon came to help. They slid the curtains to the side and used the moonlight to advantage.

"Nessie," Walter said, "War will soon be upon us. I am mighty surprised that we are not already engaged in the massacre. I'm saying this because I don't know when travel will be possible for me again. It had been my plan to escort another group north before spring, but with the way each side is hurling flammable words at each other, I just don't know how safe it will be."

Agnes put the roasted chicken aside and gave her brother a tearful hug. "I had not realized how much I missed you until I saw you drive up in that old wagon. Walter, I don't know how I can part from you again. Can't you stay?"

"Oh, Nessie, if only wishes were horses," he whispered into her ear and gave her a deeper hug. "You know I have to return to my responsibilities. But before I depart with Cicero and the Stanleys, I have a little story to tell and a gift for my favorite niece, Hannah."

"I will give it to her first thing in the morning," Agnes promised.

"Ah," her brother said as he guided her to the kitchen table. "That's not how I had it planned. This gift comes with a story and conditions. There is just enough time to tell both before I leave."

He requested Jeremiah join them at the table and sit between Agnes and Matthew. "My boy, I will be so proud to tell your parents how you have grown into a splendid example of manhood. I have had the honor to witness your bravery and good sense these past few days. In the coming strife, they will become very necessary. You will soon realize why I have said these things to you, after you have also heard the story."

Through the dim light, Agnes could just make out Walter leaning back in his chair for the telling. She heard the familiar sounds of him filling his pipe with tobacco and tamping it down. Every action made her miss him more, and he wasn't even gone yet. A flare, the flame waxing and waning as he puffed, and then his words came from the darkness and smoke.

"We stopped outside of Guilford after leaving Baltimore. Cicero, as you know, is light enough to pass, so I requested that he accompany me to the local tavern. Another set of eyes and ears is always good for reconnoitering. After about an hour, I had decided to leave since very few customers were there. Then a man about forty, a very rough forty, slunk beside me. He kept his slouch hat down over his eyes, and the white hairs along his unshaven chin caught the light. His ancient shirt had aged to gray, his vest frayed around the pockets, and his black trousers streaked with dust. He looked around to make sure no one was paying any attention to us."

Walter stopped to fumble in his pockets, and Agnes thought he was going after more tobacco. Instead, he pulled out something that became recognizable after the moonlight grew stronger through the window. His open palm revealed a small cloth bag with its drawstring firmly knotted.

"The man," Walter continued, "called himself Edmund Chapman and opened this very bag to reveal..."

Agnes, along with Matthew and Jeremiah leaned closer to see Walter open the bag and pour out a small pin set with red crystals arranged in three stars. She picked it up and moved to the window for a closer look in the moonlight.

"It's pretty enough, I guess, sir, but there's not much sparkle to it."

"That, Jeremiah, is because those are garnets, deep blood-red stones. Chapman told me how they are fabled to capture the love of two people and keep them safe. He had bought the piece from a widow who claimed the jewelry had been in her family for generations. She said her great-grandfather gave it to her great-grandmother before he went off to fight with Washington at Valley Forge. Did you know blood garnets symbolize faith, loyalty, and truth? But more than that, they protect the giver and receiver from harm and a broken heart."

Jeremiah gave him a suspicious look. "Why'd she sell it?"

"Chapman told me it was all she had left to sell. She owed taxes on her little house in Endicott City. So he bought it from her. He said he even paid her too much, but felt it was his Christian duty to help widows and orphans. He put it in my hand and requested that I examine the family treasure closely. He was confident that the brooch would make parting from my loved one easier when war came since it was a charm to keep me and mine safe. He predicted it would become a treasure to pass on to my oldest daughter someday."

"How much did he take you for, Walter?" Matthew asked.

"Matthew," Agnes scolded and moved away from the window.

Walter laughed and said, "I bargained with him and told him if he included the cloth bag, I'd give him five dollars. He did tell a mighty fine story."

She saw him hand the empty bag to Jeremiah. "My intention was to make it a gift to you, Nessie, with the hope you would pass it to Hannah. However, I have been watching young Jeremiah here the last few days, and even an unromantic soul like me recognizes how he loves your daughter. So, with your permission, Matthew and Nessie, I wish to bestow the garnet brooch on Jeremiah with the fervent hope that before he goes off to war, he asks Hannah to marry him and gives her the brooch."

Chapter 33

Part 4

Jasper Mill, Ohio, July 1862

Gnats and flies slowly agitated the peddler. He tried to pay them no heed. He also tried to ignore the heat shimmering off the fences and wagon-grooved road. A quick glance at his pocket watch reminded him that he had about thirty minutes to pitch the dirt-streaked tent and arrange the stock before the first raw recruits would reach the huge, old maple tree shading the Sabina Road.

His sources had let him know, for a small fee, that the 90th would begin enlisting the locals near the mill. Each new soldier would walk away enriched with twenty-five dollars bounty money. Not with bank drafts, but with an assortment of banknotes, war tokens, and odd coins the army seemed to collect. The man knew most of his potential customers had never held such a sum in hand before.

"Some of that ready money's going right into my pockets before they reach the tavern," Edmund Chapman vowed softly.

He knew the combination of his past experience in the infantry and his natural eye for presentation made him one of the best provisioners around. He posted the sign promising free water to lure the thirsty men in so they could turn the merchandise over. The knives and pistols always snared their attention, but the best profit came from the extras of war. The splashy uniform embellishments of buttons and braid appealed to the new recruits' sense of what being soldiers meant- brave, strong, and courageous.

Chapman had straightened the last row of hand-tooled holsters when voices joined the constant hum of the cicada chorus in the background. He removed his slouch hat and knocked the morning's dust away. After he wiped the moisture from his face, he tucked in his shirt tails. He took a seat on the camp stool near the entrance to the tent and waited, patient, like a spider.

Five men, engaged in horseplay, laughed and shoved as they approached. Dressed like the farmers Chapman knew they had to be, they walked along the rural road toward Sabina. Their steps stirred up tiny dust clouds and broke the illusion of time standing still.

"What fine specimens of soldiers you are," Chapman murmured. "Not rich cause you're on foot. Not poor. Looks like you've eaten regular. Even had your bath last Saturday."

The men neared, and he noticed their clothes were their Sunday best. The boots, though worn and a little dusty, were not on the verge of falling off their feet.

Chapman sized them up. "Oh yes, you'll be able to spare some of that bounty money."

From their boisterous jests full of bravado, he knew he had found some customers. "Come closer and allow me to relieve you of some of your burden," he said under his breath.

He moved toward the tree and waved the men over. "Hey there, my brave fellows. Stop in for some cool water, gratis."

They left the road, and as soon as they joined him, Chapman began the sales pitch, "You'll be a needin' knives and pistols for close in work." He pointed to his weapon display case inside the tent. "I know all about that sort of thing. I'm a veteran myself, fought under Zack Taylor when we went up against General Santa Anna. You'll need a pistol when you don't have time or space to reload the long gun, and," he paused, "a knife when the pistol runs empty."

He had their attention, and all but the youngest stepped farther in the tent. That one hung back by the water barrel and did not even glance at the displays of knives and uniform buttons. Intrigued by the challenge, the salesman stayed with the reluctant man and noticed he was probably sixteen if he was a day. He smiled and jested with the others, but his smile never reached his serious dark eyes.

The peddler extended his hand in greeting, "The name's Chapman, Edmund Chapman, purveyor of fine goods to our brave fighting men. And you are?"

"Parris, James." The short-statured teen with the ruddy complexion and brown hair took the offered hand.

They shook, and Chapman realized that Parris was different from his friends. The look in his eyes telegraphed that he had a notion of what he'd face after he returned next month to muster in with his regiment.

Parris must have heard war stories, real and unvarnished, most likely ones about the Fort Henry and Shiloh battles.

Chapman, an experienced pitchman from way back, knew that his customer was trapped in every soldier's dilemma. He wanted to do his duty and yet stay home with his loved ones.

The oldest recruit, probably just barely twenty, waved a Bowie knife with an antler handle and yelled from the most interior display case, "Hey Jimmy, look at this knife."

Chapman spoke up, "Be with you in a few minutes," and returned his attention to Parris who volunteered that he was not looking to buy weapons.

"Got all I need at home. But maybe something for my sister?"

"Mr. Parris, let me show you a special piece of jewelry. Bought it from a widow lady in Cincinnati. She lost her only son at Fort Donnelson back in February. She claimed it has been in her family ever since her great-grandmother received it from her sweetheart before he set off for Valley Forge to serve with Washington. "

Chapman retrieved a black velvet jewelry case from his vest pocket. "Tell me what you think of this?"

When he and the young man agreed to the price of three dollars, he congratulated himself on the sale and story. The previous week in Cincinnati, he had bargained a price of twenty-five dollars for his usual shipment of fifty assorted brass brooches set with various colored glass. The other young men bought knives along with a handful of shiny buttons and walked on to Sabina and their families.

By the time the crickets began their evening song, Chapman had taken in nearly forty dollars. "It'll pick up tomorrow," he predicted and led his packhorse away.

Margaret's Family Tree

1. Jeremiah Fielding Garrett b. 1842 Virginia to Jeremiah and Mercy Garrett d. 1883 OH m. 1863 Hannah McConkey b. 1845 VA to Matthew McConkey (1818-1905) and Agnes Clopton (1820-1906) d. 1915 OH Daughters Emma, Lida, and Minnie died in infancy

2. Esther Garrett b. 1864 OH d. 1926 m.1881 Harry Thompson b. 1860 OH d. 1924 OH Lived in Clinton County, Ohio

3. Sarah Jane Thompson b. 1882 OH d. 1930 d. OH m. 1899 Isaac Guymon b. 1880 OH d. unknown. Disappeared 1919. Her natural father was Noah McConkey. Divorced January 10, 1930 married Richard Steele, January 10, 1930

4. Mollie Elizabeth (Betsey) Guymon b. 1903 OH d. 1960 m. 1920 John Hussong b. 1897 d. 1965

5. Louise Hussong b. 1922 d. 1932

5. Marie Hussong b. 1924 d. 1961

3. Jeremiah Thompson b. OH 1885 d. 1966 OH m. 1905 Nila Merriman b. 1886 d. 1958

2. Cornelius Garrett b. 1875 OH d. 1957 OH m. 1896 Catherine Evinger b. 1876 d. 1964.

3. Jeremiah Garrett b. 1900 OH d. 1985 OH never married

3. Havilla Garrett b. 1910 OH d. 1995 CA m. 1935 Diana Cummins b. 1912 d. 1997.

2. Charles Garrett . b. 1880 OH d. 1898 Spanish American War

2. Hattie Garrett b. 1880 OH d. 1959 IN m. 1899 Robert Brown b. 1879 KY d. 1958

3. Castella Brown b. 1905 IN d. 1959 m. 1923 Russell Dakin b. 1905 d. 1958

    4. Timothy Dakin b. 1925 d. 1980

    4. Margaret Dakin b. Oct 7, 1927 d. July 1, 2010 m. Mark Julian b. 1925 d. Dec. 15, 2005

        5. Lauren Julian b. 1950

        5. Beth Julian b. 1952

    4. Miriam Dakin b. 1931 m. Henry Pierce b. 1929

    4. Mary Rose Dakin b. 1935 m. Christopher Hensley b. 1930

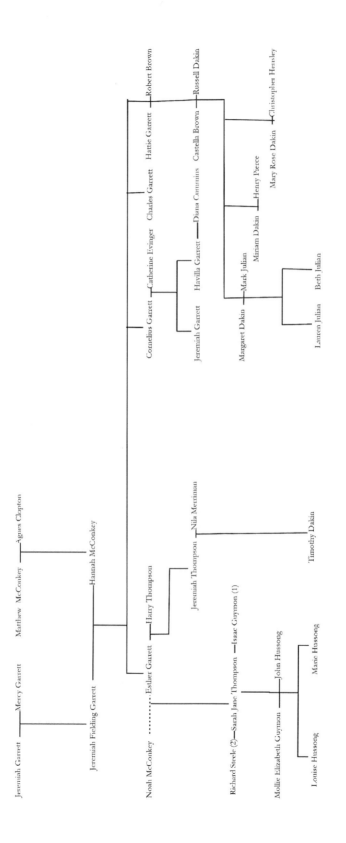

Book Club Questions

1. Margaret helped Martha Julian, a mother of a soldier who eventually became her husband. This chance meeting changed the course of her life. In fiction, of course, it is very easy to bring chance into the plot. Have you had a similar experience in life?

2. Hattie consoles Margaret with the phrase that grief is a gift. Do you agree? Did Hattie's life demonstrate that she believes grief can bring some wisdom?

3. What do you think Castella's life was like after Margaret and Tim were no longer in the house?

4. What makes Marie a pivotal character in the story?

5. Was Betsey really unhinged by grief over her daughter's death? Or was she so damaged from her unrealized love for her cousin Jeremiah that she was moving toward insanity all along?

6. Keeping in mind that in the 1880s interracial marriage was illegal, did Hannah and Jeremiah make the right decision to try to keep Sarah Jane's true parentage a secret? What responsibility did they owe to Sarah Jane and her children and their children?

7. Sarah Jane had to face the dual stigmas of being not only a wife deserted by her husband who was a known gambler but also a divorced woman. Was Richard Steele really looking out for her best interests when he wooed and convinced her to divorce?

8. Esther had a tough decision to make. Was her decision ethical?

9. Our ancestors' experiences might determine who we have become. What is your opinion about which has more influence? Our ancestors or our deeds and actions.

10. Hannah and Jeremiah's promise to each other when they became engaged was to never keep secrets from each other. This grew out of Hannah's anger over Jeremiah enlisting without discussing his

decision with her. What were the ramifications of this promise? Should they still have been bound by this promise made when they were so young?

11. Agnes' life dramatically changed when she and Matthew moved to Ohio. In your opinion, what would have been the most difficult change to accept?

12. Which character do you think was the bravest? Why?

Acknowledgements:

I inherited the garnet brooch along with the appraiser's comments that "Those weren't garnets, just red glass." I was so glad my mother never knew the truth since she wore the brooch so proudly with its companion piece, the paisley shawl. This story began as a challenge from my husband after I found pictures of an elder cousin and her mother both wearing the garnet brooch. He spurred me on with the comment that there was a good story buried in the garnet's history, and if I didn't write it, he would. Thank you, Randy, for your encouragement and support while I plunged into the writing.

I have anchored the story in Webster, Indiana where the post office still exists though it moved out of the back corner of the general store a while ago. The general store/post office was the gathering place for adults as well as children. If you have ever lived in a small town or a neighborhood where everyone knows everything and everyone else, I hope my story resonates with some of your experiences, and yes, Petey did sing in the background during party line calls.

Many of the surnames used in this book are from my genealogy research. I gleaned facts and glimpses into the way of life from antebellum times through World War Two from the file cabinets full of wills, deeds, tax records, pension files, family Bibles, military records, and my father's letters written to his mother while he served in the Air Corps during WWII. James Parris, the new recruit in the epilogue, is named for my Civil War ancestor killed at the Battle of Stone's River in Tennessee. I offer a special thank you to the park rangers there who shared their expertise and helped me gain a better picture of where and how he died.

All of the photographs are from my family with the exception of:

"I'm in this war too! WAC 1841-1945, p. 27 courtesy of The National Archives, Record Group 44, Records of the Office of Government Reports, 1932-1945, World War II posters.

"Your Victory Garden counts more than ever!" p. 58 poster, courtesy of The National Archives, Record Group 44, Records of the Office of Government Reports, 1932-1945, World War II posters.

"Depot of the U.S. Military Railroads showing the engine *President*." 111-B-4869 p. 212 courtesy of The National Archives, City Point, Virginia 1864. Civil-War-084.

I offer a well-deserved shout out to my writing groups. I repeat again that I have gained more than I gave to them. They generously offered suggestions and searched for errors and places where my words and story arc didn't quite work out as I had planned.

My editor, Vicki Van Brocklin, helped tremendously and gave terrific guidance.

My ideal reader, Megan Wilson, gave her valuable time, right-on suggestions, and the willingness to read and reread.

I leaned on my good friend, Jean Airey, for final layout guidance.

I thank all of you.

Of course, any errors and mistakes are mine alone.

Please visit my web page at: www.heirloomseries.com

You may contact me at: katenixon01@gmail.com

Made in the USA
Charleston, SC
25 October 2014